I0666691

DON'T CRY OVER KILLED MILK

(A Damon Lassard Dabbling Detective Mystery)

by

Stephen Kaminski

This book is fiction. All characters, events, and organizations portrayed in this novel are the product of the author's imagination or are used fictitiously. Any resemblance to actual persons—living or dead—is entirely coincidental.

Copyright © 2013 by Stephen Kaminski

All rights reserved. No parts of this book may be reproduced or transmitted in any form or by any means, electronic or mechanical, including photocopying, recording or by any information storage and retrieval system, without written permission from the author, except for the inclusion of brief quotations in a review.

For information, email **Cozy Cat Press**, cozycatpress@aol.com or visit our website at: www.cozycatpress.com

COZY CAT
P R E S S

ISBN: 978-1-939816-18-4
Printed in the United States of America

Cover design by Karri Klawiter
http://artbykarri.com/cover-art/e-book-print-cover-art-design/

1 2 3 4 5 6 7 8 9 10

For my parents: Art and Yolanda

A Special Note
To all—like me—who have endured the effects of
Amniotic Band Syndrome (ABS) or any other digit or
limb difference, stand proud. You can rise above any
challenge life throws at you and thrive!

Chapter 1

His fingers looked like baby carrots—orange, round, and stubby.

Damon Lassard strained his eyes to avoid staring at them. Standing opposite him, Jeremiah Milk was speaking in an animated manner, gesticulating with his right hand while the left remained planted firmly on the desktop between the two men.

Jeremiah was afflicted with a congenital condition known as amniotic band syndrome. In less than one-tenth of one percent of pregnancies, a portion of a woman's amniotic sac ruptures, leaving fibrous bands that can entangle and squeeze off parts of a fetus' developing body. Jeremiah had been lucky in a relative sense—his umbilical cord could have been severed. Instead, the stringy strands had limited their wrath to his extremities, and Jeremiah was born with each of his fingers individually pinched off like a mini sausage link.

"You need to take action," Jeremiah said with pleading tones.

"Like what, Jeremiah?" Damon asked, leaning back into his utilitarian swivel chair behind the library's reference desk.

Jeremiah's lean towering figure pitched forward to close the space Damon had just created. "I don't know what, but my crepe myrtles are getting eaten alive. My neighbors are having the same problem." The pink and white flowering trees were pervasive in Hollydale, a close-knit community in Arlington, Virginia, just west of Washington, D.C.

"Why don't you get someone to come out and spray?"

"I already told you," Jeremiah insisted. "I have a company to do that. Last week, they applied their most powerful solution—an organic one, mind you. The insects went away for a couple of days and then came right back."

Damon shifted in his chair. Not only did he volunteer at the library in Hollydale but he also served as president of the neighborhood's citizens association. The latter role compelled Damon to indulge the locals and their sundry grumblings. He usually relished helping his neighbors but Damon was stumped as to how he could assist Jeremiah Milk.

"I'll tell you what, Jeremiah," Damon said after a moment, "I'll post a notice on Hollydale's Internet listserv and see how many others in the community are having the same problem. Maybe we'll see a geographical pattern."

Jeremiah ran a hand through his light frizzy hair. He looked to Damon like a mop standing on end. "Okay, thanks. I guess that's a start. We have a naturalist on staff at the park, and he's never heard of a bug that keeps returning to eat crepe myrtles."

Jeremiah worked as a ranger at Tripping Falls State Park, a haven for soaring oaks and a magnificent natural waterfall. The majority of parkland rested in nearby Fairfax County, but fifty acres in the southeast corner trickled into Arlington. The park's land didn't stretch to the Hollydale neighborhood, so Damon's experience with it was limited to hiking as a visitor.

"Can the naturalist come out and take a look at your crepe myrtles?" Damon asked.

"I took a branch into work yesterday. He examined it and suggested I treat the trees with heavier chemicals."

"So why don't you?"

"Because I'm not going to kill the Earth to make my plants beautiful, that's why." Jeremiah Milk turned his lanky frame and strode out of the Hollydale branch library.

Damon sighed heavily. His volunteer shift would be over in less than an hour, and he planned to spend the upcoming evening obsessing over the details of the date he had arranged with Bethany Krims for the following day. After initially rebuffing Damon, the stunning evening weather girl from one of the local television networks had agreed to join him at a Washington Nationals baseball game.

* * *

Minutes later, Rebecca Leeds trounced through the library's doors. Damon's best friend tracked wet footprints across the blue-gray carpet. Mid-September brought frequent afternoon bursts of rain to Hollydale.

"Thanks for adding to the wet dog smell in here," Damon said with a smile.

"Better than that cologne you started wearing," Rebecca teased, squeezing droplets from soggy strands of dark brown bangs.

Damon laughed. Rebecca's athletic legs shone under the harsh glare of the library's yellow lights.

She set a plastic-wrapped tin on the rough-hewn desk in front of Damon. "Leftover spinach lasagna from this afternoon's class," Rebecca said. She ran The Cookery—a school for aspiring chefs located just blocks from the library.

"Thanks," he said and tore off two sheets of paper towel that the head librarian, Mrs. Stein, kept under the desk. He handed them to Rebecca. "You just missed the tirade I had to endure from Jeremiah Milk." Damon filled her in on the case of the bug-infested trees.

"I hope you weren't too hard on him," Rebecca said. "That man's had a rough life."

"I wasn't obnoxious. Has his life been difficult because of his fingers?" Damon had moved to Hollydale less than three years earlier and didn't know the histories of all of the longtime residents.

"Not that. Though I'm sure he's had to endure all kinds of things—people constantly staring, for one." She finished wiping the last bits of rain from her face and neck. "I meant what happened to his wife and son. I can't believe Mrs. Chenworth hasn't told you."

Mrs. Chenworth was Hollydale's persistent gossip. She held high court at Cynthia Trumbell's salon next door to The Cookery. Cynthia, a gaunt woman with stringy blond hair, also served as Damon's second-in-command for the citizens association.

Damon was interested. He had been introduced to Jeremiah Milk at a Labor Day parade the previous year by Bethany Krims' father, Jackson. But that was the extent of his interaction with Jeremiah until today's ambush.

"So what happened to his wife and son?" Damon asked.

Rebecca scanned the library's bowels. Two pre-teens huddled on a sofa, texting. A middle-aged woman in a green rain slicker sat on the floor in the travel section among heaps of thick glossy guides.

Rebecca lowered her voice. "They both died. On the same night."

"Were they in an accident or something?" Damon asked.

"No. That's just it. Their causes of death were completely separate."

Damon let the information sink in. "How did that happen?"

"It was about four-and-a-half years ago. Jeremiah had been married for just over a year. I remember how happy everyone in town was for him. He's not bad looking, but I don't think he ever had a girlfriend while he was growing up." Rebecca moved a stool from one of the computer kiosks to the front of Damon's desk and perched cross-legged on it.

"It was an emotional wedding," Rebecca said with a smile. "Even the cake was in tiers."

Damon slapped his forehead.

"Sorry, that wasn't very nice, given the context," Rebecca said and continued. "He married a woman named Kathryn. She worked at Tripping Falls with him, though I don't think she was a ranger. Kathryn got pregnant a couple of months after the wedding. They lived with Jeremiah's mother, Dottie, in the house he grew up in. It's just down the street from here. Jeremiah still lives there, but shortly after the deaths, Dottie moved to a retirement community in Arizona."

"Rough way to start a marriage," Damon observed. "Living with your mother."

"Well, if he wanted to stay in Hollydale, they didn't have much choice." Given its proximity to Washington D.C., housing costs in the small Arlington neighborhood were exorbitant.

"So they're living with Mom, and Kathryn is pregnant," Damon recapped.

"Yes. She had a boy. Samuel. I met him when Kathryn took him in a stroller to the picnic area here in town. Cute kid. Big brown eyes. It was February when they died. I remember because it was a rough winter, and the snow was four inches deep at the time. But the weather wasn't a factor—they both died in their sleep."

Damon raised his eyebrows.

Rebecca glanced around her. "Kathryn went to bed before Jeremiah that night. According to Mrs. Chenworth, he stayed up to watch a movie in the living room. Dottie had gone to sleep an hour earlier, and Kathryn nursed Samuel just before she went to bed at ten o'clock. By the time Jeremiah went upstairs, it was close to midnight. He tucked in beside Kathryn and kissed her cheek."

"Was it cold?"

"I don't know. The story I heard is that Kathryn was a noisy sleeper, and seemed unusually quiet that night. When Jeremiah checked more closely, he noticed that she wasn't breathing. He flipped on a bedside light and saw right away that her face looked pallid."

"What did she die of?"

"Sudden cardiac arrest."

"That's horrible," Damon said and stood up to stretch his lower back.

"Jeremiah called 911 and tried CPR, but it was too late. The paramedics took Kathryn to the hospital to see if an emergency room doctor could jumpstart her heart. It didn't work. Jeremiah went with her and left Dottie with Samuel. The baby slept through the whole ordeal. Before he left to follow the ambulance, Jeremiah peeked into Samuel's room and saw him sleeping peacefully in his crib with drool dribbling from his mouth."

"So Samuel was still alive, and Dottie was awake."

"Yes. Jeremiah woke up his mother from her downstairs bedroom right after he called 911 and tried to resuscitate Kathryn. She stayed home with the baby while Jeremiah went to the hospital. He came home just before the sun came up, and Dottie was sitting in the living room looking grim."

"That would be expected. Her son just lost his wife."

"That's what Jeremiah thought," Rebecca said. "Until Dottie told him the news about Samuel."

"He died while Jeremiah was at the hospital with his dead wife?"

"You got it. Apparently, Dottie couldn't fall back asleep after the ambulance left. She stayed up in the living room, knitting. A couple of hours later, she realized that Samuel hadn't woken up crying to be fed, as was his routine. She went upstairs to look in on him and he was lying motionless—no breath, no heartbeat, dead."

"Did she call 911?"

"According to Mrs. Chenworth, she didn't. She didn't call Jeremiah on his cell phone, either. Instead, she got down on her knees, said a prayer, and waited stolidly for her son to return home so she could deliver the news."

Damon exhaled loudly. "That's crazy."

Rebecca folded her hands in her lap. "The doctors confirmed that Samuel died of SIDS, and I heard that Jeremiah had some sort of mental breakdown. Other than the joint funeral, no one saw him for months. Dottie moved to Arizona, and I don't know whether Jeremiah had himself admitted for psychological assistance or just stayed cooped up in that old house like a prisoner in solitary confinement."

"He didn't have friends to check on him?"

"He lived in Hollydale his entire life, but as far as I knew, he was always a loner. I don't know whether he was close enough to anyone who would look in on him."

Damon walked into the small office behind the library's reference desk and poured hours-old coffee dregs from a timeworn pot into his mug. He forced the scalding syrup down his throat. It tasted burnt.

"I think I lost my appetite for the lasagna," he said, returning to his place across the desk from Rebecca.

"I can't imagine what that man's gone through," she said.

"Neither can I. Did the police ever get involved?"

Rebecca eyed him curiously. Damon recently helped his friend, Detective Gerry Sloman, solve the murder of a traveling carnival owner at the fairgrounds in Hollydale. It was the first homicide committed in the neighborhood's cozy confines that anyone could remember.

"I don't think so," Rebecca said. "Are you itching for another investigation, Damon?"

She knew him well. Perhaps that was the reason Damon's mother continually pushed him to date Rebecca. His best friend had intimated that she'd welcome the proposition, but he didn't feel the right level of physical attraction.

"No, I'm not interested in another murder," Damon said. Deep down, he knew he was lying.

Rebecca cocked her head. "It is coincidental," she said. "But Jeremiah wasn't there when Samuel died, and I can't imagine Dottie would kill off her daughter-in-law and only grandchild. Besides, I never heard anything to suggest that the deaths weren't natural."

As Rebecca left the library, Damon let the information about Jeremiah Milk's wife and son sink in. He couldn't imagine the trauma that such a series of events might cause. The least he could do for the man, Damon thought, was to try to discover what was harming his crepe myrtles. Before closing the library for the day, Damon posted a query to the Hollydale listserv to find out how many of the locals had been having out-of-the-ordinary insect troubles.

* * *

Lasagna tin in hand, Damon made his way four blocks to his mother's townhouse. He and Lynne Lassard-Brown had a standing Friday evening commitment if neither had other plans. Despite being a widow, Lynne had no shortage of Friday night outings– –a graceful neckline and a dearth of wrinkles enticed a number of fifty-year-old-plus bachelors in Arlington.

Damon had fewer dates than his mother. His blue eyes, which several women had described as striking, were offset by a receding hairline with a widow's peak. But Damon was in a fortunate financial position. A seven year stretch catching in the Japanese professional baseball league and advertising money from an overseas chewing gum campaign allowed Damon to live modestly in his 1940s duplex without a paying job. Given his frugal spending habits, Damon's investment income sufficed. Volunteering at the library and serving as Hollydale's citizens association president filled the majority of his days without providing any accompanying stress.

Damon knocked on the front door and pushed through it into his mother's narrow brick townhouse. Lynne was tucked into the corner of a scarlet love seat. She looked up over the top edge of a scrapbooking magazine.

"You brought food?" she asked, noticing the tin in Damon's hands. "I made Indian for dinner."

Damon edged around a mass of bicycle parts strewn about the center of the room—Lynne had a proclivity for creating clutter. "Rebecca stopped by the library. It's lasagna, but it can keep until lunch tomorrow. Indian sounds good." Damon pecked his mother's cheek.

Over dinner in the cramped dining room, Damon described the crepe myrtle situation and recounted his conversation with Rebecca about Jeremiah Milk. "Did you hear much about the deaths?" he asked.

"It was all anyone talked about for weeks," Lynne said. "Poor Jeremiah. Jack dated his mother Dottie for a short spell before I came along." Jack Brown had been Lynne's second husband. Both he and Damon's father had passed away.

"What did Jack say about her?"

"About Dottie? Not much. They were both in their fifties at the time, went out for a couple of weeks, and then Jack broke it off. He said she wasn't lively enough for him."

"Rebecca said she moved to Arizona shortly after Kathryn and Samuel died."

"It was strange. She lived her entire adult life in Hollydale—personally, I think Jeremiah pushed her out."

"Any idea why?"

"Jack had a theory, though I didn't agree with him. I still don't." Lynne spooned homemade chana masala onto her plate.

Damon nibbled buttered naan as he waited for her to continue.

Lynne said, "Jack thought Jeremiah wanted Dottie out of the house so he could plan some sort of grand revenge on the world."

"The blowing-up-a-building kind of revenge?"

"Something like that. Or becoming a serial killer. No one saw Jeremiah for quite some time after the joint funeral. Jack thought he was holed up in the basement eating canned food and making homemade weapons. I told Jack he was being ridiculous: Jeremiah was just grieving."

"Rebecca said he may have sought psychological counseling," Damon said.

"It's possible. But he lives close to Mrs. Chenworth, and the old bird kept an eye on the Milk house. She said she never saw anyone going in or out."

"Well, he seems to be doing all right now," Damon said. "He spent fifteen minutes this afternoon complaining to me about his gardening."

"I'm glad to hear that. I know he returned to his duties at the park the summer after Kathryn and Samuel died."

After dinner, Damon insisted that his mother relax while he washed dishes. Lynne followed him from the dining room to the kitchen and sat at a small table covered in scrapbooking paraphernalia.

"Can I tell you what happened to me last night?" Lynne asked.

Damon, standing in front of the sink, twisted his neck to look back at her. "Something good?"

"Not exactly. A taxi driver put his hand on my thigh."

Damon dropped a plate into the sink. Soapy water splashed over his wrists. "What?"

"My taxi driver hit on me. He was pretty aggressive."

"I'll say. Did you call the police?"

"No, Damon, I didn't. It was partially my fault. I sat in the front seat."

"Mother, it's not one bit your fault if you didn't invite it."

"I didn't," she said softly. "I was coming back from meeting a friend for dinner in Dupont Circle. I had taken the metro downtown because I planned to have a couple of glasses of wine, and I didn't want to drive. After dinner, I decided to catch a cab home."

"You were by yourself?"

"Yes. Sherry lives near the restaurant, and I walked her home. We flagged a taxi from her front stoop. The backseat was crammed with old suitcases."

Damon looked at the disarray in his mother's home. "That should have made you feel right at home."

Lynne smiled. "Touché, Damon. The taxi driver said he hadn't intended to pick up any more customers for the night but saw us waving. He offered to put the suitcases in the trunk. I told him not to bother, I could just sit in front."

"Do you think he planned it in advance?"

"To lure a naïve fifty-three-year-old woman into his passenger's seat? I don't think so."

"So what happened?" Damon dried his hands on a dish towel.

"I made some mild conversation as he started the drive. My skirt had ridden up a bit from the way I was sitting. Just after we crossed over the Key Bridge into Arlington, he clamped a sweaty paw down on my left thigh. It felt like a wet jellyfish. He didn't say anything or even look over."

"Mother, that's molestation."

"It was more like loutish flirtation. I just grabbed his shirtsleeve, picked up his arm, and shunted it back to his side of the console." She grinned. "Don't look so dismayed, Damon. I can handle myself and I did."

"Did you get out?"

"No. He didn't say another word. He drove me home and I paid him. I didn't leave a tip. No big deal."

"Except now he knows where you live. I should call Gerry Sloman."

"Damon, I don't need the police. Save the chivalry for Bethany Krims."

Chapter 2

Damon walked home through the clammy evening air. David Einstaff, his duplex neighbor, greeted him with a tip of his whiskey glass from the front porch they shared. Damon nodded and continued inside.

He plunked down at the kitchen table in front of his laptop and logged onto the Hollydale listserv. It had only been three hours since he posted his message but he already had four replies. Each conveyed a story similar to the one articulated by Jeremiah Milk. Insects were eating away at crepe myrtles throughout the neighborhood despite the best efforts of the tree care companies. One gardening enthusiast pointed to several species of aphids and Japanese beetles as possible sources of the problem. But that didn't explain why insecticides had failed to keep away the bugs for more than a few days at a time.

As Damon was logging off, a new posting came through. Melanie Dumfries, whose name Damon didn't recognize, had been treating her two crepe myrtles with a store-bought pesticide and had no problems with insects.

* * *

The following morning, Damon opted against taking a run through his neighborhood in favor of a hike at Tripping Falls State Park. He hadn't been to the land reserve in over a year, and meeting with Jeremiah Milk the previous day reminded him of its splendor. Taking in the scenic falls would relax his brain, which had started to race with apprehension. He was meeting Bethany later in the day.

It took Damon less than fifteen minutes in his ten-year-old Saab to reach the park. At nine o'clock on a Saturday morning, the parking lot was almost empty. Damon pulled in close to the visitor center. The two-story structure's weather-beaten siding stood camouflaged against the woodlands. Opened doors welcomed visitors and flies alike, but Damon skirted the outer flank of the building. He strode through the brisk morning breeze to the first of three overlooks offering breathtaking views of the eighty-foot falls plunging into the Potomac River.

Damon closed his eyes and breathed in deeply. Fumes of wet moss filled his nostrils—earthy, not fetid. Delicate autumn mist cooled his face. The massive waterfall sounded like dishes crashing onto antique floorboards. Damon peered beyond the low metal railing at the majesty of nature. A six-year-old girl screeched with delight as she held her father's hand and approached a vantage point near Damon. Her older brother raced up a cluster of rocks and hurled pebbles into the abyss.

Damon stepped down from the wooden platform and considered an oversized sign displaying a labyrinth of hiking paths. The diagram reminded Damon of a map at a ski slope—each trail was imprinted with a corresponding degree of difficulty. The lone double diamond route was dubbed "Zazel's Summit." Damon opted against taking the demanding course in favor of "Cherubim's Run," a hike of moderate difficulty.

Halfway into the six mile trek, he stopped at a bend that bordered a calm spot on the river upstream from the falls. There were no rails or fences, just a warning sign directing hikers to refrain from entering the water. Downstream from the falls, the river narrowed to one tenth of its upstream width, creating a deadly gorge where bullheaded adventurists perished every year. Damon was not so bold, even upstream. But he squared his lean backside on a length of tree root peeking out of the damp riverbank and stripped off his sneakers and socks. Damon sank his feet into the edge of the cold river and wiggled his toes in silt.

Five minutes later, he rinsed his feet and climbed to a flattened boulder fifteen feet above the riverbank. From that position, Damon could see fifty yards back up the trail. He hadn't encountered another hiker all morning. But as he rested and allowed his bare feet to dry in the morning sun, two uniformed figures crested the rise of the trail, making their way toward him. When they passed, Damon noted patches on their sleeves with the words "Park Police." One stared at Damon's bare feet and soundlessly pointed to the warning sign.

* * *

After finishing the circular hike, Damon entered the visitor center in search of a water fountain. The interior of the cavernous building was trisected into equal-sized areas open to the public. The lobby housed vending machines, a small gift shop, and a rangers' desk obscured by masses of pamphlets. A theater accommodated flat benches, a stage, and a projection screen. The final area featured dated science exhibits. Closed double doors bearing the words "Park Management" stood at the east end of the lobby.

Damon located a water fountain near the gift shop. As he rose from taking a drink, Jeremiah Milk shepherded a cluster of Girl Scouts into the lobby from the exhibit hall. Damon listened as he finished speaking to the girls on the subject of butterflies native to the park. Jeremiah handed off the troop to a tall wiry ranger bearing a name tag that read "Milt," who led the group outside.

Jeremiah spotted Damon and raised a hand to him. Damon tried not to stare at his fingers.

"Beautiful morning for a hike," Jeremiah said, placing a binder on the rangers' desk.

"It is." Damon moved toward him. "I just finished Cherubim's Run."

"That's one of my favorite hikes. Are you here about the crepe myrtles?"

"Actually, I just wanted a change of scenery for my morning exercise. But I sent a post to the listserv yesterday. By last night there were already a number of responses. It seems you're not alone in having an insect problem."

"Well, I knew that," Jeremiah said testily. "Are they all crepe myrtles?"

"As far as I can tell, yes. One of the posters thinks it could be aphids or Japanese beetles."

"That's what Lawrence said. He's the naturalist here. But it doesn't explain why they keep coming back."

A spritely honey-blond in her early-thirties emerged from the doors marked for management and approached the rangers' desk. She stopped several feet away, presumably waiting for Jeremiah to finish speaking with Damon. Her narrow hips were accentuated by a vertical-striped sundress and tight ponytail.

Jeremiah waved her closer. "Alex, this is Damon Lassard. He's a neighbor of mine."

Damon extended his hand, and Alex shook it firmly. "Hi, Damon. Welcome to Tripping Falls." She studied his sweat-soaked shirt. "Looks like you've already had a chance to take a good hike this morning."

"I did," he said and wiped a bead of perspiration from his forehead. "It's a beautiful day, and you all keep the park so clean."

"Thanks," she replied crisply. Damon wasn't certain of Alex's responsibilities at the park, but she had the air of a person who was tasked with oversight.

A tall elderly man approached the group and interrupted the conversation. He looked at Alex. "Ms. Rancor, I want to hold another fundraiser for the park at my home next month. Do you have moment to discuss the details?"

Alex excused herself and shuttled the older man toward the management wing.

"Sorry he butted in like that," Jeremiah said to Damon. "Mr. Bertlemann has a home that backs into the parkland and he acts like he owns the place. He's constantly hiking before the park even opens, but he's one of our largest donors so we tolerate a few minor transgressions."

Damon nodded and excused himself. Less than five hours until his date with Bethany.

* * *

Damon met Bethany Krims on the Ballston metro station platform in Arlington forty-five minutes before the first pitch of the Washington Nationals baseball game. Mid-thigh cuffed shorts coupled with low-heeled sandals accentuated the length and tone of Bethany's legs. She wore a shapeless blue blouse, but a knot tied at one hip tugged the cloth with dramatic effect. Shoulder length chestnut hair flared-out under a fitted red Nationals ball cap. They jostled into a crowded train and, given the crush of riders, kept conversation to a minimum.

Located in Southeast D.C., Nationals Park was a testament to modern luxury. Their seats were excellent—in the lower level, fifteen rows behind first base. The pair settled down between a salt-and-pepper-haired man with hooded eyes who was listening to headphones and a harried mother trying to control three grade-schoolers. Damon's knees touched the seat in front of him. He struggled to maintain a two inch gap between his legs and Bethany's.

"I haven't seen you in the library lately," Damon said. Bethany was a regular reader of thrillers.

"I started training for a marathon," she said. "That's been taking up a lot of my free time. I'm surprised you put in so much time at the library. It must get a little boring."

"Sometimes it does, but I enjoy talking to all of the regulars. A lot of them think of me more as a bartender than a library volunteer."

"Mrs. Chenworth would be jealous!" Bethany said with enthusiasm. They both laughed. "What kind of stories do you hear?" Bethany asked.

Damon regaled her with a tale from a distraught mother who had taken her toddler to a local eatery and was served a chicken tender that resembled a male private-part. "Apparently, the manager apologized, swept away the plate of food, and crammed the tender into his mouth on his way back to the kitchen."

Bethany snickered, and Damon hailed the attention of a soda vendor who tossed him two plastic bottles of Diet Coke.

"Yesterday, someone cornered me at the library to discuss another interesting situation," Damon said. He cracked open his soda and described the neighborhood insect incursion. Damon had checked online before meeting Bethany: there had been three more postings—all citing similar problems as the first group.

"You should ask all of the people who are having problems who they use to spray their crepe myrtles," Bethany said when Damon finished.

Damon turned to face her. She whisked a loose strand of silky hair behind her ear. "You mean which company?" he asked.

"Yes. Jeremiah Milk said he used an organic company, right?"

Damon nodded.

"So maybe they're all using the same company," Bethany said and sipped her soda.

"And their chemicals are no good?"

"Probably. If the woman who used the store-bought solution isn't having problems, maybe the organic chemical company is using a faulty batch of product."

The crowd groaned collectively as a Nationals batter hit into a double play.

"Damon," Bethany said suddenly and grabbed his forearm. "What if it's something more nefarious?" Her eyes glowed a radiant auburn.

Damon's insides quivered at Bethany's touch. He steadied his nerves and considered her comment. "Maybe a disgruntled employee is spraying water instead of chemicals so the company loses customers," he said.

Bethany shook her head. "That doesn't work. You said after spray is applied, the insects disappear for a few days before they come back."

"True," Damon said. "So maybe the employee's diluting the spray. It works for a few days but doesn't solve the problem."

"I suppose, but I had something else in mind."

"Something more *nefarious*, right?" he asked.

She leaned in close to Damon's ear. "What if a competitor to the organic spray company is repopulating the insects?"

Damon could feel the heat from her breath. Their faces were only inches apart. "So Pesticides-R-Us is tired of losing business to the environmentally-friendly contingent in Hollydale?"

"Exactly," Bethany said, excitedly. "The pesticide company is trying to make it appear that the organic spray doesn't work on crepe myrtles."

Damon took a drink of his soda, then said, "But there are dozens of garden treatment companies that serve Hollydale. Even if the perpetrator could figure out which residents use a company that specializes in organic sprays, how could he be sure the clients would move to his company instead of a competitor?"

Bethany considered the question. "I don't know. I suppose the idea was a bit fantastic."

They passed the remainder of the game with pleasant and flowing conversation but without any further flirtation. By the time they returned to Arlington, it was nearly eight o'clock.

"Would you like to have dinner somewhere?" Damon asked.

Bethany declined, insisting that she was still full from the nachos she'd eaten during the seventh inning. Damon settled for walking her home from the metro station.

When they reached the door to her condominium building, Bethany gave Damon a hug. "I had a very nice time," she said, and hastily turned. Her swift motion eliminated any possibility of a goodnight kiss. She's used that move before, Damon thought sulkily as he walked away.

Chapter 3

The following morning, Damon called his friend Gerry Sloman. Damon knew the dogged Arlington County detective would be interested to hear about the dying crepe myrtles.

"Hi, Damon, I don't have time to speak right now," Gerry said quickly after picking up on the third ring. "Is it urgent?"

Damon sensed Gerry's tension. "It's not. Jeremiah Milk and some of the other Hollydale residents are having a suspicious insect problem."

"Jeremiah Milk?" Gerry parroted with disbelief. "I don't think he'll be worried about bugs anymore." Gerry hesitated, and then added, "He was murdered at Tripping Falls last night."

"Murdered?" Damon shouted into the receiver, "I just saw him there yesterday."

"You saw Jeremiah at the park yesterday?"

"I went for a hike in the morning and saw him when I went into the visitor center for a drink of water."

"What time was that?"

"I finished hiking at around eleven," Damon said.

"Which trail were you on?"

"Cherubim's Run."

"Damon, can you come down to the park right now?" Gerry asked. "We want to speak with everyone who saw Jeremiah at the park yesterday. And if you were on Cherubim's Run, the sooner you can get down here, the better."

* * *

A bespectacled patrolman met Damon's Saab at the Tripping Falls gate and motioned for him to turn around. Damon relayed the reason for his presence. After a brief exchange over a walkie-talkie, the officer directed Damon down the tree-lined drive to the parking lot.

It was just before nine o'clock in the morning. Five sparkling white police cars were parked side by side in tight formation at the front of the lot. Damon recognized Gerry's blue sedan in the quarterback position behind the center cruiser.

The visitor center was cooled with overhead fans in lieu of central air. Damon scanned the lobby and spotted a top-heavy redhead who he recognized as Lieutenant Margaret Hobbes—Gerry's supervisor. Her furrowed brow protruded angrily toward two uniform-clad men standing in front of her.

Gerry sidled up beside Damon and said, "She's not a happy camper right now."

"I'm sure murder doesn't sit well with her," Damon responded.

"True, but that's not why she's livid. The small man standing near her is the chief of the Fairfax County police department and the officer sucking in his gut is with the park. They're having a pissing match over jurisdiction."

"Are you trying to win or lose?" Damon asked with a smile.

Gerry laughed and clapped his hand on Damon's shoulder. "Good question. The body was found on the small piece of parkland that lies in Arlington. Between that and the fact that Jeremiah Milk was a Hollydale resident, we'd like to take the lead. The rest of the park sits in Fairfax County. The Department of Conservation and Recreation cops—the Park Police—have jurisdiction over the day-to-day matters here. But they don't have the resources for a murder investigation."

Through the opening connecting the lobby to the theater, Damon could see a cluster of people gathered on benches. "Is that the staff?" he asked, looking in their direction.

"Yes. We'll be interviewing them just as soon as we figure out who gets to be in the room." They heard Margaret Hobbes bark at the man from Fairfax.

"I have free reign to interview anyone else who saw Jeremiah at the park yesterday," Gerry said. "Let's go into the rangers' lounge."

Gerry led Damon into the wing marked "Park Management." Beyond the entrance stood closed doors on either side of a green-carpeted hallway. One door was marked "Head of Operations," and the other, "Education Specialist." The end of the short passage opened into a communal area, which was empty. Gerry and Damon sat across from one another on mismatched cloth sofas adjacent to a kitchenette.

"First, tell me everything you know about Jeremiah Milk," Gerry said.

Damon filled him in on what he knew of the man's back story, the majority of which Damon had just learned himself.

"Did you find his body on Cherubim's Run?" Damon asked when he finished.

"A man named Colin Scott did. He's a retiree. At seven-fifteen this morning, just after the park opened, he saw Jeremiah, stripped down to his boxer shorts, right on the trail. We found his uniform nearby—crumpled into a ball and a little stiff, as if it had been wet then dried in the overnight air."

"Do you know how he died?"

"Grace Chu, the medical examiner, is with the body now. I saw it earlier. I think Jeremiah may have been burned to death."

"Burned?"

"His face, arms, and chest are covered with welts and gashes," Gerry said. "But it's a little strange. I've seen burn victims before and their flesh is always blackened. Jeremiah's gashes are clean."

"Do any of the park buildings have fire damage?"

"Margaret has Richard, one of our seasoned officers, making the rounds right now with a woman named Alex. She's in charge of operations here. Other than the visitor center, there are thirteen structures in the park—mostly maintenance and storage sheds."

"I met Alex yesterday," Damon said. "Nice looking woman."

Gerry shook his head at his friend. "You never cease to pick up on these things, Damon." Damon wondered how Gerry could fail to notice attractive women—probably because he had a remarkable wife at home.

"Even with the burn marks, the park workers were able to identify Jeremiah?" Damon asked.

"They were," Gerry said. "We know that he was the last staffer here yesterday. I think the rangers take turns closing down the park after it gets dark. A Park Police officer makes a quick patrol of the parking lot and visitor center once during the overnight hours but doesn't go down the trails."

"The officer didn't see any cars in the lot?"

"I haven't had the chance to ask yet. Hold on." Gerry paced out of the room. While he was waiting, Damon noticed a woman in her mid-thirties enter, and seconds later, exit the nearby room designated for the education specialist.

Five minutes later, Gerry returned.

"Margaret is going to start interviewing the staff," Gerry said. "Fairfax County is out. We're taking the lead with the Park Police as support. I have to get in there with Margaret in a minute, so tell me about your hike yesterday."

Damon quickly provided the details of his vanilla visit.

"You didn't see anything unusual on the trail?"

"No. The only people I saw were two Park Police officers," Damon said. "Did you find out if there were any cars in the lot during the overnight hours?"

Gerry hesitated. Damon had lent him an ear on a recent murder case—the strangulation of a traveling carnival owner—and had uncovered details unknown to the police. But Damon had also overstepped boundaries by interviewing suspects on his own.

Gerry inhaled deeply. "There was one car," he said. "It was Jeremiah's, which makes sense."

"The Park Police didn't look into it?"

"They didn't. I spoke with one of the officers—Davida Harkens. She said that over the past three months, Jeremiah's car has been in the lot overnight once or twice a week. She doesn't know why he was leaving it here, but the officers knew the vehicle was his and never considered its presence out of the ordinary."

Gerry thanked Damon for his time and excused himself to join Margaret in the theater.

* * *

Damon stepped through the back door of the rangers' lounge to a small patio space. It was barren save for a cracked plastic table, a full ashtray, and three folding chairs. Cigarette butts littered the area's stone pavers.

Damon sat for a moment to consider the implications of Jeremiah Milk's car. Why would a ranger who lived less than fifteen minutes away spend a couple of nights a week at the park? Had Jeremiah been concocting a destructive plan, as his mother's second husband Jack had envisioned? Perhaps Jeremiah hadn't been murdered, and an explosive he was building had prematurely detonated and burned him to death. No. Jeremiah was found on the trail in his boxer shorts. An accident didn't fit.

Damon was about to take a path that led from the patio to the parking lot when he heard voices. A small group had entered the rangers' lounge. There were no windows between the patio and the lounge, so Damon couldn't see who had entered. But they couldn't see him, either. He contemplated the door leading inside. He had fortuitously left it ajar. Damon selected a cigarette stub from the ashtray—if anyone walked outside, he would pretend to be finishing a smoke.

Damon recognized the voices of Gerry and Lieutenant Margaret Hobbes. There was another male voice as well.

"So let's hear it, Richard," Margaret said curtly. "You pulled us out of an interview, so it better be good."

"I went to all of the buildings in the park with Alex, the operations manager, like you asked," Richard said.

"And what did you find?" Margaret demanded.

"There's one place that Alex thought looked strange. It's a storage shed on a small path connecting Cherubim's Run and one of the other trails. The shed is halfway in between, about fifty yards from either one."

"Is the path wide enough for a vehicle?" Gerry asked.

"Not a car," Richard said. "But the golf carts that the park staff use would fit."

"Okay," Margaret said. "What's in this shed?"

"On ground level, it's just a single room that houses equipment. There's a basement, too. Alex said it's usually pretty sparse down there—mainly cleaning supplies and small disposable items like batteries and paper towels. But when we went into the shed, all of the basement gear was piled in a corner on the main level. Other than a utility sink, the basement was totally empty."

"Was there any evidence of a fire in the basement, like a charred smell?" Gerry asked.

"Just the opposite," Richard said. "It was as clean as a whistle. The whole room seemed damp."

"Was there a drain in the basement floor?" Gerry asked.

"I believe there was," Richard replied, sounding confused.

Gerry put two-and-two together for him. "Someone may have recently mopped the place up with water from the utility sink."

"We'll get Forensics down to that basement and see if we can establish if it's where Milk was murdered," Margaret said. "Anything else out of place?"

"Not out of place," Richard said. "But Alex noticed something. It may be a coincidence." There was a pause before he continued. "The electrical outlet on the ground level is shorted out. The shed doesn't have an overhead light, just an old lamp without a shade. I noticed that the bulb was out—it was sitting on the table next to the base. Alex screwed it in but it didn't work. She found a package of new bulbs in the pile of supplies from the basement. Alex put in a new one, and it didn't work either. It looks like the outlet needs to be fixed."

"Are there any other outlets in the shed?" Margaret asked.

"There's one in the basement over the utility sink. I walked the lamp with the new bulb down there and plugged it in. It worked fine. The old bulb worked, too, down there."

"Okay, maybe it's a coincidence," Margaret said. "Is that all, Richard?"

"There's one more thing. Alex pointed out a chart tacked to the back wall of the shed's main floor. Every night, the last ranger at the park initials the chart and denotes the time to indicate that he or she made a series of inspections—the trash has been emptied, there are no illegal campers. Things like that. You could see a month's worth of initials. Mr. Milk's are there every fourth day, always around ten o'clock at night. The other initials correspond to the other three rangers. Alex said there are similar charts in two other sheds in the park."

"They're on a fixed schedule," Gerry concluded. "Jeremiah Milk closed down the park every fourth night. He probably drives around in a golf cart, makes his inspections, and enters the sheds to sign off. If the killer knew the rangers' schedules, he'd know that Jeremiah would be in the shed near Cherubim's Run by himself at a certain time on a certain night. Easy pickings."

"That limits the suspect list," Margaret said. "It has to be someone who's familiar with the schedules of the rangers. There can't be more than a handful of people who fit that description."

"Unless the killer didn't specifically have Mr. Milk in mind and just murdered whoever came by first," Richard said.

"That's possible," Margaret conceded. "But let's start by focusing on the park staff who would know the rangers' schedules."

Gerry ticked off names. "Alex Rancor, the operations manager. Three rangers: Milt Verblanc, Lawrence Drake, and the female ranger, Aylin Erul. The other two on staff are the education specialist and the maintenance worker—I don't know whether they would know the rangers' schedules or not." Gerry paused. "There are also two Park Police officers who do patrols. They'd probably know the schedules."

"That's true," Margaret said. "Even though we're running this investigation, we have to keep the Park Police in the loop, so let's tread carefully with them."

"Was there a lock on the door of the shed?" Gerry asked.

"Yes," Richard replied. "But Alex said the rangers routinely leave it unlocked. If someone wanted to wait for Mr. Milk inside the shed, it would have been easy."

"Good job, Richard," Margaret said. "Detective Sloman and I will take it from here. Gerry, let's get back to those interviews and crack this case wide open."

"You bet, boss," Gerry said. "One last thing, Richard: Did Jeremiah initial the chart last night?"

"You know what?" Richard responded. "He didn't."

Chapter 4

On his way home, Damon stopped in front of Jeremiah Milk's house. He longed to search it but knew the police would be along soon, and he didn't want to disrupt evidence. The Milk home was landscaped decently but otherwise in disrepair by Hollydale standards. Paint peeled from wood siding. Sunlight glinted through a crack in an upstairs window. Edging the right side of the house stood three bedraggled crepe myrtle trees.

An hour later, Damon and Rebecca were sitting in matching rockers on Damon's front porch. He summarized his morning excursion.

"The police think it's probably one of the park employees," Damon said in closing.

Rebecca sipped fresh-squeezed lemonade through a straw. "That makes sense," she said. "Though it could have been anyone who knew his work schedule."

"But you told me he was a loner," Damon countered.

"That was certainly true years ago. It's possible he changed."

"There's his mother, of course," Damon said. "But she lives in Arizona."

"I'm sure she'll be back in Hollydale soon enough to coordinate a funeral and tie up Jeremiah's affairs. You could ask her if he had any friends. Assuming they were on speaking terms."

Damon thought about Dottie Milk. Would the police ensure she had an alibi for the night her son was murdered? Damon couldn't imagine a mother killing her own child. But Dottie had been in the Hollydale home when her daughter-in-law and grandchild died.

Rebecca interrupted his thoughts. "What's happening up there in your head?" Even when the two were sitting, Damon hovered five inches above Rebecca.

"I was thinking about what you told me the other day. Dottie Milk didn't inform the police after her grandson died." Damon had forgotten to pass along that snippet of information to Gerry when he spoke with the detective earlier in the day.

"You don't believe that Kathryn and Samuel died of natural causes," Rebecca said incredulously. "And you figure that Dottie flew from Arizona to Arlington and finished wiping out the family by burning her own son to death?"

Damon smiled grimly. "You did ask me what I was thinking about."

* * *

Hours later, when the sun began to dip toward the horizon, Damon dialed Gerry's number.

The detective picked up and said, "Thanks for the background information this morning. Lieutenant Hobbes and I are making good progress."

"That's wonderful. When we spoke, I forgot to mention something about the deaths of Jeremiah's wife and son. Are you interested in coming by for a late dinner?" Damon could have summed up the point in a matter of sentences, but he wanted to see if he could glean more information from Gerry. Damon was too interested in the case to leave it to the professionals.

"I grabbed a bite here at the station," Gerry said. "But I'll swing by on my way home if you make some coffee."

Gerry arrived at Damon's white HardiePlank duplex half an hour later. "I can't believe I have another homicide," the detective said, sitting down at Damon's eat-in kitchen table. Gerry toyed with a gold cross dangling from a chain at his open collar.

"You did so well with the last murder investigation, I'm not surprised Lieutenant Hobbes picked you to work this one." Damon poured Gerry a steaming mug of coffee.

"Thanks, Damon. Your instincts helped a lot. Now what did you want to tell me about Jeremiah?"

Damon relayed what Rebecca had told him about Dottie's failure to notify the police of baby Samuel's death.

"That's interesting, but I've heard stranger things," Gerry said. "People have all types of reactions when they're in shock. They don't always act rationally."

"Have you notified Dottie Milk about Jeremiah?"

"Margaret did several hours ago. Dottie's plane arrives at Reagan National later this evening. I'm planning to speak with her tomorrow morning, but I don't expect she'll have much useful information. Just to be safe though, we'll verify that she has an alibi for last night."

Damon smiled at his friend, then admitted to overhearing Gerry and the other officers from outside of the rangers' lounge.

Gerry chortled. "If it was anyone else, I'd be upset." He sipped from his mug. "We still don't know exactly how Jeremiah was killed. The lacerations in his neck and chest were deep and severe. No doubt he died from them, but the medical examiner, Dr. Chu, is certain they weren't caused by fire. They may be chemical burns. The lab will run tests, and we should know within a week. He had broken bones, too. In his fingers and toes."

"His fingers were disfigured from birth," Damon said.

"I know. So were his toes. But they still had bones, which were crushed."

"Do you think he was targeted because of his condition?" Damon asked.

"Is there a madman prejudiced against the malformed? It's possible. Or maybe the killer just wanted to torture Jeremiah before doing him in at the chest and neck."

"If Jeremiah was the last one at the park, no one would have heard him scream," Damon commented. "Especially in the basement of a shed. Could a chemical burn have caused the broken bones?"

"Margaret thinks the killer hammered down on his fingers and toes before turning to the chemicals," Gerry said. "And the use of chemicals would account for a wet uniform and the damp basement. The killer might have been trying to wash away the smell."

"So you're looking for suspects who have access to deadly chemicals," Damon surmised and wrapped both hands around his mug to warm them despite the moderate temperature of the kitchen.

"It's on our radar. But you can find acids and other chemicals that will do serious damage in a lot places. Almost every high school science lab is stocked with them."

"I heard the police caught two guys drinking battery acid," Damon said and gave Gerry a wry grin. "They were charged immediately."

Gerry shook his head with a smile.

Damon turned back to the conversation. "I suppose the park rangers have chemicals on site as well."

"They do," Gerry replied. "Let me tell you, Damon, the park staff is an interesting bunch. The operations manager, Alex, seems to be the most normal one there. That's probably why she's in charge."

Damon recalled Alex's delicate facial features.

"Jeremiah's fellow rangers didn't talk much during their interviews," Gerry continued. "Milt Verblanc—the tall wiry one—has been there for ten years and builds robots. He and Jeremiah started at Tripping Falls within a couple of months of each other. Verblanc didn't have much to say about Jeremiah. But when he started talking about robots, we heard an earful about advanced electronic systems and modular limbs."

Gerry rose and refilled his coffee cup. "Then there's Lawrence Drake, the naturalist," Gerry said. "He was prone to grunting and one word answers. The third is Aylin Erul—the name sounds Turkish if you ask me. She's carves fruit—makes watermelons and cantaloupes into animals. It was weird: she showed me a wallet full of photos, as if the carved specimens were her children."

"How about the education specialist?" Damon asked.

"Veronica Maldive. She's the one we're most interested in." He paused. "She and Jeremiah were dating."

"That's something." After a moment, Damon snapped his fingers. "Rebecca told me Jeremiah's late wife Kathryn worked at the park, too, before they were married."

Gerry waved a hand dismissively. "People have to meet somewhere. Trina was a dispatcher at police headquarters when we met."

"Do you know how long Jeremiah and the teacher were dating?" Damon asked.

"She said for several months. It was a little delicate, but I asked Veronica if Jeremiah ever spent the night at her place after work. After blushing, she admitted that he did once or twice a week."

"Which is why Jeremiah regularly left his car at the park overnight," Damon said, picking up the line of thinking.

"Correct. They'd drive in Veronica's SUV from the park to her place in Reston, spend the night, and go back to work together the following morning."

"So she would know his schedule."

"I see where you're going," Gerry said. "But if she wanted to kill him, why do it at the park? Why not murder him when they were at her place? She lives alone."

"Maybe to cast suspicion elsewhere."

"That's a possibility," Gerry admitted.

"Did Veronica mention any friends of his?"

"She said he didn't seem to have any. According to Veronica, the only person Jeremiah ever talked about was his mother."

Damon contemplated this information, then pulled himself up from the table and filled a glass with water. "Did you interview the maintenance worker?" he asked.

"We did. Emmanuel Alvarez is Dominican, but he's lived in the States for over thirty years. He's in his mid-sixties."

"I imagine he has access to all of the buildings in the park."

"He does," Gerry said. "I misspoke earlier when I said Alex Rancor was the most normal one at the park. Alvarez is pretty balanced, too. But Margaret Hobbes has been grilling him."

"Why's that?"

"There's a small cabin and garage about an eighth of a mile behind the visitor center. Alvarez uses the cabin as his personal space. He claimed he doesn't live there, but I saw a mattress inside. When we scoured the grounds around the park buildings this afternoon, one of our officers found a severed power cord in an outdoor trash bin that sits between Alvarez's cabin and garage. We showed it to him, but he said he didn't put it there."

"Is the cord important?" Damon asked.

"We don't know yet. It was of the heavy-duty variety, so cutting it wasn't a simple task. We found both ends in the trash."

"Anyone could have put it in there," Damon said.

"Theoretically, yes. Alvarez said he emptied the bin into the park's main dumpster at six o'clock last night. The park stayed open until eight, so a visitor could've put it there but it's not likely. The cabin is set back in the woods and not near any of the trails."

"So that points right back to the park staff," Damon said.

"If the cord was used to kill Jeremiah, then yes. Margaret accused Emmanuel Alvarez of committing the murder."

"How did he react?"

"He has an easygoing temperament, so he took the accusation in stride. I was impressed at how well he kept his cool. To be honest, I think someone is trying to frame him."

"Makes sense," Damon said. "If the power cord was instrumental in the murder, Alvarez would be crazy to leave it right next to his cabin."

"I agree," Gerry said. He stood and stretched his legs. "I appreciate talking through these points with you, Damon. You have a keen sense for human nature."

"Thanks. What are your next steps?"

"We have Forensics scouring the shed with the empty basement. They're looking at the power cord now, too. And our finance expert spent this afternoon digging into Jeremiah Milk's accounts. Money is always a potential motive for murder."

"Anything unusual there?"

Rather than answering, Gerry said, "I know you didn't know Jeremiah well, Damon, but did he strike you as a man with considerable means?"

Damon reflected back to the poor condition of the Milk family home. "I don't think so. After he married, Jeremiah and Kathryn lived with his mother rather than getting a place of their own. He stayed there after his wife and son died and Dottie moved to Arizona. His house is at least sixty years old, and it isn't in very good condition. No, I didn't have the impression that he had much money."

Gerry scratched the underside of his chin and gave Damon a hard stare.

Damon took it in without comment. He could see that Gerry was debating his next move. Damon was prone to interference when it came to police investigations, but it was his stirring the pot that led Gerry to collar his first murderer.

Gerry sighed. "Don't make me regret this, Damon," he said. "According to Cameron Williams at True Capital Bank, Jeremiah Milk deposited $2 million into his savings account two-and-a-half years ago. One year later, he pulled out $1.6 million in a single transaction."

Damon whistled.

"When someone gets murdered and has that kind of money," Gerry said, "there's almost always a connection."

"What did he do with the $1.6 million?"

"We don't know yet."

"I wonder if his mother will be entitled to the remaining money now that Jeremiah's dead," Damon said.

"We'll check to see if he had a will or not, but I suspect the remaining money will go to Dottie either way."

"Did you ask Jeremiah's new girlfriend, Veronica, about the money?"

"In a roundabout way. I didn't let on that Jeremiah had $400,000 left in the bank or that he either spent or moved another $1.6 million. But I danced around the issue of his money in general."

Damon waited for more.

"She didn't think Jeremiah was well-off," Gerry said after a moment. "When they went out, it was to a chain restaurant or a diner. Either he kept her in the dark about his wealth, or she's a very good liar."

"It would be interesting to know whether Dottie Milk knows about it," Damon said. "It sounds like he came into the money after she moved from Hollydale."

"I plan to ask her tomorrow morning."

Chapter 5

Damon spent the following morning helping his mother prune the rosebushes abutting the steps to her townhouse.

"Terrible news about Jeremiah Milk," Lynne said as she snipped thorny stalks.

"I didn't realize word already made its way around town," Damon replied, collecting the refuse.

"You know how fast information travels around here. Have you spoken with Gerry about it?" Lynne Lassard-Brown knew how close Damon was with the detective.

"A little," Damon said sheepishly.

Mother and son looked up at the sound of a high pitched shrieking. Mrs. Chenworth's sizable girth was hurtling down the sidewalk after a mammoth yellow Labrador retriever at the end of a flimsy leash. "Help!" she shouted as the leash broke free from her hand.

Damon sprang forward and corralled the beast into a hug on the grass beside the sidewalk. The Labrador responded with a series of sandpaper licks to Damon's face. He scratched the dog's underbelly in return.

Mrs. Chenworth caught up and bent over panting. "Thank you, Damon," she said between breaths.

Before Damon could respond, Mrs. Chenworth caught a second wind and began to prattle. "It's my niece's dog. She lives in Alexandria and had the nerve to ask me to watch him while she's on vacation. In Greece! A twelve-day trip. It's only my first day with this creature. I don't know how I'm going to handle him if he jets off every time I try to walk him."

"There's the dog park on the ridge," Lynne said, joining them. "You could let him exercise there."

"I suppose," Mrs. Chenworth replied. "But I have to get him there first!"

"I can take him out a few times this week," Damon volunteered.

"That's very kind of you, Damon. Now, what's happening in your murder case?"

"My murder case?" Damon asked.

"I know how you like to get involved in these things. As well you should. You're the Hollydale citizens association president. And Jeremiah lived in Hollydale his whole life. It's only fitting that you solve the mystery."

Damon thought the police would have been the more obvious choice to catch a murderer. He let Mrs. Chenworth continue on the subject of Jeremiah Milk while he played with the Labrador.

"He completely closed himself off from the world after his wife and son died," she said. "But I suppose for the last couple of years he's been a little more social. Over the summer, I even saw him playing catch or some nonsense at the town's picnic area."

Damon looked up with interest. "Who was he playing with?"

"I don't know," Mrs. Chenworth said. "A boy—he looked like he was a teenager. But he's not from Hollydale. I know everyone here, and I'd never seen him before."

"What did he look like?" Damon asked.

"I don't recall. I was paying more attention to Jeremiah. I was surprised he could throw the ball so nicely given how short his fingers were."

Damon reattached the Labrador's leash and handed it to Mrs. Chenworth. After chattering for another five minutes, Mrs. Chenworth marched away with a much calmer pet.

* * *

Damon went home and washed up from the yard work, then walked a half mile to the True Capital Bank branch just outside of Hollydale. Gray clouds darkened the sky. Damon had a check to deposit. He was also determined to ask the bank manager, whom he'd known for more than two years, about Jeremiah Milk.

A wave of air conditioning cooled Damon's face as he entered the unremarkable bank building. Cynthia Trumbell stood at the end of a line that Damon joined. His citizens association vice president's brow was wrinkled—she looked anxious.

"Is everything all right, Cynthia?" Damon asked with concern.

She took in his relaxed posture. "I don't know, Damon," Cynthia said. "I think I witnessed a crime this morning, but I'm not certain." She pulled strands of unkempt hair from her face and bound them into a ponytail.

"What did you see?" Damon asked, his voice lowered to a whisper.

"I didn't sleep well last night, so I was up particularly early this morning. I saw a man poking around in the Rothsteins' trees. They live next door."

"Crepe myrtles?"

"Yes. How did you know?"

Damon outlined the story about mysterious tree infestations in Hollydale. "Could you see what the person was doing?" he asked.

"No. It was just before dawn. In the light from the streetlamp outside, I saw a man dressed in a black shirt and black pants with a knapsack near the crepe myrtles.

But his back was to me, so I couldn't make out what he was up to."

"Did you call the police?"

Cynthia blanched. "I didn't. By the time I thought about calling, he was gone. He wasn't there long, and I never saw his face."

"Too bad."

"I know. I spoke with Lydia Rothstein and told her what I saw."

"How did she react?"

"She was pretty terrified. Lydia said that her crepe myrtles have been dying, so there's probably a connection."

"I'm sure there is. I'll have a word with Gerry Sloman about it," Damon said. "He's a detective with the Arlington police. They may want to interview you and Lydia."

After parting with Cynthia and taking care of his deposits, Damon poked his head through the open door of the bank manager's office. Cameron Williams had lost weight since the last time Damon saw him. But he hadn't updated his wardrobe, and his suit hung about his shoulders like loose skin.

"Cameron, do you have a minute?" Damon asked.

The bank manager looked up from his computer monitor and gave Damon a toothy smile.

"Damon Lassard," Cameron said heartily. "To what do I owe the pleasure?"

Damon shut the door to the office and sat in the tight space in front of the manager's desk.

Cameron eyed him questioningly.

"I was down at Tripping Falls yesterday talking with Detective Sloman," Damon said.

"And you want to know about Jeremiah Milk's finances," Cameron interrupted. Damon's reputation as an amateur sleuth had travelled beyond the confines of Hollydale to the surrounding neighborhoods.

Damon held up his hands. "Gerry Sloman gave me the details last night," he said. "Two million dollars came in to Jeremiah and $1.6 million went out."

"If you already know the details, I don't know what else I can tell you, Damon."

"Did he have any strange spending habits?"

"Not at all. He had $400,000 left in his account but treated it as if he only had a couple of thousand. He didn't invest it. He spent about as much as he brought in from the park's direct deposit system. It was almost as if he'd forgotten it was there."

"Can you tell me where the $2 million came in from, or what he did with the $1.6 million?"

"Sorry Damon, that would be against bank policy. Even the police need a warrant for information that detailed. They're putting one together, and once a judge signs it, we'll be happy to help them out. They should have the information in a matter of days."

* * *

After lunch, Damon headed off to offer his condolences to Dottie Milk. Even though Damon had moved to Hollydale after Dottie left for Arizona, as the local citizens association president, he felt obligated. Of course, his insatiable curiosity also pushed him along.

Damon climbed a set of creaky wooden steps to the lifeless porch of the Milk house. With his right hand, he rapped lightly on the door. His left elbow cradled a turkey casserole from The Cookery—he didn't want to show up empty-handed.

The door swung open quickly, and a wide-eyed woman stared at him with a look of confusion. She wore a loose dress that resembled a hospital gown. But Damon knew she wasn't much older than sixty.

"Mrs. Milk? I'm Damon Lassard, with the Hollydale citizens association. I knew your son. I'm so sorry for your loss." He pushed the casserole toward her.

Dottie's eyes flashed with understanding. "Come in, young man." She moved at a pace that belied her appearance.

At Dottie's direction, he placed the casserole dish in the refrigerator beside an oversized head of lettuce that looked remarkably like the shape of Mrs. Chenworth's bulbous dome.

They moved to the living room. Damon settled into an easy chair near a dormant fireplace. A picture window dominated the room and provided ample light. Cheaply-framed replica maps lined the walls—Siberia, Antarctica, and the Canadian Arctic. Dottie Milk sat on a hard-backed chair that appeared to be part of a dining room set.

"Did you know Jeremiah well, Mr. Lassard?" Dottie asked. "He's never had many friends."

"Actually, I didn't, Mrs. Milk. I've been in Hollydale for less than three years." He crossed his legs.

"Well, it is nice to have a visitor. Most of my friends from the old days have left Hollydale. And after the morning I had with the police, I could use some better company."

Damon straightened up. "The police were hard on you?"

"The male detective, Mr. Sloman, wasn't. But the female lieutenant was merciless."

"Margaret Hobbes," Damon said.

"That's the one. I just lost my only child and she started grilling me about what I was doing two nights ago. How could she act like that? I live in Arizona for goodness' sake."

Margaret must know about the deaths of Jeremiah's wife and daughter, Damon thought. He spent several minutes placating Dottie Milk to gain her trust.

"Hearing that Jeremiah was murdered was so distressing," Dottie said.

"I can't imagine what you must be going through, Mrs. Milk."

"The only other time I had a shock like that was on the day Jeremiah was born." Dottie fixed her eyes squarely on Damon.

He noticed that she left out the night her daughter-in-law and grandson died.

"Obstetricians back then didn't have the fancy testing equipment they have now," Dottie continued. Her voice was melancholy. "I had no idea Jeremiah would be born with abnormalities. He had four surgeries before he was a month old. And another six by the time he turned sixteen."

"That must have been incredibly hard on you and your husband," Damon said.

"My poor husband never got to see Jeremiah," Dottie whimpered. "Roger was in the military. He died in a training exercise accident three months before Jeremiah was born."

Damon considered the woman facing him. She had lost her husband, daughter-in-law, grandson, and now her only child, each in a tragic event.

Dottie said, "Thankfully the government paid Jeremiah's medical expenses. But he had such a hard life growing up."

"Was it difficult for him to do the same things that other children did?" Damon asked with interest.

"Well, that part wasn't too bad. He learned to make do with the curveball God threw him." She crossed herself.

Damon nodded.

"I meant he was teased incessantly," Dottie said. "Kids can be downright mean."

Damon thought about his own childhood. A group of girls in his middle school had so badly bullied a girl who wore a back brace to treat her scoliosis that her parents transferred her to a private school.

"When Jeremiah was in kindergarten, the other children were curious," Dottie said. "Why were his fingers so short? Why didn't he have any fingernails? The questions bothered Jeremiah, but they were innocent. Jeremiah cried a few times, though I could still soothe him with a trip to Baskin Robbins. Then, around the time he started second grade, the other boys lost their inhibitions."

She coughed and inhaled several quick breaths. "Mr. Lassard, would you be a dear and get my asthma inhaler? It's next to the sink in the upstairs bathroom."

Damon bounded up the narrow flight of steps two at a time. He could see four closed doors from the landing. He tried the closest door first. It opened into a makeshift office stocked with a desk, a metal two-drawer filing cabinet, and more maps on the wall. The next door led to a bathroom, where Damon quickly located a yellow and white inhaler. He picked it up with a tissue and brought it downstairs.

Dottie greedily sucked in the elixir, and her breathing recovered.

"Thank you," Dottie said. "Where was I? Second grade. It started when one of the other boys tied Jeremiah's shoelaces together. The class was watching a film strip in the dark, and Jeremiah didn't see the boy crawl under his desk. When the film ended and the class raced outside for recess, Jeremiah tumbled to the floor. Every child in the room laughed at him." Dottie knitted her brow. "Dominic Freeze. A malicious little kid—he was the ringleader. After that day, Dominic and his group of little cronies made it their mission to torture my sweet baby. It wasn't just the pranks that got to Jeremiah. It was the name calling. They made up the most awful names, which I refuse to repeat to this day."

"That's terrible," Damon said.

Dottie went on, sniffling. "He came home in tears almost every day. Even the kids in class who didn't tease Jeremiah wouldn't befriend him—they were probably afraid they'd get ridiculed for consorting with him."

"How long did it last?"

"For three years. I implored Jeremiah to take up sports. He could play soccer well, and I thought that proving his athletic prowess would shut up those boys." Dottie Milk took another puff from the inhaler. "But that didn't fit Jeremiah's personality. He went in the exact opposite direction, Mr. Lassard—he holed up and became a hermit. Jeremiah didn't speak a word to anyone. He just stopped reacting to the teasing and became nonexistent. By the end of fourth grade, I think the novelty of making fun of him finally wore off."

"I suppose that affected his personality as he grew up," Damon said.

"It did, Mr. Lassard. He was emotionally scarred. I imagine he had suicidal thoughts as a teenager, though I never saw evidence of it. Jeremiah didn't have a single friend until he got a summer job outside of town when he turned sixteen. I suspect he never kissed a girl before he met his wife."

"I heard he had a new girlfriend at Tripping Falls."

"He mentioned that on the telephone a few weeks ago. Good for him. It takes a special woman to look past a physical imperfection and into the heart of a man."

After several more minutes of discussion, Dottie relayed that she didn't know of any friends her son had as an adult. "He had his fellow rangers at the park, but I believe they were colleagues rather than friends," Dottie said. She asked if Damon had met Jeremiah's girlfriend.

"I was at the park recently," he said, "but I didn't meet her."

"Even so, Mr. Lassard, would you do me a favor? Would you ask her to come and see me before the funeral? I'd like to meet this woman who was so good to my son."

Damon didn't hesitate. "I certainly will."

As he rose to take his leave, Damon asked, "Mrs. Milk, do you know anything about a large sum of money Jeremiah came into about two-and-a-half years ago?"

Dottie Milk looked straight into Damon's eyes and replied, "No. The police asked me the same thing. But I don't know anything about it."

Chapter 6

Damon stopped by The Cookery for a midday treat. He knew Rebecca's schedule well, and she would be cleaning up between classes.

He poked his head through the door and saw Rebecca bent in half. Her head was inserted fully into an industrial-sized oven.

Damon crept up beside her. "How's the weather in there?" he shouted.

Rebecca jumped and smacked her head on the oven's roof.

"You scared the daylights out of me," she said, pulling her torso laterally from the depths of the oven. She delicately touched the crown of her head.

"Sorry about that," Damon said.

"As if I wasn't scared enough sticking my head in there."

"I suppose as far as phobias go, that one's pretty reasonable."

Rebecca grinned. "I was going to buy a book on phobias." She waited a beat. "But I was afraid it wouldn't help me."

Damon laughed and gave her a friendly hug.

Rebecca pulled away after a moment and said, "When I saw you yesterday, I was so engrossed with Jeremiah Milk's death that I completely forgot to ask you about your date with Bethany."

Damon knew the subject was a sore one for Rebecca. "I'm going to be honest, it's a little weird to talk about it with you."

"No problem." She immersed her forearms into a suds-filled sink. "So did you take that casserole over to Dottie Milk?"

"I just came from there. Thanks again for the food."

"Did she look guilty?" Rebecca asked.

"Of being a serial murderer who picked off her family members one by one?" Damon set a towel next to the sink for Rebecca to use. "No, I changed my mind. I think she's just had a really tough life."

"Is anything else happening in Gerry's investigation?"

Damon held back the information Gerry and the bank manager had provided about Jeremiah's windfall. Despite raising it with Dottie, he suspected the information wasn't meant for a wider audience. Rather, he said, "Dottie asked me to speak with the teaching specialist at the park. She and Jeremiah had been dating, so I'm going over there now."

* * *

As Damon sped toward Tripping Falls State Park, he plugged in a hands-free device and dialed Bethany's number. He hadn't spoken with her since their date two days earlier.

Bethany greeted him pleasantly.

"Thanks again for going to the game with me the other day," Damon said.

"I had fun," Bethany said. "You have an ear to the ground in Hollydale, and it makes for a change of pace for me. I spend a lot of time talking about news and weather at the station."

"It turns out your instincts are pretty sharp," Damon said in an attempt at flattery. "Before daylight this morning, Cynthia Trumbell saw someone dressed in black messing around in her neighbor's crepe myrtles."

"No way! That's scary. Did she recognize him?"

"No, she didn't get a look at his face. But there's definitely something sinister happening. I'm planning to call Gerry Sloman with the county police and let him know. Maybe they can set a trap."

"How exciting," Bethany said with liveliness. "I wish I didn't have to leave town."

Damon's heart crashed. He slammed on the Saab's breaks, narrowly avoiding a minivan that had turned onto the road just in front of him.

"You're leaving?" he spluttered.

Bethany didn't pick up on his anguish over the phone. "Tomorrow morning. The station is sending me to Nebraska to do live coverage on the aftermath of yesterday's tornado. It's my first long distance assignment."

Damon breathed a sigh of relief then chastised himself for feeling respite when hundreds in the Great Plains had been devastated by a brutal twister. He wished her good luck, then said with apprehension, "Maybe we could go to dinner when you get back."

Bethany was silent. After a moment, she said, "Give me a call in a few days. I should be back in town by then."

It wasn't a resounding yes, but it wasn't a rejection either.

* * *

Tripping Falls had reopened to the public, although a handwritten note on the trail map marked Cherubim's Run as "closed until further notice." Damon stepped inside the visitor center. It was empty but for an older couple perusing the exhibit hall and the ranger named Milt. The thin and muscular ranger looked to be in his late-forties. He greeted Damon.

Damon introduced himself as Jeremiah Milk's neighbor.

"Just awful, that was," Milt said.

"Did you know him well?"

"He was here just about as long as I've been—ten years," Milt said. "I suppose I knew him well enough. He came to work almost every day, except for a little while after his wife and son died."

"That must have been terrible for him," Damon said.

"I suppose, but he never talked about it with me. I know it was hard on Veronica. She's the teaching specialist here. Veronica and Jeremiah's late wife were close."

The statement startled Damon. Jeremiah Milk's wife had been friends with his current girlfriend.

Milt Verblanc registered Damon's surprise. "Kathryn was the head educator here before Veronica," he explained. "Years ago, when we had better funding than we do now, Veronica was Kathyrn's assistant. Then, after Kathryn had the boy, she stopped working and Veronica took over the primary teaching role."

Damon filed the information in his memory bank. He needed to think through the implications, if there were any.

"I heard Jeremiah and Veronica recently started dating," Damon said.

Milt shrugged. "Alex and Aylin say the same thing, but I never noticed."

Damon told Milt that Jeremiah's mother had asked him to speak with Veronica. Milt authorized him to proceed and pointed to the set of doors leading to the management wing.

The door to Veronica Maldive's office was closed, but across the short hall, Damon noticed Alex Rancor in her office. She was busily pecking away at a keyboard. Sensing his presence in the hall, Alex looked up sharply. A determined face instantly transformed to a manufactured smile.

"You're Jeremiah's friend, right?" she asked.

"Yes, his neighbor," Damon replied and took a step into the frame of the open door.

Alex had abandoned the tight ponytail from earlier in the week in favor of neatly groomed hair tucked beneath a turquoise headband. The style took five years off of her already youthful face.

A framed photograph of Alex in blue dress uniform was mounted on the wall behind her desk. She stood beside an aircraft wing.

Alex caught his line of sight. "I was in the Air Force," she explained. "Can I help you with something?"

"I'm looking for Veronica Maldive. Jeremiah's mother asked me to speak with her."

"She should be in her office." Alex pointed to the door across the hall. "Just knock. She keeps the door closed when she's preparing lesson plans." Alex paused. "I saw you speaking with Detective Sloman yesterday," she said cautiously.

Damon stepped inside Alex's office. "We're friends, and I was hiking on Cherubim's Run the morning before Jeremiah was killed. He wanted to pick my brain."

"I remember you had worked up quite a sweat. Do you know whether the police are close to finding the murderer?"

Damon raised his eyebrows.

"I have some personal interest here," Alex offered and held up her hands in an innocent gesture. "The Park Police don't like me for some reason. Since I took the management position here three years ago, they've been looking for ways to make me look bad in front of the Board of Overseers—that's the group of heavy hitters that makes the major decisions for the park. If the murderer turns out to be one of the staffers here, the Park Police will try to shift the blame onto me. As if it could have been my fault. Other than Aylin, who I hired six months ago, every one of them was already here when I started."

"That hardly seems fair," Damon said. "Why don't they like you?"

"I have no idea," Alex said and looked away. "I think they're just surly."

Damon left Alex to her deskwork, crossed the short hall, and tapped lightly on Veronica's door.

"Come in," called a throaty voice.

Damon opened the heavy wooden door. Veronica Maldive was on her knees in front of a large whiteboard laid flat on the carpet. Papers covered the rest of the floor. From his standing position, Damon could see down her blouse. After a moment, he pulled his eyes away.

Veronica stood and adjusted a knee-length navy blue skirt. She was heavy but had curves in the right places.

Damon introduced himself as Jeremiah's neighbor. "I just came from speaking with his mother," he said.

"She must be devastated," Veronica replied. She invited Damon to sit while she wedged in behind her desk.

"Sorry for the mess," she continued. "I'm behind on prepping, and September's one of my busiest months." She explained her role as a jack-of-all-trades instructor for school and other groups that came to the park on field trips. "The rangers take the kids into the park and provide some special lessons. Especially Lawrence— he's our naturalist. Most of the instruction I provide is on the park's history and ecology."

"I have a favor to ask," Damon said, looking into Veronica's heavily-mascaraed eyes. "Jeremiah's mother, Dottie, would like you to visit her before the funeral. She's staying at Jeremiah's house."

"Of course, I will. Jeremiah must have told her that we had been dating."

"I believe he did." Damon decided against asking Veronica about her relationship with Jeremiah's late wife, Kathryn.

"Do you know when the funeral will be?" Veronica asked.

"I'm not sure," Damon said. "I don't know how long it'll be until the police release Jeremiah's body."

Veronica's expression saddened. "It was hard talking to the police. I didn't even know Jeremiah died until I arrived at work yesterday. The police were already swarming the visitor center."

"You hadn't gone out with Jeremiah the previous night?" Damon asked.

She gave him a questioning look. "No. Jeremiah had late duty on Saturday night, and I had that day off."

"I heard the police were questioning all of the park staff," Damon said. "Is there anyone you can think of who would want to hurt Jeremiah?"

Veronica took a deep breath and exhaled. "I've been thinking about that a lot. Jeremiah was very reserved. I don't know of any friends he had, let alone anyone who would want to harm him. Once you penetrated his shell, it was clear he was a wonderful man. Last winter, we had a holiday party. Jeremiah dressed up as a snowman. All night, he kept saying, 'Is it just me, or does it smell like carrots in here?'" She laughed.

"It was very endearing," Veronica continued. "I had never considered dating him until that night, then a few months later I asked him out." Her eyes took on a distant look.

Damon waited for more. After an awkward silence, he gathered himself to stand up.

"Hold on a minute, Mr. Lassard," Veronica blurted out. She took a moment to compose her thoughts.

"There's an outsider that I thought of this morning. I called and told Detective Sloman about him." Veronica opened her top desk drawer, removed a business card, and slid it across the desktop to Damon.

Damon examined the card. It was plain white with a phone number below four words: Marcus Pontfried, Private Investigator.

Veronica flattened her palms on the desk. "He came by the visitor center about nine months ago. It was during a morning that Jeremiah had off. Alex and the rest of the park staff were in the field, so I was filling in behind the rangers' desk in the lobby."

"Had you seen him before?"

"No. He looked like he had a pinch of Native American blood. But I might have just thought that because he had long dark hair. Who knows with a name like Pontfried."

"Did he want to see Jeremiah?"

"I don't think so," she said. "That's what made me suspicious. I'll tell you what I told Detective Sloman. Mr. Pontfried handed me his card, but instead of asking for Jeremiah, he started asking me questions about him. He wanted to know if Jeremiah was the same Jeremiah Milk who grew up in the Hollydale neighborhood of Arlington. I got a little scared."

"That's understandable," Damon said. He scratched his jaw. "Did you answer his question?"

"No. Mr. Pontfried came to the park before Jeremiah and I started dating, but I knew that he lived in Hollydale because I had been friends with Kathryn, his late wife. I asked Mr. Pontfried why he wanted to know. He said he was working for a client and couldn't provide me with any more information, then told me it would benefit Jeremiah if I could answer his questions. I'm not the smartest person in the world, but I knew that he was trying to pull one over on me. If finding out about Jeremiah's background would be so beneficial, why was the private investigator talking to me instead of him?"

"Is that what you said to Pontfried?" Damon asked.

"I wish I had that kind of chutzpah. I just said I didn't know the answer to his question. That frustrated Mr. Pontfried, but he plastered on a phony smile and began to talk about money. He asked me if I knew whether Jeremiah had made any million dollar transactions." She looked down at her pink-painted fingernails. "That question stumped me. I've been working here for seven years, and I've never seen any indication that Jeremiah had much money. He drove a Chevy that had over a hundred thousand miles on it, and he brought a sack lunch to work every day."

"And you told Marcus Pontfried as much," Damon said.

"I did. Before he left, Mr. Pontfried asked me if Jeremiah's fingers were malformed. I didn't see how I could deny that, so I told him they were."

Veronica pulled out a bottle of water from a desk drawer for herself and offered one to Damon. He declined and then asked whether she discussed the private investigator with Jeremiah.

"I had to. It's only natural."

She drank and wiped a trickle of water from her chin with a tissue. "Jeremiah took it in stride," Veronica said. "He laughed when I told him that Mr. Pontfried asked about million dollar transactions. Jeremiah said the private investigator must have been looking for a different person. I doubted that but didn't press the point. After I hung up with Detective Sloman this morning, I recalled a strange thing that Jeremiah said at the time. He asked me if Mr. Pontfried had inquired about anyone else. 'By name?' I asked. He said yes but wouldn't give me a particular name. He said he didn't have anyone specific in mind, though I suspect he did."

"That does seem strange," Damon agreed. "Have you seen Marcus Pontfried since then?"

"No. A couple of weeks after Mr. Pontfried's visit, I asked Jeremiah if he had heard from him. Jeremiah said he hadn't. I let it drop after that and didn't think about it again until now."

Veronica Maldive took a small sip of water, then shook her head. "I shouldn't fib," she said and looked at Damon with puppy-dog eyes. "I *have* thought about my conversation with Mr. Pontfried. And about the money. I'm not a gold digger, Mr. Lassard. The prospect of money had nothing to do with my dating Jeremiah. But I admit that I thought about it. I fantasized about marrying Jeremiah and him telling me on our wedding night that he was fabulously rich." She rubbed her eyes. "I snooped a bit. There's an office upstairs in his house. One day when he was picking up some take out food, I went up there and looked inside the desk drawers. I didn't see anything other than household bills. But there's a filing cabinet in the office, too. It was locked, so I wasn't able to look inside."

"It was a natural reaction," Damon reassured her.

"Thanks for letting me get that off of my chest, Mr. Lassard."

A few minutes later, Damon left Veronica to her class preparations. He walked away from Veronica's office convinced that Jeremiah Milk was hiding a massive secret from those who knew him—a secret that almost surely led to his last breath. And the involvement of a private investigator suggested that an outsider was involved. Perhaps the killer wasn't a fellow park employee after all.

Chapter 7

Before heading home from the park, Damon stole through the woods to Emmanuel Alvarez's stomping grounds. The cabin wasn't marked on the trail map, but Gerry had roughly described its location. Damon found it at the end of a narrow dirt path, nestled among towering oaks and unkempt brush. A sloped roof and stovepipe chimney highlighted the rustic log cabin—it looked as if it had grown in place from roots. The smell of cannabis was patent.

Once past the surrounding undergrowth, Damon faced a bare cement porch. To one side of the cabin sat a freestanding single-car garage. A waist-high metal trash bin stood between the structures—Damon assumed that was where the police found the severed power cord. He walked toward the garage's raised door, then paused and listened for signs of life. But for rustling that sounded like a small animal, the air was silent. Damon stepped in close to the edge of the garage and scanned its interior.

A mix of maintenance equipment and eclectic gear was scattered on the floor and on shelves lining the garage's three walls.

"See anything interesting?" a deep voice intoned with mirth.

Damon was so startled he nearly jumped. He turned to see a dark-skinned man in a ribbed gray undershirt and long jean shorts. Wrinkles lined his neck, and small red spots dotted the creases.

"I'm sorry.... I was just looking around," Damon stammered.

"And what are you looking for, young man?"

"I don't exactly know," Damon admitted. "Are you Emmanuel Alvarez?"

"I am."

Damon introduced himself as Jeremiah Milk's neighbor. "I heard the police found a severed power cord in the trash here."

"They did." He smiled widely, showing white teeth with sizable gaps between them. "It was mighty convenient for those pieces to be left right where I spend most of my time." Emmanuel pointed at the nearby trash bin.

Damon concurred. "It looks like someone was trying to point the police in your direction."

"On one hand, finding the cord there makes it look like an obvious frame-up," Emmanuel said. "On the other, the police could think I put it there on purpose to draw away suspicion—on account of the fact that only a moron would put it so close by." He paused. "Explain to me again why you're here."

Damon recounted his limited history with Jeremiah, and explained that Dottie Milk had asked him to come see Veronica.

"Okay," Emmanuel said, considering Damon with shrewd eyes. "That clarifies why you're at the park. So you heard about the power cord and decided to snoop around a little."

Damon blushed.

"Your curiosity is understandable. Do you want to hear my theory on how Jeremiah was murdered?" Emmanuel asked bluntly. "I plan to tell the police later today, but Lieutenant Hobbes has been pretty rough on me, so I haven't been in a hurry."

Damon said he'd love to hear the man's idea.

"First, let's grab a couple of beers. I have a fridge in the garage. I'd offer to share a joint with you, but I have to keep my wits about me. I'm sure after I relay my ideas to the police, they'll question me again."

Damon followed Emmanuel into the garage and accepted a cold can of Miller Lite. "Do you live here?" he asked.

"I don't technically live in the cabin, but one could if one needed to," Emmanuel said and winked at Damon.

Damon popped the top on his can and sipped foam. He leaned his shoulder against an interior wall of the garage. Emmanuel straddled a sawhorse, legs dangling.

"The police showed me the power cord pieces they found," Emmanuel said. "It was a heavy duty orange one I keep in this garage." He pointed to a series of hooks along the back wall. One in the middle jutted out, unadorned. "If the killer needed a power cord, and Jeremiah was murdered in the basement of the shed near Cherubim's Run, why take the cord from here?" Emmanuel asked rhetorically. "Other than a weak attempt to frame me."

"There are power cords kept closer to the shed?"

"Yes, in two other locations. The police found the severed cord in my trash bin, out here off of the beaten path, so I figure the killer knows park grounds well. If that's the case, he or she probably also knows that there are other power cords housed closer to the shed off of Cherubim's Run. That got me thinking."

Emmanuel drank half of his beer in a single gulp and continued without taking a breath. "I suspect the reason the murderer took the cord from my garage is because there are two other items he or she used that are kept here, and only here."

Damon surveyed the garage's interior.

"The first is the electric hedge trimmer," Emmanuel said. He pointed to an orange and black device with a blade that resembled the oblong snout of a saw shark. "I think the killer used it to blow the electricity on the first floor of the shed. Jeremiah would figure the light bulb in the lamp up there had gone out and go down to the basement where we keep spares."

"I heard that all of the gear from the basement had been stacked into a corner on the main floor," Damon said.

"Alex, our operations manager, told me the same thing. But Jeremiah wouldn't have seen the pile in the dark. He'd have felt his way down to the basement, where I believe the killer was waiting for him."

"So how do you short an electrical socket with a hedge trimmer?" Damon asked with curiosity.

Emmanuel smoothed the hair on the back of his knuckles. "You plug one end of a power cord into the wall socket and the other end into the electric trimmer. Then you power up the trimmer and slice straight through the cord. In an old shed, it would immediately fry the circuitry in the socket."

Damon nodded. "So Jeremiah enters at about ten o'clock to sign off on the daily chart and the lamp doesn't work. He unscrews the bulb and walks downstairs to look for a replacement. Not an easy task in the dark."

"That's true," Emmanuel agreed. "I tip my cap to Mr. Edison. If it wasn't for electricity, we'd all be watching television by candlelight." He guffawed.

Damon was too busy thinking for the joke to register. "Wouldn't Jeremiah be carrying a flashlight?"

"I doubt it," Emmanuel said, still laughing. "All of the places he checks have lights inside and the golf carts have headlights. I think Lawrence and Aylin use flashlights, but I've never seen Milt or Jeremiah with one."

The maintenance man certainly knows a lot about the rangers, Damon thought. "So Jeremiah walks down the basement steps in the dark," he recapped. "Then what?"

"Watch this," Emmanuel said and led Damon out of the garage. He directed Damon to stand ten feet back from group of oak trees. The elder man wheeled a menacing-looking machine from the garage. Its body was a two-and-a-half-foot box on wheels featuring a large motor and gas tank. It had an appendage that resembled a gun attached to the end of a long wand. Emmanuel connected one end of a hose to the machine's base and the other to a spigot on the side of the garage. He turned on the water. Then he flicked a switch on the machine, pressed the choke, and pulled violently on a long rip cord. The machine jumped to life with a tremendous roar. Emmanuel pointed the gun at one of the trees and pulled the trigger. A ferocious jet of water obliterated the oak's bark and tore into its pulp like a food processor puréeing summer squash.

Emmanuel released the throttle after fifteen seconds and the two men approached the oak's pummeled trunk. It had a gash two inches deep.

"My gosh," Damon said, staring at the tree's wound. He turned and looked at Emmanuel. "That's a pressure washer, right?"

"It is," Emmanuel said in a serious tone. "The police told me what Jeremiah's body looked like and that the basement of the shed was damp. I think a pressure washer was used to do the deed. The water would have gone down the drain." He lifted the machine's gun. "This one is gas powered. We use it for major jobs, like stripping paint and cleaning the asphalt in the parking lot. I ripped apart that oak tree using the medium setting."

"That could definitely kill a man. Could it break bones, too?"

"Easily," Emmanuel replied.

Damon paused. "You probably shouldn't have used it. The police will want to look at it."

"The killer didn't use this one," Emmanuel said confidently. "I let a buddy of mine borrow it a week ago, and he didn't return it until this morning. So it wasn't at the park when Jeremiah died. I think the killer used our electric pressure washer. It's in there now." Emmanuel nodded toward the garage but Damon couldn't see the machine from his position near the trees.

"That one's not quite as strong as the gas powered washer," the maintenance man said. "But it has more than enough juice to murder a man if the person wielding the water gun knew what he was doing."

"Electric," Damon said. "So it would have to be plugged in."

Emmanuel cut him off. "Alex told all of the staff here what she saw in the shed. Only the outlet on the main floor was fried, not the one in the basement. And the electric pressure washer has its own cord."

"But how could the killer have known both outlets wouldn't blow when he cut the power cord with the hedge trimmer?"

"I don't know. I don't have enough experience in circuitry. You could ask Milt Verblanc. He's a whiz with electronics. Builds his own robots."

Interesting, Damon thought. Was Emmanuel subtly suggesting that Milt Verblanc was the killer? And did Emmanuel really lack the requisite circuitry knowledge? He seemed fairly astute when describing how the killer could have shorted the outlet on the main floor of the shed.

* * *

Damon's head was swimming with information when he left Emmanuel Alvarez and made his way to the Tripping Falls parking lot. Emmanuel's theory about the instrument of murder made sense. A pressure washer could leave horrific marks and break bones, without charring skin. And it would account for Jeremiah's wet uniform and the damp basement.

Damon's mind wrinkled. If Emmanuel lived in the cabin, how could the killer have spirited away, and then brought back, the pressure washer, hedge trimmer, and power cord without Emmanuel's knowledge? Perhaps the maintenance man was involved in the crime somehow.

As Damon returned to his car, he noticed Gerry Sloman in the parking lot speaking with a pair of park rangers. One was a solid man with tree-trunk legs and powerful shoulders. A thick brown moustache lined his upper lip. The other was a wisp of a woman. She had green saucer eyes and straight blond hair with dark roots. Damon tentatively approached the trio. Gerry looked up.

"Hi, Damon," he said and introduced Lawrence Drake, the park's ranger who doubled as a naturalist, and Aylin Erul. Gerry asked Damon what he was doing back at Tripping Falls.

Damon stopped himself from blurting out that he hoped to speak with Gerry alone—to get the detective's thoughts on the private investigator, convey Emmanuel's theory of how the murder was committed, and discuss the man Cynthia had seen poking around her neighbor's crepe myrtles. Given the presence of the rangers, he instead said, "I paid Dottie Milk my respects this morning on behalf of Hollydale. She asked me to touch base with Veronica Maldive and arrange a meeting between the two of them prior to Jeremiah's funeral."

"Too bad for Veronica," Aylin said. "I think she liked Jeremiah a lot."

"Was he an affable person?" Gerry asked.

Aylin hesitated. "To be honest, I didn't know him very well. He was reserved. When we interacted, we only spoke about work. But he wasn't unpleasant."

Gerry turned and looked at Lawrence Drake.

The big man shrugged his massive shoulders. "He was okay," Lawrence grunted.

"What the hell is *he* doing here?" Margaret Hobbes thundered. She strode out of the visitor center and toward the group in the parking lot. Hobbes jabbed a finger in Damon's face. "You're not a police officer, Mr. Lassard," she shouted. "You interfered the last time I had a murder investigation, and it looks like you're up to your old tricks. If you want to help the police, enter the academy or join the Crime Solvers group." She turned to face Gerry and lowered her voice. "Detective Sloman, I know Mr. Lassard is your friend, but you are not to speak with him about this investigation. Do you understand me?"

Gerry nodded, and Margaret shooed Damon away.

* * *

A disappointed Damon left the park. Despite her gruffness, he knew that Margaret Hobbes was right. He wasn't a police officer.

Hobbes' suggestion to join the Arlington County Crime Solvers was a good one, Damon thought. It was a local non-profit group staffed by Arlington citizens who monitored an anonymous tip line for county crimes. They maintained a semi-formal relationship with the police.

Damon's duplex neighbor, David Einstaff, was smoking a cigarette on their shared front porch when he arrived home. It was just before five o'clock in the afternoon.

"Early day today?" Damon asked. David was an engineer in his fifties who had been fighting a bout of depression. Damon also suspected that the man had been drinking liberal quantities of whiskey since his divorce was finalized earlier in the year.

"Yes," he said. "I told my partners I had a personal matter to attend to, but I just needed to get out of there."

"Are you having problems at work?" Damon asked.

"There's nothing in particular. But I think I've had enough. I've been a wastewater engineer for thirty years. It might be time for a change."

Damon put a hand on the man's shoulder. "Have you considered talking to a professional about this depression you're having, David? Maybe a psychiatrist who could prescribe something? Don't make a drastic decision that you might regret later."

"I'll think about it, Damon. Thanks for looking out for me. Are you up for a drink?"

Damon wanted to eat a quiet dinner by himself and mull over the information on Jeremiah Milk he had learned during the day. But his neighbor was struggling, and Damon didn't think he had a support system. "I'm not in the mood for anything alcoholic," Damon said. "But I make a mean fruit smoothie. How about I whip up a couple?"

David agreed, and the two men spent the evening on the porch drinking strawberry-banana smoothies, eating Lebanese take out, and debating the prospects for the Redskins' football season.

Chapter 8

After lying awake during the overnight hours and thinking about Jeremiah Milk, Damon resolved to spend his Tuesday making two stops. First, he decided to join the Arlington County Crime Solvers. Second, he was determined to gather any information he could from the private investigator, Marcus Pontfried. He justified the latter stop to himself. Technically, Margaret Hobbes had only forbidden Gerry and Damon from discussing the murder with each other.

Before driving to the Crime Solvers' office near the southern border of Arlington, Damon dialed their anonymous tip line. He reported that a man wearing black had been seen fiddling with the Rothsteins' crepe myrtles in Hollydale the previous morning. Damon had promised Cynthia that he would alert Gerry Sloman. Providing an anonymous tip wasn't ideal, but the police would still receive the information.

The Arlington County Crime Solvers operated out of a single room on the first floor of a derelict two-story office building. Damon knocked gently on the door.

It was opened by a young man wearing a wrinkled T-shirt, cargo shorts, and flip flops. He introduced himself as Jessie and invited Damon inside. A box fan clicked steadily and blew hot air in the direction of a small metal desk.

"What can I do for you, sir?" Jessie asked and sat behind the desk.

There was no guest chair, so Damon remained standing. "Call me Damon. I'd like to volunteer with Crime Solvers."

"Great." Jessie's eyes passed around the windowless office. A CRT television stood atop a square of four inverted crates, and a stark white refrigerator rested in one corner. "This is it," he said. "Actually, the office is a new addition. Until three months ago, we operated remotely and calls were transferred to an on-duty volunteer. Arthur Jenkins is in charge of Crime Solvers in Arlington and owns this building. When the prior lease on this office expired and the tenant moved out, Arthur decided to start using it for the Crime Solvers team."

"Do all of the volunteers work from here?" Damon asked.

"No. We can still take calls remotely, but I like coming to the office. I'm taking criminal justice classes at Marymount, and I share an apartment with three other guys, so I come here to study. You're the first visitor I've ever had. Crime Solvers mans an anonymous line, so people call in their tips."

"So why have the office?"

"Arthur says it's so we can put a sign on the outside of the building for neighborhood publicity and to keep files, but that's not the real reason. Arthur wanted an excuse to get away from his wife a couple of nights a week. He comes here to watch television in peace."

"How often do calls come in?" Damon asked.

"Usually two or three times a day. I just took one fifteen minutes ago."

Damon looked away and hoped Jessie didn't recognize his voice.

The younger man didn't appear fazed. He said, "We take down the tip and pass it along to the police. Then we give the caller an identification number so he can call back a few weeks later to see if his tip led to an arrest. If it did, we issue a reward. A lot of the calls are bogus but some really work. I took a tip two months ago that led to the arrest of an armed robber who hit three restaurants in Shirlington."

"That's really cool," Damon said. He definitely wanted to give it a try. "How do I sign up?"

Jessie gave Damon Arthur Jenkins' e-mail address to schedule a training session. Arthur also coordinated shifts for the volunteers, most of whom worked two four-hour stints each week.

Damon walked away from the Crime Solvers office with a sense of excitement. The confines of the room might be dreary, but the prospect of taking his first anonymous tip thrilled him.

* * *

Before leaving that morning, Damon had looked up directions to the office of Marcus Pontfried, Private Investigator. He was based in York, Pennsylvania—one hundred miles north of Arlington. Damon made the trip in less than two hours.

York was blue collar to the bone. Old buildings shared worn down streets with dilapidated houses. A Harley-Davidson assembly plant supplied much needed lifeblood to the town that was the original home of the peppermint pattie.

Damon parked his Saab in a strip mall parking lot. Pontfried's address corresponded to an end unit adjacent to a nail salon. Its glass door was etched with the words, "Private Investigator. No Appointment Needed."

Damon stepped into a tidy lobby. It was empty. Neatly framed prints of Impressionist flora hung on the walls. Magazines rested on a low table surrounded by fabric-covered chairs. Coat and umbrella stands occupied one corner.

A young brunette poked her head through an interior window between an inside hallway and the lobby. Small frameless glasses balanced on a pinch of a nose. "Are you here to see Mr. Pontfried?" she asked Damon.

"I am," Damon replied. "I didn't call ahead, but I just drove up from outside of Washington, D.C. Is there any chance he's free?"

"He's eating lunch in his office right now, but let me see if he can spare a few minutes. What's your name?"

Damon supplied it, and the woman disappeared from view.

She came back less than a minute later and waved him inside. "Come this way." She wore a form-fitting pink blouse and flared black pants. Damon followed her down an empty hallway into a spacious office with deep pile carpet. A man in his late-forties with creases crossing his forehead looked up but didn't rise or extend a hand. His eyes were jet black slits and his mouth had an air of truculence. Dark hair was pulled back into a neat ponytail.

The brunette exited and shut the office door. Damon sat across from the man, who slowly wrapped foil around a half-eaten sandwich.

"Are you here to hire me?" he asked Damon without preface.

"No," Damon said with caution. "I'm trying to gather some information. A neighbor of mine was murdered. I believe you knew him."

"Are you a police officer, sir?" Marcus Pontfried asked with skepticism.

"No," Damon admitted. He took a breath. "I understand you were investigating a man named Jeremiah Milk less than a year ago. He's been killed."

Marcus Pontfried winced. "I know. I have an interview with a lieutenant from Arlington, Virginia, at noon tomorrow."

Damon gulped and recalled that Veronica Maldive had shown Gerry the private investigator's card.

Pontfried continued. "I can't help you and I won't be able to help the police, either. As a matter of procedure, I shred all paper files and permanently destroy all electronic records six months after I close a case." He narrowed his eyes to razor-thin lines. "And I have an absolutely terrible memory."

"But surely you can remember who hired you and why," Damon protested.

Pontfried emitted a biting laugh. "I wish I could," he said with derision and tapped his forehead. "But I can't recall a thing about it." The private investigator stood and pointed toward the door. Damon followed the cue and walked out, unsatisfied.

He headed straight to his Saab, resigned to making the long drive back to Hollydale. But as Damon approached the car, Pontfried's receptionist bolted out of the office's front door. With an outstretched hand, she motioned for him to stop, then walked briskly in his direction holding a finger to her lips.

She pointed wordlessly at the Saab's interior. Damon unlocked his vehicle and climbed into the driver's side. The receptionist scurried into the passenger's seat. She quickly introduced herself as Sheila Ranch and asked Damon to drive to the far side of the strip mall.

Damon followed her direction, parking in front of a 7-Eleven.

Sheila pushed her glasses up to the bridge of her nose. "I overheard you and Mr. Pontfried talking," she said.

She must have had her ear to the door, Damon thought. He waited for her to continue.

"It's true that we destroy all of the files, but of course he doesn't forget his clients or the work he performs for them." She gave Damon a captivating smile. "He charges three times the regular price in exchange for a convenient lack of memory," Sheila said. She lowered long-lashed eyelids and nibbled delicately on the nail of a forefinger.

Damon felt heat spreading to his ears. Sheila's perfume, redolent of jasmine, infused the air between them. He fought to recover his composure. "Have the police ever arrested him?" he asked.

"Mr. Pontfried?" Sheila laughed. "No. He's much too savvy for that. He went to law school and knows how to dance around legalities."

So why are you here? Damon wondered. As if reading his mind, Sheila said, "I have more scruples than my boss does. I heard you say that Jeremiah Milk was murdered. That's just awful. I don't know what Mr. Pontfried did for his client, but I remember the man who hired him to investigate Mr. Milk."

Damon almost jumped out of his seat. He leaned in close with eagerness. "Who was it?"

Sheila closed her eyes and tipped her head toward him, her lips only inches from Damon's neck. His arousal was conspicuous. Damon quickly placed a ball cap he kept on the dashboard in his lap before Sheila opened her eyes.

"I can tell you," Sheila purred, her eyes remaining shut. "But I need something from you."

"Anything," Damon heard himself replying.

"I remember the man's name and hometown. I'll let you have them for three hundred dollars." She opened her eyes and gave Damon a look of self-reproach. "This job pays next to nothing," she said quietly.

Damon was momentarily stunned into silence. He considered the proposition, then said, "Okay. I just need to find an ATM."

Sheila pointed to a bank across the street. Damon exited the Saab, still holding the cap. He dodged oncoming traffic on foot, and minutes later was back in the car with a pocketful of bills.

Damon handed the wad of cash to Shelia. She pushed up her glasses and pecked Damon on the cheek. "His name is Shin Ho-Pyong." She spelled it out. "He lives in Hanover. That's about twenty miles southwest of here."

Sheila folded the money into a pants pocket and held a finger to her lips. After a moment, she touched the same finger to Damon's lips and then rushed out of the car.

Damon digested the information. A man named Shin Ho-Pyong had hired a private investigator to find out if the Jeremiah Milk who worked at Tripping Falls as a ranger was the person by the same name who grew up in Hollydale.

Damon savored the lingering wafts of jasmine before they dissipated, then went into the 7-Eleven and asked a clerk for directions to Hanover.

* * *

It was close to two in the afternoon when Damon arrived in the small town. Hanover was dominated by a pair of massive snack food factories: Snyder's pretzels and Utz brand potato chips.

Damon stopped for lunch at a deli counter. The air smelled of salt. He ordered roast beef with mustard on rye and sat in a corner of the timeworn restaurant. Damon debated calling Gerry Sloman—he had vital information that the police might not otherwise obtain. On the other hand, Margaret Hobbes would blast Damon for interfering if she found out he had approached Marcus Pontfried. He decided to take a couple more steps on his own. But before proceeding, he called Rebecca and let her know he was in Hanover.

If Shin Ho-Pyong was a murderer, Damon wanted someone to know his whereabouts.

"What exactly are you doing there, Damon?" Rebecca asked.

"I'll tell you later. If you don't hear from me by tonight, tell Gerry Sloman where I am and to find Shin Ho-Pyong." He spelled the name.

"Damon, you're freaking me out. I'm calling Gerry now."

"No, Rebecca. You'll get me and Gerry in a heap of trouble. I'll be fine."

A frustrated Rebecca hemmed and hawed, then finally gave in.

Damon dialed directory assistance from his cell phone and obtained Shin Ho-Pyong's number. The deli was bustling, and the clamor of voices facilitated privacy. He sipped ice water then called the number.

"Hello." The voice on the other end of the line had a heavy Korean accent.

"Is this Shin Ho-Pyong?" Damon asked.

"No. This is his roommate. He's at work."

Damon thought quickly. "I owe him some money. Where does he work?"

"Who is this?" the roommate asked with suspicion.

Damon was caught off guard. "Just a friend of a friend."

"Hmm…" the man said. "He's at the barber shop." Click.

Damon's heart was pounding. Maybe he wasn't as good at detective work as he thought. He finished lunch and asked the man behind the deli counter if Hanover had a barber shop. There were two, but according to the counterman only one was operated by Koreans.

It was located a half mile from the deli, across a railroad track in a poor part of town. A sign marked "BARBER" hung from a post at the corner of the glass-fronted shop. Next door, a pub advertised itself as "The Pour Judgment." Damon cracked his knuckles nervously and stepped into the barber shop. Near the entrance, a young Korean woman was shaving the back of an elderly black man's neck. At the shop's rear, a man in his thirties and an aged woman were playing cards at a folding table.

Damon was in luck. The man at the back of the shop stood rather than the woman.

"Need a trim?" he asked. His Korean accent was faint.

Damon's thinning hair didn't need a cut. "I have an interview tomorrow," Damon said by way of explanation, "so I just need it cleaned up."

Damon was seated in an open chair. As the barber sculpted his meager locks, Damon internally debated whether to broach the subject of Jeremiah Milk. The man, who could be a murderer, was wielding sharp scissors inches from his jugular vein. There were others in the shop, but witnesses weren't much help for a dead man.

"Are you Shin Ho-Pyong?" Damon asked cautiously.

"I am," he said without hesitation. "You've heard of me?"

"A friend told me you give the best haircut in Hanover," Damon said. He didn't enjoy lying.

"Word of mouth is big in the haircutting business," the man said casually. "Who's your friend?"

Damon was stuck. Not only did he not relish lying, he wasn't very good at it. He made up a name. "Toby Flynn. He was just here one time on business at the pretzel factory."

The barber didn't respond. By the time he finished Damon's trim, the elderly customer had departed, and the two women were seated at the back of the shop, conversing in Korean.

Damon paid Shin Ho-Pyong, then summoned his courage. "Mr. Ho-Pyong, I'd like to ask you something."

The barber smiled. "Actually, Shin is my family name. Some Koreans westernize their names and reverse the order, but I haven't."

"Sorry, Mr. Shin," Damon said. "Can you tell me how you know Jeremiah Milk?"

A puzzled look crossed the barber's youthful face. He washed his hands and dried them on a towel. "Sorry, I don't know anyone by that name."

Damon tried again. "He lives in the Hollydale community of Arlington, Virginia. It's just west of Washington, D.C."

"Sorry," Shin said coolly. "I've never been to Virginia. You must have me mixed up with someone else."

Frustrated, Damon left the barber shop. He considered his options as he walked toward his car. An idea struck and Damon changed course and stepped into the pub next door to the barber shop. The Pour Judgment was dark and reeked of stale cigarettes. Smoking hadn't been banned in Pennsylvania establishments that served more alcohol than food. Damon ordered a Bass Ale from the bar and picked up a discarded crossword puzzle from a booth. He chose a stool at a tall table in front of the only window in the pub. From his position, Damon could see the street in front of the barber shop. He hoped Shin's shop didn't have a rear exit.

Damon spent the next three hours nursing his beer and eyeing the street. Just minutes after six o'clock, Shin and his two co-workers emerged from the barber shop. Damon waited until they passed the pub's window and then he stepped outside. The barber shop trio loaded into a tan Corolla. Damon jogged to his Saab and followed the Corolla at a reasonable distance. Shin and his colleagues stopped at an Asian grocery, then proceeded to an apartment complex on the periphery of town. Damon parked in the complex's lot and watched Shin and the two women enter a garden style apartment building.

Damon sat in his car with the windows down. The crisp evening air felt like aftershave against his cheeks. Shin would likely be home for the evening, he thought. Damon closed his eyes. He could sit in the parking lot all night, hoping the barber would emerge. But what did he expect to see—Shin Ho-Pyong loading a pressure washer into the trunk of his car? Even if he was the killer, the pressure washer was back in Emmanuel's garage. The more he thought about it, the more Damon felt he needed to know where Emmanuel Alvarez had been on the night of the murder. If he lived in the cabin and the instruments used in Jeremiah Milk's death had been temporarily pilfered from his garage, there were only three possibilities: Emmanuel was the killer, he was an incredibly deep sleeper, or he hadn't been in the cabin on the night of the murder.

Damon's eyes flew open as he heard the slam of his passenger's side door. He turned to see Shin Ho-Pyong brandishing a kitchen knife six inches from his face. The man had unlocked the door through the open window. Damon reflexively shrank back.

"Why are you following me?" Shin demanded.

Damon didn't know whether to scream for help or to try to jump out of the car. His seat belt was still latched. "I'm trying to find out who murdered Jeremiah Milk," Damon gasped. "Don't kill me. I'll do whatever you want."

A look of angered confusion came onto the Korean's face. "What the hell are you talking about? I told you this afternoon, I have no idea who Jeremiah Milk is." He pulled the knife back from Damon's face but kept it at the ready. "This knife is for *my* protection. I've never had anyone follow me home before."

Damon quickly considered the man's position. Damon, a stranger, had come into his shop asking bizarre questions and hours later followed Shin to his apartment. Damon had clearly not followed the Corolla surreptitiously enough. In the face of limited alternatives, he opted for honesty.

"Jeremiah Milk was murdered at Tripping Falls State Park in Virginia a few days ago," Damon spat out. When Shin didn't respond, he continued. "About nine months ago, a private investigator was looking for him."

"Is that what you are?" Shin asked, "A private eye?

"No," Damon clarified. "I live in Jeremiah's neighborhood, and I'm helping the police." *Without their knowledge*, Damon thought. "The private investigator's name is Marcus Pontfried. And I was told that you hired him."

Shin Ho-Pyong burst out laughing. The eruption startled and stupefied Damon. Was the man insane?

"Let me guess," Shin said after gathering his laughter under control. He laid the knife down in his lap. "Sheila Ranch?"

Damon blanched. "Yes. How did you know?"

Shin cackled. "She was my girlfriend. We broke up a month ago."

Damon's face still registered confusion.

Shin explained. "While we were dating, Sheila told me that she suckered people for money. Every few weeks, someone would show up in Pontfried's office looking for information. Pontfried's mouth is a vault, but his walls are thin. Sheila listens in on his conversations. When she hears Pontfried tell someone to go pound sand, sometimes she'll follow the person out of the office."

"This sounds familiar," Damon said.

Shin grinned. "She tells the person that she has vital information," he said. "Then she asks for cash and, in exchange, feeds the sap a phony name. After the person finds out that Sheila made up the name, most of the time, he or she just leaves well enough alone. A few times, Sheila said, the person demanded their money back. She would just say she had no idea what they were talking about. And the person she conned was stuck. It was her word against theirs."

"Someone could have told her boss," Damon said.

"I suppose, but Pontfried is intimidating. Once he tells a person to get lost, not too many people want to encounter him again." Shin shook his head. "Our break up last month was pretty bad. I guess rather than making up a name, she decided to mess with me."

Damon sat, speechless.

"Sorry for pulling a knife on you," Shin said. "And sorry Sheila screwed you."

Shin Ho-Pyong returned to his apartment building. Damon admonished himself for giving Sheila Ranch three hundred dollars. He felt relieved that he hadn't told Gerry Sloman about Shin. It would have wasted police resources to track down the false lead. He drove away from the apartment complex and parked in a motel lot. Damon punched Rebecca's number into his phone.

"I'm glad you're alive, Damon," she said after he recounted his afternoon's goose chase.

"Me too," he said. "I was scared to death when Shin was holding that knife in front of my face—I thought he was a murderer."

Rebecca was silent for a moment. "Any chance he is?" she asked.

"He just invented the story about the private investigator's receptionist as a jilted girlfriend?"

"You never know," Rebecca said.

"I suppose it's theoretically possible," Damon admitted. "But you should have seen him laugh when I mentioned Marcus Pontfried's name. It looked genuine to me. "

Chapter 9

Before driving home to Hollydale, Damon took a detour back to York. It was eight-fifteen in the evening when Damon passed into the town's city limits. Except for lights in the parking lot, the 7-Eleven, and a twenty-four hour Laundromat toward the far end, the strip mall housing Marcus Pontfried's office was dark. Damon parked, walked up to the office, and peered through the glass door. He couldn't see anything and didn't sense any movement inside.

He crept to the back side of the strip mall and was greeted by a desolate alley wide enough for a single vehicle. An overhead light illuminated a dumpster behind Pontfried's office. A pick-up schedule posted by the garbage company indicated that trash was collected every other day, including seven o'clock the following morning. Marcus Pontfried told Damon all of the Milk files had been destroyed months earlier. But had the private investigator taken a final sweep ahead of his upcoming meeting with Lieutenant Hobbes?

Damon looked around—seeing no one, he pushed the dumpster's sliding metal door backward and appraised the inside. Three neatly-tied black plastic garbage bags and two white ones were heaped on a scattering of loose trash. Damon crawled inside and tossed out all five bags. He retrieved his car and parked it in front of the dumpster to serve as a makeshift shield. If someone approached, they might see the car, but they wouldn't immediately know that Damon was digging through refuse.

Damon readied his nose and tore into the bags. The two white trash bags contained waste from the nearby nail salon. The black bags were from the private investigator's office. One was filled with food scraps, soda cans, and soiled tissues. The other two were stuffed with paper.

Damon spent an hour sifting. Most of the paper was shredded with crumpled balls and torn scraps mixed in.

Eureka! Halfway through the second bag, Damon found a handwritten reference to Jeremiah Milk on a ripped corner of a page of lined notebook paper. A curved arrow directed the name "Alistair Atwater" to "J. Milk." The symbols "$?" were positioned over the arrow. The note appeared to question whether money had flowed from Atwater to Milk. Was it the $2 million Jeremiah received two-and-a-half years earlier?

Damon racked his brain. The name Alistair Atwater sounded familiar but he couldn't place it. Damon could text with his phone, but the device lacked Internet access, so he wouldn't be able to look up Atwater until he returned home. Damon vowed to purchase a smart phone.

He spent another thirty minutes combing through the remaining debris but didn't find anything further of interest.

* * *

Bleary eyes clouded Damon's vision after an exhausting day. It was close to midnight when he turned the corner onto his street and noticed a miniscule flickering light on his porch. Damon parked the Saab at the curb, four houses from his own. He killed the car's lights and stared out into a darkness abated by a handful of streetlamps. Damon could distinguish a figure crouching in front of his door with a pen-sized flashlight. Was someone trying to break into his house?

Within seconds, the prowler straightened up and hastened down Damon's front steps to a sedan directly across the street from his duplex. In the glow from the streetlamps, Damon recognized the figure. It was Aylin Erul, the female ranger from Tripping Falls.

Aylin's car jerked away from the curb and disappeared into the night. Leaving his car in the street, Damon slowly approached his porch, eyes peeled. At the top step, he dropped to his knees and inched toward the base of the door. Nothing seemed amiss. Still kneeling, Damon unlocked his front door and pushed it open.

He missed it at first. Only after standing and flicking on the lights in the foyer did Damon spy the plain white envelope on the floor, just inside the door. Aylin must have slid it under. He opened the envelope's flap carefully, then removed and unfolded a sheet of white paper. It bore a single typewritten sentence: "Lawrence Drake is obsessed with Veronica Maldive."

Damon crawled into bed. His head was pounding. Drake was the ranger who doubled as the park's naturalist. Damon didn't know much about him—just that he appeared to be a strong man who spoke little. As a ranger, Drake would have known Jeremiah's schedule and—provided Emmanuel Alvarez was correct on the cause of death—where to locate the equipment that was used to kill him. *Obsession* is a strong word. If Lawrence Drake was infatuated with Jeremiah's girlfriend, he had to be considered a significant suspect. But if Drake was the murderer, how did Marcus Pontfried fit into the equation?

Damon's attention turned to Aylin. She had been present at the park the previous day when Margaret rebuffed him. So why would Aylin provide Damon, rather than the police, with information about Drake? And if she didn't feel comfortable notifying the police, why surreptitiously deliver the news to him by way of an anonymous letter?

* * *

Damon woke at seven o'clock on Wednesday morning. He resolved to call Gerry Sloman at nine o'clock sharp and tell him about Aylin's secret message. He had a training session with Arthur Jenkins from the Arlington County Crime Solvers later in the morning. A volunteer shift at the library rounded out Damon's plans for the day.

He brewed a pot of strong coffee and sat down at the kitchen table in front of his computer. Damon typed "Alistair Atwater" into Google and was deluged with hits.

Atwater was the chief executive officer of the largest commercial construction company in the Washington, D.C., metropolitan area. Photos showed a man in his seventies with a shock of white hair and an unassuming smile. He was cited scores of times in *The Washington Post* and had several quotes in *The Wall Street Journal*. That's why I recognized his name, Damon thought. Society pages coupled him with governors, senators, and a bevy of youthful fashion models. Forbes listed Atwater as the 375th richest person in America, with a net worth just topping $1 billion. He lived in Bethesda, Maryland, less than ten miles north of Hollydale. Atwater also kept residences in Manhattan, Palm Beach, and Cape Town, South Africa.

Damon tapped his fingers nervously against the table. Did this mogul pay Jeremiah Milk $2 million? Unless Jeremiah doubled as a closet hit man, Damon couldn't conceive of a reason for such a payout.

* * *

Damon popped into The Cookery as Rebecca was preparing for her morning classes. He filled her in on the latest details of his investigation into Jeremiah

Milk's death. And this time, he decided to clue her in to the vast sum of money Jeremiah had obtained and spent.

Rebecca knew Damon too well to ask why he felt so driven to pursue the matter on his own. It was a combination of his rampant curiosity and the absence of the typical pressures of a thirty-one-year-old man—like regular work or a family life.

Wearing thin plastic gloves, Rebecca partitioned allotments of lamb meat for a cassoulet her students would be making later in the day. "So, as I see it, you have six or seven suspects," she said. "There are six regular park employees. The manager Alex Rancor; three rangers—Milt Verblanc, Lawrence Drake, and Aylin Erul; Jeremiah's girlfriend Veronica; and the maintenance man. The seventh suspect is Jeremiah's mother. She's the dark horse, but you can't completely count her out. Even though you have some significant external factors, like the money and the private investigator, only those people would know Jeremiah's park schedule and where the pressure washer was kept—assuming that was the murder weapon."

"The two Park Police officers might know, too."

"True," Rebecca allowed as she pressed ground lamb into a glass measuring cup. "But for now, let's focus on the park workers. Go over the high points one more time for me."

"Sure," Damon said. "Veronica Maldive was dating Jeremiah and thought there was a chance he had a substantial amount of money. The police found a severed power cord in Emmanuel Alvarez's trash. Emmanuel suggested that Milt Verblanc might know how to blow the circuitry in the shed. And Lawrence Drake was obsessed with Veronica."

"I'd add that Alex Rancor said that the Park Police don't like her," Rebecca injected. "And Aylin slipping that letter under your door—that's pretty bizarre." She paused the conversation to scrub her hands in the sink.

When she turned off the water, Rebecca added, "I think you need to find out where Emmanuel Alvarez was on the night of the murder."

Damon nodded his head. "I had the same idea. All signs suggest that he lives in the cabin. It's hard to believe he's such a sound sleeper that someone could sneak into his garage, remove heavy equipment, and return it all without waking him."

"Are you planning to speak with Emmanuel again?" Rebecca asked.

"I'm not sure. I want to pursue it, but I don't want Margaret Hobbes to find out I'm discussing the murder with suspects. I *am* going to call Gerry and tell him about the note Aylin left for me last night. Margaret warned me not to speak with Gerry, but this could be a huge break for the police. Maybe while we're talking, I can ask Gerry if he knows where Emmanuel was on the night of the murder. And the police should have ample resources to track down a connection between Jeremiah Milk and Alistair Atwater, if there is one."

Damon punched Gerry's office number into his phone. It rang six times before it was picked up.

"Gerry?" Damon blurted out. "It's Damon. I know you're not supposed to talk to me about Jeremiah Milk...."

"Stop right there!" Margaret Hobbes' voice boomed through the receiver. "Mr. Lassard, this is Lieutenant Hobbes. Unless you are calling to confess to killing Jeremiah Milk, I don't want to hear from you again. Leave the detecting to real detectives." She hung up.

Damon was speechless.

Rebecca, who couldn't have missed hearing Margaret through the phone, held up her hands. "You tried, Damon. You know what they say: What goes around comes around. I'm sure Margaret Hobbes will be on the other end of a tongue-lashing herself someday soon."

Damon sighed. "You're right. My mother would say the 'Rule of Three' applies—whatever negative energy you dish out is returned to you threefold later in life."

"Is that a corollary to Cole's Law?" Rebecca asked with a straight face.

"What's Cole's Law?"

Rebecca smiled. "It's thinly sliced cabbage, silly."

Damon groaned. Thirty seconds later, he received a text message from Gerry. "Hobbes was in my office and saw your name on my phone. Sorry."

"Are you going to give up?" Rebecca asked skeptically.

"I'll stop trying to work with the police, but that doesn't mean I'm going to stop looking. I want to talk to Aylin. Any interest coming with me?"

"Damon," Rebecca cautioned, "What about Margaret Hobbes?"

"She'll be in York this afternoon. Pontfried said he was meeting with a lieutenant from Arlington at noon today. I have a training session with Arthur Jenkins at the Crime Solvers office in an hour." He briefed her on his latest volunteer activity. "After lunch, let's go to Tripping Falls and see what Aylin has to say for herself."

"I do have a break in classes between one and five. I suppose I could go with you."

"Great. I'll pick you up here at one o'clock."

* * *

Damon called Mrs. Stein at the Hollydale library and asked her to cover his afternoon shift. She readily agreed. The retired widow was happiest when tending to the routine duties of the local branch library.

At ten-thirty in the morning, Damon was back in the office of the Arlington County Crime Solvers. Arthur Jenkins was a neatly groomed man with a tight face. Growing up in Michigan, Damon had a neighbor who suffered from mild scleroderma, which caused natural stiffening of facial skin. Arthur's condition looked similar.

Damon listened intently as the Crime Solvers' coordinator explained the ins and outs of the tip line. Arthur had been the force behind the group for the past ten years and had helped the police catch a number of criminals.

Halfway through the training session, the Crime Solvers' telephone rang. Arthur adroitly handled a tip from a caller who had witnessed a recent home invasion in the western part of the county. Jenkins jotted down notes on the burglar's physical characteristics: approximate height, weight, skin color, hair color, and clothing description. He provided the caller with an identification code and asked the man to call back in two to three weeks. If the tip led the police to an arrest, the man could claim a five hundred dollar reward.

After Arthur contacted a county police employee designated to receive calls from Crime Solvers and passed along the tip information, he scheduled Damon for his first shift—that night from eight o'clock until midnight.

Chapter 10

At one-twenty in the afternoon, Damon and Rebecca walked into the Tripping Falls visitor center. Milt Verblanc manned the rangers' desk.

"You were here the other day to see Veronica," Milt observed when he saw Damon.

"I was," Damon said. "This time, I'm looking for Aylin Erul."

"It doesn't matter to me, but I heard you've been snooping around," Milt replied in a mechanical tone.

"Is that right?" Damon asked.

"Lawrence and Aylin heard the lieutenant yell at you the other day. Then Aylin looked you up on the Internet. She said you helped the police solve a murder a few months ago."

Damon blushed. Margaret Hobbes and Gerry had reaped the lion's share of credit for the collar. But Gerry, as an unnamed source, had praised Damon for his assistance in a couple of newspaper articles.

"I'm not snooping," Damon fibbed. "Aylin left me a message yesterday, and I just want to discuss it with her."

Milt shrugged his shoulders. "It doesn't bother me either way. I saw her ten minutes ago. She said she was meeting with someone from the grass cutting service out near the head of Craven's Pass."

The Craven's Pass hiking trail started near the falls' third overlook. Aylin was sitting cross-legged at a wooden picnic table examining paperwork on a clipboard. The area was otherwise desolate, save for a man walking to a nearby pickup loaded with lawn equipment.

The truck rattled away as Damon and Rebecca sat down across from Aylin. Damon introduced Rebecca. He hoped her presence would mollify the shock Damon was about to inflict. Aylin's unnatural blond hair was tucked under a brown kerchief, which matched her ranger's uniform. She looked at them nervously.

Damon cut right to the chase. "Aylin, I saw you on my porch last night."

She opened her mouth to protest, then closed it.

"You slipped a note under my door," Damon continued. "I came home late last night and saw you from my car."

Aylin's green eyes pierced Damon's. Then she lowered her gaze and came clean. "I thought I saw a car turn off its headlights. But I didn't do anything wrong. I just thought someone should know about Lawrence Drake."

"Why not tell the police?" Rebecca asked soothingly.

"I didn't want Lawrence to find out who revealed his fixation with Veronica. He's a strong man, and he has a mean streak. If I told the police, it would get back to Lawrence."

"You could have called in an anonymous tip," Damon said with Crime Solvers in mind.

"I didn't think of that," Aylin said softly. Damon thought she looked pretty, in a vulnerable way.

"So why Damon?" Rebecca asked.

"When I saw him two days ago, it looked like he knew Detective Sloman fairly well." Aylin focused on Damon. "I looked you up online. You've helped the police before. Even though the lieutenant asked you not to interfere, you were the only person I could think of to contact."

"Do all of the park staff know that Drake is in love with Veronica?" Damon asked, putting his elbows on the picnic table.

Aylin shook her head. "As far as I know, I'm the only one he told, and he doesn't act weird here at the park. I don't even think Veronica knows."

"Did Jeremiah Milk?" Damon asked.

"I doubt it," Aylin said. "About a month ago, Lawrence and I were on one of the trails clearing out a hornets' nest. I was trying to make conversation and mentioned a new lesson plan that Veronica was working on about gypsy moths indigenous to the park."

Aylin's irises gleamed under a radiant sun. "When I mentioned Veronica, Lawrence started gushing about how attractive she is and how nicely she treats him. I asked him why he hadn't asked her out before she started dating Jeremiah; they had been working together for years. He said he was too shy but that she kept him company at night in his attic. That freaked me out. 'Do you mean you have dreams about her?' I asked. He became flustered and changed the subject. But I got the impression that he had some sort of shrine to Veronica up there."

"But you didn't tell Veronica," Rebecca said.

"No way. This job is peaceful. I didn't want to stir things up. If I told Veronica, she would've told Jeremiah and caused an uneasiness between him and Lawrence."

Damon redirected his focus and asked Aylin about the other matter that was on his mind, as it was clear that the park staffers had spoken freely with each other about the investigation. "Do you know if the police spoke with Emmanuel Alvarez about some of the equipment in his garage?"

Aylin stretched her hands above her head. Rebecca kicked Damon in the calf as his eyes drifted to Aylin's breasts. He quickly pulled his gaze away.

"The pressure washer and hedge trimmer?" Aylin asked.

"Yes," Damon said.

"On Monday night, Emmanuel told the police his theory about how Jeremiah was killed. He said they brought him to the station in Arlington and interrogated him for two hours."

"He told me his thoughts on the subject, too," Damon said. "I'm not surprised the police grilled him. If those instruments were taken from Emmanuel's garage, anyone other than a very heavy sleeper would've noticed."

"Emmanuel didn't sleep in his cabin on Saturday night when Jeremiah was killed," Aylin said awkwardly. "He was with me. The police made me confirm his alibi."

Damon looked at Aylin in disbelief. What was a sixty-something-year-old maintenance man doing with an attractive young woman on a Saturday night?

Aylin registered Damon's stare and scolded him. "Don't be such a pig. I wasn't sleeping with him."

Rebecca jumped in. She had a knack for diffusing heated situations before they went too far. "Do you mind telling us what you and Mr. Alvarez were doing?" she asked.

Aylin turned to face Rebecca. "I don't mind at all. We were in Harrisonburg at my mother's house." Harrisonburg, Virginia, was a two-hour drive from Arlington.

The female ranger tapped a pen against her clipboard. "My mother has been having trouble with her kitchen sink. She doesn't have much money, and plumbers are expensive. While she was up here visiting me last month, she met Emmanuel. I could tell he took a liking to her. My mother's a fine looking woman and treats men well. The prospect of seeing her again coupled with a homemade dinner and breakfast in the morning, was enough for Emmanuel to come with me to Harrisonburg for a night."

"Emmanuel is a plumber?" Damon asked.

Aylin rolled her eyes. "He's the maintenance man for the whole park. He knows how to fix everything." She excused herself, explaining that she was scheduled to give a nature talk to the public.

"Well," Rebecca said when Aylin was out of earshot. "It looks like we're down from six suspects to four from the park staff. Unless Emmanuel or Aylin had an accomplice."

"I agree," Damon said and stood up from the picnic table. "But I still don't completely trust Aylin." He scratched behind his ear. "If she was scared of Lawrence Drake, I can understand her wanting to leave an anonymous note. But if she was the only person Lawrence told about his obsession with Veronica, Drake would know she was the source if anyone questioned him about it."

"True," Rebecca said. "Should we go find Lawrence Drake?"

Damon steadied his resolve. "Yes."

* * *

The lobby of the visitor center was empty but the doors to the management wing stood open. Down the short hall, Damon observed Lawrence Drake in the kitchenette of the rangers' lounge.

Damon and Rebecca approached him.

"Mr. Drake," Damon said. "We met a couple of days ago. I'm Damon Lassard. This is my friend, Rebecca."

"Okay," Drake said cautiously. The big man was holding a bowl of hot soup. "What do you want?"

"We were hoping to ask you a couple of questions about your colleagues here at the park," Damon said, standing just inside in the kitchenette's entryway.

Lawrence Drake set the soup on a small table and folded his arms across his chest.

"You're not the police. No way I'm talking to you. Why don't you shove off?" He sat down and picked up a spoon.

Damon held his hands up. "Sorry to bother you. But we'll have to tell the police about your obsession with Veronica Maldive." They were standing less than ten feet from the closed door of her office.

Drake looked up from his soup bowl and scowled. "What the hell are you talking about?"

Rebecca stepped forward. Damon admired her courage in the face of the angry man. "We understand that you were jealous of Jeremiah Milk. That you're in love with Veronica."

Lawrence Drake pounded a fist on the table and shot to his feet. Broth flowed over the side of his bowl. "In love with Veronica? That's bull. How dare you try to pin a murder on me? I don't want to see either of you in this park ever again."

Damon and Rebecca scampered out of the kitchenette and made a beeline for the parking lot. Seconds later, they were inside Damon's Saab, zipping away from the park and Lawrence Drake.

"Looks like we touched a major nerve," Damon said.

Rebecca agreed. "We probably shouldn't have been so direct." She paused, then asked, "So, now what?"

Damon thought for a minute. Finally, he said, "I'm going to drop you off at the police station. I can't talk to Gerry, but no one said anything about you." He glanced at her sideways. "Rebecca, you have to tell Gerry that Lawrence Drake may be in love with Veronica, and Aylin thinks he has a shrine to her in his attic."

"Lucky me," she sighed. "All right. I'll do it."

* * *

Fifteen minutes later, Damon left Rebecca at the Arlington County police station in the Courthouse neighborhood. "I'll wait for you at the pizza place on the corner," he said.

Damon ordered two slices with pepperoni and pineapple and a Mountain Dew, then sunk into a booth to wait. He was irritated, wanting to discuss the case with Gerry himself.

Damon felt certain one of the park employees had murdered Jeremiah. Dottie Milk wouldn't have known where to locate the hedge trimmer and pressure washer, so he crossed her off of his list. Emmanuel and Aylin had alibis, so that left Lawrence Drake, Alex, Veronica, and Milt Verblanc as potential killers. Unless Jeremiah had written a will leaving vast sums of money to his girlfriend, Damon couldn't see why Veronica would want to kill him. That whittled it down to Lawrence, Alex, and Milt. Unfortunately, Damon had no idea where any of them were on the night of the murder.

Damon considered the shed's electrical sockets. Emmanuel said that a person would have to possess a sophisticated knowledge of circuitry to know that slicing through a running power cord would blow the electricity on the main floor without affecting the basement socket. Milt Verblanc, who built robots as a hobby, might have that knowledge. Would Alex or Lawrence? Damon recalled the photograph in Alex Rancor's office. She had been in the Air Force, and Damon knew the military recruited engineers. If Alex was trained as an engineer, she might know a thing or two about electrical wiring.

After thirty minutes, Rebecca plodded into the pizza shop. She plopped into the booth across from Damon.

"You don't look too well," Damon said. "Let me get you a slice and a soda."

Damon retrieved a piece of mushroom pizza and a Diet Pepsi, then returned to the table. "What's wrong?" he asked.

"Gerry is upset," Rebecca said. She took a small bite of pizza and chewed slowly. "As you know, Margaret went to York to meet with Marcus Pontfried, so I was able to meet with Gerry alone in his office. I told him that Aylin tried to slip an anonymous note under your door but you saw her. When I relayed what the note said, Gerry was thrilled. He was grinning from ear to ear. I told him that's why you called this morning."

"That all sounds good," Damon said and sipped his soda.

"It was. I said we went to the park to ask Aylin about the note because Margaret wouldn't let you talk to the police. When I mentioned that Aylin thought Lawrence Drake had a shrine to Veronica in his attic, Gerry's eyes lit up. I think he was ready to hug me. Then I told him that we spoke with Lawrence about it."

Damon leaned forward. "Does he think we made a break in the case?"

"Just the opposite," Rebecca sulked. "Gerry thinks we ruined his chances of blowing it wide open."

Damon sat back and slumped down in the booth. "How so?"

"Gerry would've taken the information we received from Aylin and used it to get a search warrant for Lawrence Drake's attic. That way, the police could've sprung the warrant on Lawrence before he had the opportunity to clear the place out. They'll still get one, but Gerry's certain the attic will be empty by the time the police can legally inspect it."

Damon knocked his knuckles against his forehead. "I never thought of that. So Gerry's really mad?"

"He is. But more at Margaret than us. If she would've allowed him to speak with you this morning, the police could've questioned Aylin themselves and gotten a warrant before Lawrence knew what hit him."

Damon grumbled, and the amateur detectives ate in silence.

After he finished his pizza, Damon asked, "Did you happen to ask Gerry about Emmanuel's alibi?"

"I did," Rebecca said. "He said that Aylin's story checks out. Emmanuel and Aylin were in Harrisonburg on the night Jeremiah was murdered. Aylin's mother confirmed the story as did a cashier at a nearby gas station. They stopped to fill up before driving back to Tripping Falls."

Rebecca licked tomato sauce from her fingers. "Gerry also told me that Forensics is certain Jeremiah was killed in the basement of the shed off of Cherubim's Run by Emmanuel's electric pressure washer. And the power cord was severed by his hedge trimmer."

"So Emmanuel's theory on how Jeremiah was murdered was dead on," Damon said.

"Yes," Rebecca replied, "dead on is right."

Chapter 11

At eight o'clock in the evening, Damon installed himself at the Arlington County Crime Solvers' desk. Despite feeling exhausted, his fingers danced with excitement on a fresh pad of paper. He stared at the telephone and willed it to ring.

After an hour of absolute silence, Damon turned on the television but couldn't concentrate on any of the programming. His mind was fixed on an image of the corporate headquarters of Atwater Enterprises, which he and Rebecca had agreed to tackle the following morning.

During the third hour of his shift, Damon's thoughts veered to the crepe myrtle mystery. It had been several days since he'd checked in on the situation, so he logged onto the Hollydale community listserv. A flood of posts filled the online board. Insects were continuing to devour Hollydale's crepe myrtles despite the best efforts of home owners and lawn care companies.

Reading through the posts, Damon learned that affected citizens had organized their efforts to gather information. One local resident, Diana Sauerbrun, had gathered the names and addresses of the Hollydale residents who had posted on the subject and asked them a series of questions: Did the resident use a professional service to spray, or did they treat their trees themselves? For those who used professionals, which company was used? For those who did their own spraying, what product was employed? Diana also asked for the number of days between the date their crepe myrtles were sprayed and the date the insects returned. Finally, she asked for pictures of the pests.

Diana had collated responses from thirteen Hollydale residents and posted the results. The infestations had started almost three weeks earlier and were not limited to any particular geographic location in Hollydale. Of the thirteen homeowners, ten had used professional companies, and three had done their own spraying. Four different professional companies were used: two organic and two standard pesticide companies. The three store-bought products were all different. And the number of days between spraying and the infestation returning ranged anywhere from two to five days. It all amounted to a lot of information that didn't answer any questions. Interestingly, even the insects weren't the same. Diana collected photos from eight of the households. Comparing the pictures to images from various websites, Diana surmised that some crepe myrtles had Japanese beetles, others were infested with crepe myrtle aphids, and one person's trees appeared to be covered with a bug called the primrose flea beetle.

Damon shook his head in frustration. There didn't appear to be any rhyme or reason to the infestations. The only consistent point was that crepe myrtles were under attack.

Damon was relieved of his Crime Solvers duties at midnight by a night watchperson at a high-rise condominium who would have the tip line forwarded to her cell phone. Damon hadn't fielded a single call all night, except one from Arthur Jenkins to check in and ask if Damon could fill in for a sick volunteer the following night.

* * *

Damon wore his best coat and tie on Thursday morning. He picked up Rebecca, who was dressed in business formal attire, from her 1950s brick bungalow. They parked near a metro station in Arlington, then took mass transit into downtown Washington, D.C.

Atwater Enterprises dwelled in the heart of lobbyist country. A crush of suits and briefcases met Damon and Rebecca as they emerged from the metro's escalator. Weekday morning commuters plowed forward on the sidewalks along K Street, which itself was jammed with vehicles. The thoroughfare was flanked by office buildings gleaming in the bright morning sun. Newspaper dealers, food truck vendors, and panhandlers all claimed valuable square footage on the street corners.

The commercial property behemoth was headquartered in a twelve story building on K alongside Farragut Square. Rebecca and Damon strolled through the street-level revolving doors of the Atwater building. Employees waved identification badges in front of a scanner at a security booth and proceeded to a bank of elevators. The Hollydale residents walked with bravado toward a guard positioned behind the booth.

"We're here to see Pamela Reeves," Damon said. Reeves was Alistair Atwater's executive assistant. Rebecca had found her name on the Atwater Enterprises corporate website.

"Your names?" the bored security guard asked.

Damon provided their names. He wasn't sure what would happen next. The security guard's fingers clattered across his keyboard, and then he punched a number into his telephone. Damon and Rebecca listened to one side of a brief conversation.

"I have a Mr. Damon Lassard and a Ms. Rebecca Leeds here to see you, Ms. Reeves," the guard said into the receiver.

After a brief pause, he repeated, "Lassard and Leeds."

The guard looked at Damon. "Do you have an appointment?" he asked.

"No," Damon admitted, "but it's very important that we speak with Ms. Reeves. It concerns Mr. Atwater."

The security guard shrugged his shoulders and repeated Damon's plea word for word into the telephone. He listened for ten seconds, then hung up. "Sorry," the guard said. "You need an appointment."

"Can you give us Ms. Reeves' telephone number to set one up?" Damon asked. "I would have called it, but it's not available online."

"Sorry, sir," the security guard said. "I'm not permitted to give out the direct telephone numbers of any of the employees. But if you call the main corporate number, they can connect you."

Damon and Rebecca left the Atwater building and found a Starbucks on the same block.

"I suppose if anyone could get into the executive suite without an appointment, they'd have a lot of unwelcome visitors," Rebecca said over a cup of hazelnut coffee.

Damon conceded the point. "Do you want to call the corporate line, or should I?"

"Let me try," Rebecca said. She looked up the number on her iPhone, dialed, and asked the operator to connect her to Alistair Atwater. Damon smiled. She was going straight to the man at the top. Rebecca picked up her coffee cup and walked around the booth to sit beside Damon. She turned up the phone's volume and leaned toward his ear so he could hear both sides of the conversation.

"Alistair Atwater's office." The voice was female.

"Good morning, I'd like to make an appointment with Mr. Atwater," Rebecca said in a clipped tone.

"Who would like to meet with him?" The woman must have assumed Rebecca was someone's administrative assistant. No one important enough to see the CEO would set up his or her own appointment.

"Mr. Damon Lassard," Rebecca said without missing a beat.

"Who is he with?" The woman sounded skeptical.

"Arlington County," Rebecca improvised, but the confidence in her voice had waned.

There was a pause on the other end of the line. "This is Mr. Atwater's assistant, Pamela. Were you just at the security desk in our lobby?"

Rebecca breathed in deeply and renewed her vigor. "We were. Mr. Lassard and I really need to speak with Mr. Atwater. Someone he knows was murdered." Damon admired Rebecca's pluck.

After a moment's hesitation, Pamela Reeves asked, "Are you with the police?"

"No, we're neighbors of the deceased man."

"And what exactly was this man's connection to Mr. Atwater?"

"We don't know. But we have information suggesting that he and Mr. Atwater had a business relationship."

"I'll pass along your names to Mr. Atwater," Reeves said and requested Rebecca's telephone number. "He can decide if he wants to call you back."

Rebecca thanked the assistant.

Before hanging up, Pamela Reeves asked for the name of the murdered man.

"His name was Jeremiah Milk," Rebecca replied. "He lived in the Hollydale community of Arlington."

* * *

"Do you think he'll call?" Rebecca asked Damon as they passed through Bethesda, Maryland. The pair had returned to Hollydale on the metro to retrieve Damon's car, then promptly headed north to the upscale suburb. They wanted to take a look at Atwater's home.

"It probably depends on his relationship with Jeremiah," Damon said. "If Atwater paid Jeremiah two million dollars to do something illegal, I'm sure we won't hear from him. If their relationship was aboveboard, my guess is that he'll either call us back or contact the police."

Damon turned onto Atwater's street and drove slowly past the magnificently manicured lawns of houses spaced hundreds of yards apart. He pulled his Saab to the curb across from Alistair Atwater's estate. Unlike a majority of the neighboring homes, his drive wasn't barred by a gate.

The Victorian-style mansion was covered in ivy and dominated by cupolas and elaborate gables. Flower gardens in the large front yard were crafted to perfection. A governor's driveway circled in front of a veranda highlighted by intricately-carved columns.

"Should we see if anyone's home, or give him a few hours to call us?" Rebecca asked.

Damon tapped his thumbs on the steering wheel. "Let's give it a shot. I'm sure he's at work, but he could have a wife at home." After Damon spoke the words, he recalled the photos of Atwater with women much younger than him on the Society pages.

Damon parked the Saab in front of a five-car garage and the pair approached glass-inlaid double front doors. Damon rang the bell.

A uniformed housekeeper answered. Her dark hair was pulled into a severe bun.

Damon asked whether Mr. Atwater was home.

"Mr. Atwater is at work," the woman said with a slight German accent. "But Glenda, I mean the missus, is here."

Rebecca said they would love to see her.

The housekeeper left them on the doorstep.

"I didn't think he was married," Damon whispered to Rebecca and quickly described the newspaper pictures he had seen of the billionaire.

"His wife could be forty years younger than he is," Rebecca murmured.

Thirty seconds later, a gray-haired woman came to the door. She was dressed in loose, comfortable clothing but wore a stern expression. Large jewels dangled from her ears and wrists. "May I help you?" she asked stiffly.

"Good morning, Mrs. Atwater," Damon said. "We were hoping to speak with your husband about someone he knew who recently passed away."

The older woman smirked. "It's *Ms.* Atwater. You don't know Alistair well, do you?"

"Not at all," Damon admitted.

"If you did, you'd know he'd never have a wife as old as me. He prefers girls closer to her age." She grimaced and nodded toward Rebecca. "I'm his sister, Glenda."

"Perhaps you can help us," Rebecca said using her sweetest voice. "We live in Arlington. A neighbor of ours died recently, and we came across a document with Mr. Atwater's name on it."

"Who died?" Glenda asked.

"A man named Jeremiah Milk," Rebecca said.

Glenda Atwater put a hand to her mouth. "Oh my." Her tone softened considerably. "You two had better come inside."

※ ※ ※

They sat in a spacious living room adorned with Italian furniture and Persian rugs. The housekeeper brought in tea and chocolate chip scones.

"How did Jeremiah die?" Glenda asked after Damon and Rebecca formally introduced themselves.

Damon looked at Rebecca, then turned to Glenda
Atwater. "He was murdered. Someone killed him at the
state park where he worked."

"Goodness!" Glenda's face registered shock. "Who
would do such a terrible thing to such a good-hearted
man?"

"We don't know, ma'am," Damon said. "The police
are investigating."

Glenda Atwater reached for a cup of tea, then
changed her mind. She pulled a phone from her pants
pocket and punched a series of buttons. "Pamela?" she
said into the phone a moment later. "This is Glenda
Atwater. I need to speak with my brother immediately."
She waited a beat. "Get him out of the meeting. This is
important family business, and I need him at home right
away." Damon nibbled on a scone in silence.

After two minutes, Glenda said into the phone,
"Thank you, Pamela." She hung up and turned to
Damon and Rebecca, "Alistair will be home in thirty
minutes. This is terrible. Jeremiah was so very good to
our family."

Rebecca nudged her. "Ms. Atwater, would you mind
telling us how you knew Jeremiah?"

"Not at all, dear. Jeremiah Milk practically saved my
grandson's life." Glenda smiled warmly. "My late
husband and I had two children—a son, Adam, and my
daughter, Liliane. I kept the Atwater name and gave it
to my children as well—it goes a long way in the
circles we travel in. Adam's a free spirit and a world
traveler. He never settled down. But Liliane is more of
a homebody. She's married to a wonderful man,
Geoffrey Katz. They live nearby in Potomac. Geoffrey
is one of my brother's best executives. Alistair's
grooming him to take over Atwater Enterprises in a
couple of years." She picked up her tea cup. "Liliane
and Geoffrey have two children. Their oldest, Rachel, is

a well-adjusted young woman. She's in school at Dartmouth." Glenda dabbed at the corners of her mouth with a napkin.

"Liliane and Geoffrey's son, my only grandson, is named Matthew. He's fifteen now. He was born with...." She stopped and searched for the correct words. "Physical imperfections." Damon and Rebecca looked at each other. "You're aware of Jeremiah's condition?" Glenda asked.

Damon and Rebecca were seated next to each other on a divan. They nodded in unison at Glenda who sat opposite them in an armchair.

Glenda went on. "Matthew was born with amniotic band syndrome disfiguring each of his fingers and toes. Just like Jeremiah. Alistair loves my grandson very much—he never married and has no children of his own." She coughed. Damon interpreted the expression as disbelief that Alistair had never impregnated one of his young girlfriends. "So Alistair made damn well sure that Matthew had every advantage he could provide. My brother found the world's leading pediatric hand surgeon to perform the necessary medical procedures. He bought Geoffrey and Liliane a large home nearby so he and I could spend more time with Matthew." She explained that she'd lived with her brother, for the sake of companionship, since her husband had passed away.

"Alistair even tried to convince Geoffrey to give up working," Glenda said. "When Matthew was born, Geoffrey was a partner at a large accounting firm downtown. The hours were brutal. But Geoffrey thought having a layabout for a father would be a bad influence on the children. So he and Alistair compromised, and my brother gave Geoffrey an executive-level position with Atwater Enterprises. That way, Geoffrey could reduce his workload and take time off whenever he needed to."

Glenda crossed her legs. Her back was ramrod straight. "When Matthew began to walk, Alistair hired a physical therapist to work with the boy. I don't think he needed the help—Matthew's arms and legs have always worked just fine. But he did have to learn how to take on certain routine tasks with his fingers in ways that are different from the norm. For example, he can type on a computer keyboard, but he pecks with his middle fingers. There are, of course, a few things he can't do. He never could swing across monkey bars as a child— the bars were too thick for him to grip."

A tear started to drip from Glenda's eye. Despite her upright posture and strict deportment, she was a grandmother to a boy who had dealt with difficulties his entire life.

"Things were all right until he hit first grade," Glenda said. Damon recalled Dottie Milk reciting the problems Jeremiah had as an elementary school student.

Glenda Atwater described the teasing Matthew endured despite the best efforts of his teachers. "Alistair sent him to three different private schools," Glenda said. "But it didn't matter. Kids of that age will be kids. When Matthew was ten years old, before he started fifth grade, Alistair convinced Liliane to pull him out of school. My brother hired a team of teachers to homeschool him. Unfortunately, it didn't solve his emotional problems."

Glenda Atwater stood and retrieved a tissue box from a shelf. She brought it back to her chair and blew her nose gently. "Matthew went into a shell. He stopped speaking to everyone, including his parents and sister. Including Alistair. Including me." She started to cry.

Damon thought that other than the private teachers and physical therapist, Matthew's upbringing sounded eerily similar to Jeremiah's.

Rebecca walked over to Glenda, crouched down beside her chair, and put a soothing hand on her knee. Glenda Atwater grasped it firmly, then recovered.

"For the next year-and-a-half," she said, "Alistair hired a parade of specialists to see Matthew. He had psychologists, psychiatrists, and even a woman who claimed to be a 'mind-healer.' Nothing worked. Matthew would listen to his teachers and do his homework, but there was no other conversation between them. He spent all day, every day, in his bedroom. He'd order science fiction books online and have them mailed to the house. And he spent countless hours on his computer. Matthew didn't go outside, and after a while, he didn't even go downstairs for dinner."

Glenda thanked Rebecca for her comfort and said she could rejoin Damon on the divan. Rebecca crossed the room and sat down beside Damon.

"Then I met Jeremiah Milk," Glenda said. "It was almost three years ago to the day. I was at Tripping Falls State Park on a beautiful Saturday afternoon. I hadn't been there in years, but one of the charities I support was hosting a luncheon at the park's visitor center. Jeremiah gave a talk to our group about land conservation. I noticed his fingers right away. They looked similar to Matthew's. I had never met anyone else who had been born with the same deformities."

"So you spoke with Jeremiah?" Damon asked.

"Yes, after the question and answer period. I didn't ask about his fingers right away. Small talk first—I wanted to get a feel for him. He was naturally shy but pleasant. I asked him if he was married. Liliane and I were worried that Matthew would never have a girlfriend. Jeremiah said he had been married but his wife had passed away." Glenda cleared her throat. "The charity had a nice buffet for us. After lunch, when the crowd cleared, I found Jeremiah in the exhibit section of the visitor center. This time, I told him about Matthew. He seemed sympathetic, so I asked if he would come to Liliane's house to meet my grandson."

"And he accepted?" Damon asked.

"He did. He went to see Matthew the following morning. Liliane and I were in her kitchen having coffee when Jeremiah arrived. Liliane hadn't told Matthew he was coming. She directed Jeremiah to Matthew's room and left them alone. That first morning, Jeremiah spent almost three hours with Matthew. I have no idea what they talked about—neither Jeremiah nor Matthew ever told anyone. But Jeremiah came back two days later. For six months, he spent two or three mornings a week with Matthew, depending on his work schedule. And Matthew slowly came out of his shell. First, he started to have dinner with his family. Then, he began talking with his parents and sister. Two months after Jeremiah first visited, Matthew ventured out of the house and came here." Glenda looked around the room. "By the end of six months, Matthew was largely back to his old self—shy but not a zombie. He insisted on going back to school, and for the past two-and-a-half years, he's been doing reasonably well. He's not the captain of the football team, but he joined the math club, and he runs cross-country."

"It sounds like Jeremiah helped him a great deal," Rebecca said.

"He was a godsend. Once Matthew started back at school, Jeremiah's visits became less frequent. First, he scaled back to once a week, then twice a month. In the past year, they probably only saw each other seven or eight times. I believe Liliane even took Matthew to visit Jeremiah in Arlington once or twice."

Damon recalled Mrs. Chenworth's story about Jeremiah playing catch with a boy at Hollydale's picnic facility. It had probably been Matthew.

Damon shifted in his seat uncomfortably. "Ms. Atwater, thank you for being so open with us. It sounds as if Jeremiah helped not just Matthew but your whole family."

"Oh, he did." She smiled sadly. "I can't believe he was murdered."

Damon filled her in on the details that the police had made public. "If you wouldn't mind, Ms. Atwater, I'd like to ask you a question that's a little sensitive."

Glenda folded her hands in her lap. "Go ahead, Mr. Lassard."

"Did you or your brother give Jeremiah a large sum of money? Two million dollars, to be exact?"

Glenda Atwater smiled. "Alistair gave him the money. He was so grateful to Jeremiah."

Chapter 12

A door slammed. Seconds later, a thin man with white-tufted hair crossed into the living room. He waved away the housekeeper who had approached to ask if he wanted a drink.

"What's going on here?" Alistair Atwater asked his sister.

Glenda introduced Damon and Rebecca.

Alistair directed his attention at them. "Just after Glenda called, my assistant told me that you two tried to see me this morning." His voice was impatient but not unwelcoming. "Jeremiah Milk was murdered?"

"Yes, sir," Damon said meekly.

Glenda stepped in and recounted the conversation she'd been having with Damon and Rebecca.

Alistair Atwater tousled his hair with a wrinkled hand. "I'll have to tell Matthew."

"Oh my," Glenda said. "I hadn't even thought about that."

"He'll be devastated," Alistair said. "Milk wasn't a sociable man or even particularly interesting, but Matthew sure connected with him."

Alistair remained standing and tapped a foot against an expensive rug. "Have you spoken with the police, Mr. Lassard?"

Damon said that he had, but his knowledge of their activities to date was limited. "The police know that Jeremiah received two million dollars about two-and-a-half years ago. And that a year later he spent $1.6 million of it. Last I heard, the police were planning to get a warrant to find out where the money came from and went."

"Hmm…" Alistair mumbled as he sat down in an antique hard-backed chair. "I didn't know Jeremiah spent most of the money." After a moment's silence, he said, "It may take the police a while to figure out that it was me who gave him the $2 million."

"Why's that, Ali?" Glenda asked. "Didn't you set it up as a gift?"

"I did," Alistair said to his sister. "But I paid out the money through a subsidiary of Atwater Enterprises. Twice, my personal tax filings have been leaked to some of my competitors and the press. I didn't want the gift to become public for the sake of Matthew's privacy. So I set it up with a complicated structure. Don't worry, Glenda. Everything was perfectly legal."

"So what would the bank's records show?" Damon asked.

"Probably just the name of the subsidiary. But we closed down that company last year so it could take several days to piece it all together and get back to me. It doesn't matter. I'll call the police and tell them I was the source of Jeremiah's money. How did you happen to find out about me, Mr. Lassard?"

Damon told Alistair about Marcus Pontfried.

"A private investigator?" Alistair asked rhetorically. "Now that's curious. Why would someone hire a private eye to follow Jeremiah Milk?"

"I don't know," Damon said. "But I'd be surprised if it wasn't directly linked to the murder."

"I agree with you there," Alistair said. "This Pontfried fellow probably followed Jeremiah and watched him go to Liliane and Geoffrey's house. From there, he could guess that I was the source of Jeremiah's wealth." Alistair Atwater stood. "Let's call the police."

Damon provided the executive with Gerry's cell phone number. After a brief exchange with Gerry, Alistair hung up. "Detective Sloman is coming right over."

While they waited for Gerry, Alistair excused himself, relocating to his study to call Liliane. He'd tell Matthew in person later in the day. Glenda disappeared into the kitchen to provide the cook with instructions for lunch.

"Nice digs," Rebecca said, looking around, when she and Damon were alone.

"That's for sure. At least we know where Jeremiah's money came from. Too bad Alistair doesn't know how Jeremiah spent it. I wonder if Gerry has found out yet."

Thirty minutes later, Gerry arrived at the Atwater mansion. He eyed Damon and Rebecca, shaking his head with incredulity. Glenda invited the group into the informal dining room for Camembert sandwiches and pâté tartines.

Alistair provided Gerry with an abridged version of the history between Jeremiah Milk and the Atwater family, including the enormous financial gift Alistair bestowed on Jeremiah.

"Thanks for letting me know, Mr. Atwater," Gerry said. "We executed a warrant for Jeremiah's financial records, but we hadn't yet linked the payment to you. We would've tracked down your gift eventually, but it's always best to get information as soon as possible in a murder investigation."

"What else can I do?" Alistair asked.

"We'll want you to come down to the station in Arlington and provide a formal statement," Gerry said. "And if you could give us back-up documentation on the payment you made to Jeremiah, that would be fantastic. We'll keep everything strictly confidential."

"Consider it done," the commercial real estate billionaire said.

* * *

Damon and Rebecca left the Atwater home with Gerry. In the driveway, Gerry asked how they found the link between Jeremiah Milk and Alistair Atwater.

Damon relayed the chain of events, leading up to the search of Marcus Pontfried's dumpster.

Gerry didn't question Damon's visit to York. "Pontfried is crafty," he said. "He told Margaret that all of his investigation files on Jeremiah Milk had been destroyed, and he doesn't recall any part of the investigation or who hired him."

"Can you charge him with obstruction of justice?" Damon asked. "If he lies in front of a judge and says he doesn't remember anything, couldn't you get him on perjury?"

"Possibly, but Pontfried's not an amateur. He had an experienced attorney deflecting questions when Margaret met with him. If he sticks to his story, we don't have any evidence to contradict him."

"Yes you do," Rebecca said with excitement. "Damon, do you still have the scrap of paper? The police could match the handwriting to Marcus Pontfried's."

Damon blanched. "I accidently left it in the pocket of my pants when I washed them yesterday," he said sheepishly.

Gerry and Rebecca moaned in unison.

"Gerry," Damon said with uncertainty, "I know you're not supposed to discuss the case with me...."

"But you want to talk about it anyway," Gerry interrupted.

Damon kicked the ground near his car. "I just want to know if you found out from the bank records what happened to the $1.6 million a year-and-a-half ago."

Gerry didn't respond. He looked up. Damon followed his gaze. A faint midday moon graced the sky.

"You know Einstein developed a theory about space," Damon said. "It was about time, too."

Gerry laughed. "RDF Corporation," he said a minute later. "I can't tell you anything about the company because we don't have any additional information yet. All we know is that about a year after receiving two million dollars, Jeremiah wired $1.6 million to RDF. Our initial search revealed RDF as an empty corporate shell. We can't find any record of employees, property, or anything else."

"Wow," Damon said. "Too bad RDF is a dead end."

"It is so far, but we'll keep looking. And I think it goes without saying that this conversation never happened."

"Absolutely," Damon said, and Rebecca nodded in agreement.

"By the way," Gerry said. "We got a warrant to check Lawrence Drake's attic."

"Let me guess," Damon said. "It was empty."

Gerry's cell phone squawked. He unclipped it from his belt and peered at the screen. "Gotta run, sorry."

"The attic?" Damon asked as Gerry bolted toward his sedan. "Was it empty?"

The detective looked back. "Worse. His house doesn't have an attic."

* * *

During the drive back to Hollydale, Damon and Rebecca decided that either Lawrence Drake lied to Aylin when he divulged hints about having a shrine to Veronica, or Aylin had fibbed to Damon and Rebecca. Neither explanation made sense. If Drake was the murderer, why fabricate a story about an obsession with the victim's girlfriend a month before committing the crime? And what did Aylin have to gain by casting suspicion on Lawrence Drake? She had a rock-solid alibi for the night of the murder. Was she trying to save a colleague by diverting police attention to Lawrence? Or perhaps she knew Lawrence was the killer but had no proof, so she devised a falsehood to shift the focus onto him.

Damon dropped off Rebecca at The Cookery then spent two hours on the Internet looking for information on RDF Corporation. He came up empty.

That night, Damon returned to the Crime Solvers' office armed with a book to while away the hours. By ten o'clock, he was up to his wrists in Buffalo chicken sauce from delivered hot wings. The Crime Solvers' telephone shrilled.

Damon's heart raced. He quickly wiped greasy fingers on a napkin and snatched up the receiver. "This is the Arlington County Crime Solvers' Tip Line," he said with as much professionalism as he could muster.

There was a male voice on the other end of the line. "I have a name for you. Beauregard Snead."

"And what crime is this regarding?" Damon asked, as he wrote the name in his notepad.

The man was silent. Damon could hear rapid breathing.

Damon tried again. "Can you describe what you saw, sir?"

"Beauregard Snead," the man repeated and hung up.

Damon stared at the name on his notepad. He hadn't provided the caller with an identification number or asked him to call back in case the tip led to an arrest. The man hadn't given him the chance.

Damon connected with the Crime Solvers' liaison at the police station and described the call.

"We can't do anything unless the name is tied to a particular crime," said the officer.

"He wouldn't tell me what the crime was," Damon protested.

"Why don't you call him back and try again?"

"He didn't leave his number. Can't you at least talk to Beauregard Snead?"

"We're not authorized to do that, sir."

Damon ended the call, unsatisfied. Who was Beauregard Snead and what crime had he committed? Could he have killed Jeremiah Milk?

A quick Google search yielded a single hit. An online White Pages site provided Snead's address. Not only was the man from Arlington, but he lived in Hollydale. Yet, the name Beauregard Snead didn't ring a bell.

* * *

Damon walked to his mother's townhouse the following morning. He hadn't called ahead. Lynne Lassard-Brown answered the door in a fuzzy pink bathrobe and slippers. Her delicate gray hair was covered by a towel.

"Damon, what a pleasant surprise," she said. "Let me put some clothes on and dry my hair. Can you make coffee?"

Damon agreed and waited for his mother in her cluttered kitchen. The air smelled of silver polish.

Ten minutes later, Lynne sat at the kitchen table across from her son. He handed her a mug of hot coffee laced with milk.

"Thank you, Damon. What brings you by so early?"

Damon wrapped his hands around his mug. "I wanted to know if you know of someone named Beauregard Snead. He lives in Hollydale."

"Of course I know him. So do you."

Damon arched his eyebrows.

"No one calls him Beauregard," Lynne explained. "He works at the garden center in Oakdale. Everyone calls him Clementine."

Damon nodded with recognition. He knew Clementine as a certified master gardener. Almost everyone in Hollydale bought plants from him at The Garden Grove in neighboring Oakdale. Damon's mind immediately jumped to the crepe myrtle trees.

"He helped me pick out a few shrubs when I moved into the duplex," Damon said. "But I don't know much about him. Do you?"

"A little," she said. "Why the interest?"

"I suspect he may be the person responsible for the crepe myrtle infestation."

Lynne sipped her coffee. "That wouldn't surprise me. I probably should have thought of Clementine myself."

"Why's that?"

"Well, he knows more about plants and trees than almost anyone in the area. And he's always struck me as devious, though there's nothing in particular I could point to."

"My best guess," Damon said, "is that under the cover of night, he's repopulating destructive insects on Hollydale's crepe myrtles. Do you have any idea why he would do that?"

Lynne considered the question. "He doesn't own The Garden Grove, so I doubt he'd be doing it to drive sales. I suppose if he was a glory hound, he could be planning to swoop in and save the day with his gardening expertise."

"Maybe. Does he have a grudge against the citizens of Hollydale?"

"I've never heard anything like that," Lynne said. "You're certain he's the culprit?"

"I'm not positive." Damon refrained from revealing that he was acting on a tip that came into the Crime Solvers' line. He hadn't asked Arthur Jenkins, but surely there was a tacit prohibition against doing anything with a tip other than passing it along to the police.

After finishing his coffee, Damon kissed his mother goodbye and drove to The Garden Grove. He spotted Clementine in the spacious outdoor area helping a customer in the herb section.

Damon feigned interest in a row of emerald and golden Euonymus plants. He wondered how Clementine's moniker had originated. The man was in his late forties. His thin black hair was gelled and combed straight back over his scalp. Beady eyes rested in deep sockets above gaunt cheeks and a weasel-shaped nose. Damon left the garden center before Clementine had the opportunity to ask him if he needed assistance. Watching the man at work, Damon thought, wouldn't accomplish anything.

Chapter 13

After passing the early afternoon hours volunteering at the library, Damon decided to pay Dottie Milk another visit. The police had finally released Jeremiah's body, and his funeral was slated for the following morning. Dottie might be busy planning the details, but Damon wanted to ask her delicately about RDF Corporation.

"I'm sorry to bother you, Mrs. Milk," Damon said when Dottie opened the door to the Milk family home, "but I was hoping to ask you one more thing about your son."

"Come in, Mr. Lassard." Dottie didn't look as wild-eyed as the first time Damon had seen the woman. She was dressed plainly in slacks and a sweatshirt. Damon followed Dottie to the same living room he sat in days earlier.

"Thank you for speaking with Veronica," Dottie said. "She came over and we talked for almost two hours. It was so nice to have a conversation with someone who had feelings for Jeremiah. I think she and I are the only living souls who knew him more than casually."

Damon nodded but mentally added Glenda Atwater's grandson, Matthew, to the list of people who knew Jeremiah well.

"I'm glad Veronica came to visit," Damon said, sitting down.

"It really lifted my spirits. I was so distraught when I found out Jeremiah died. My friend Bernice in Phoenix had to drive me to the airport and physically walk me to the security line." Before sitting, Dottie asked, "Can I get you some tea?"

Damon declined. "How are the funeral arrangements coming along? Is there anything I can do to help?"

"Thank you for offering, but there's nothing that needs to be done. The funeral director is handling everything. There will be a short service at the funeral home before the burial, but I'm not having anything here at the house. I expect the gathering to be small. Veronica will come, and I suppose some of his colleagues from the park will feel obligated to attend. I have a sister who lives in Philadelphia; she's driving down. You've been so kind, Mr. Lassard. I'd be happy if you could come as well."

Feeling bad that attendance would be so sparse, Damon agreed. Besides, it would give him another chance to observe the park workers. And Damon thought self-indulgently, if Gerry went to the funeral, maybe he could ask him about alibis for those other than Emmanuel Alvarez and Aylin Erul. The previous day, Gerry had been called away from their conversation in the Atwaters' driveway before Damon had the chance to inquire.

"Now, what was it that you wanted to know?" Dottie asked, interrupting Damon's thoughts.

He leaned forward. "Have you ever heard of a company called RDF?"

She answered quickly. "I haven't, sorry."

"Jeremiah never mentioned it?"

Dottie shook her head.

"Okay, sorry to bother you. It's just that I think RDF could have something to do with Jeremiah's death."

Dottie cocked her head to one side. "How's that?"

"If you remember, when we met earlier this week, I asked you about Jeremiah coming into a substantial sum of money. It looks like he did. But then he turned around and passed the majority of it along to RDF Corporation. The problem is RDF doesn't appear to be anything except a corporate shell."

"That does sound strange," Dottie said and glanced around the room.

Damon had a premonition. He envisioned a secret stash of papers hidden in a safe behind one of the framed maps adorning the walls.

"You're welcome to look through the papers in his office," Dottie said. "The police have already been through them. They said they didn't find anything out of the ordinary."

"That would be great," Damon said. "Thank you."

Dottie excused herself. She said she had been planning to go to the grocery store and the pharmacy. But she gave Damon permission to cull through Jeremiah's papers while she was out.

* * *

After Dottie left, Damon gently lifted removed each of the maps from the living room walls—nothing but painted drywall. He quickly rehung them and then checked behind the framed pictures hanging throughout the rest of the house. No luck. Dottie had only given him permission to go through Jeremiah's office files but Damon first quickly searched the other rooms of the house. After striking out, Damon turned to the office.

He focused on the desk and filing cabinet, which was unlocked, presumably by the police. Damon methodically combed through the dead man's papers—credit card bills, property tax statements, and retirement account records. Nothing suggested that Jeremiah Milk had any money other than a moderate income from Tripping Falls State Park.

Damon spent another five minutes in vain, checking the rest of the room and every surface of the filing cabinet and desk for a secret compartment. If Jeremiah had a stash of papers detailing the comings and goings of the money he received from Alistair Atwater, they didn't appear to be in the man's home.

Damon wondered if Jeremiah kept files at Tripping Falls. The rangers didn't have offices, but Jeremiah could have hidden something in the rangers' lounge or in any of the other park buildings. For that matter, he could have buried a shoebox full of papers—finding it would be like looking for a needle in … eight hundred acres of parkland.

Before giving up, Damon took one last look around the room. Inside a closet hung a collection of old sport coats and dusty suits. Damon patted down the pockets of each. When Damon pressed against a houndstooth-patterned jacket crammed against the side wall of the closet, he felt something small and hard. His heartbeat quickened. He instinctively looked toward the door of the office. The house was still quiet.

Damon reached into the inside pocket of the jacket and pulled out a small box designed to store cufflinks. He was momentarily disappointed. Then he opened the box. Inside lay a small key and a yellow sticky note with an address and the number "47" written in pencil.

As Damon tucked the box and its contents into his pants pocket, he heard the home's front door open.

"Are you still here, Mr. Lassard?" called Dottie from downstairs.

"I was just finishing up," Damon replied and hopped down the steps.

"Find anything?"

Damon fudged the truth. "All of Jeremiah's financial paperwork looked pretty standard to me. Nothing unusual." He thanked Dottie for her graciousness, helped her lift two grocery sacks onto the kitchen counter, and made his way home on foot.

As he walked, Damon's mind raced. If the key opened a safe deposit box, Damon thought, he wouldn't be able to get inside. At a minimum, he'd need Jeremiah's driver's license. Most banks required a signature card as well. He neither had those items nor did he look anything like Jeremiah.

Back at his duplex, Damon punched the address from the sticky note into his computer. He smiled at the result. It matched the location of a fitness center in Frederick, Maryland—an hour's drive from Hollydale.

He contemplated whether to tell Gerry about the key. Did Margaret Hobbes' ban on discussion of the case between the two men still apply after Damon led the police to the source of Jeremiah Milk's wealth? It probably would in the lieutenant's mind. Recalling his misguided run-in with Shin Ho-Pyong, Damon decided to see what fruit the fitness center bore before disclosing his find to Gerry.

Damon glanced at the clock. Ten minutes after six. According to its website, the fitness center closed at seven o'clock on Friday evenings—not enough time to make it to Frederick. Damon would visit the gym after Jeremiah's funeral the following morning. It could wait—he had other detective work he wanted to do in the meantime.

* * *

At seven-thirty in the evening, darkness began to settle over Hollydale. An hour later, Damon pulled on black pants and a black zip-up fleece. He tucked a digital camera and sportsman binoculars into the fleece's pockets and drove to Beauregard "Clementine" Snead's house.

Clementine lived two blocks from the Fish Barrel, an unpretentious bar and grill along the primary commercial street in Hollydale. Bethany Krims' father, Jackson, owned the eatery. Clementine's home was a two-story, brick-fronted row house, positioned in the center of a strip of five identical residences. Damon parked his Saab on a street perpendicular to Clementine's block. From that vantage point, he had a clear view of Clementine's front door and the car parked in his driveway. Damon shut off his engine and waited.

It wasn't a well-executed stakeout. Given his proximity to the Fish Barrel on a Friday night, dozens of people parked on the nearby streets and took the sidewalk past Damon's car en route to and from the restaurant. Damon pretended to be sleeping when anyone passed by on foot.

At nine-thirty, Damon heard heavy footsteps coming down the sidewalk behind his car. He snapped his eyes shut. Fifteen seconds later, there was a rapping on his driver's side window. He cracked open an eye. Mrs. Chenworth's face was pressed against the glass. Damon instinctively jerked his head back.

"What are you doing in there, Damon?" she shouted.

Damon urgently put a finger to his lips. He tried to slide down the window. It didn't budge—the power was off. He cracked the driver's side door. "Shh!"

Mrs. Chenworth looked from side to side. She tried to whisper but sounded like a frog. "Who are you hiding from, Damon Lassard?"

"No one, Mrs. Chenworth. Just keep walking."

She looked at him through the gap in the car door. "Why are you wearing all black?" she croaked. Her hands were planted on considerable hips.

"I'll tell you later, Mrs. Chenworth, I promise. Please go."

The look of frustration on the gossipy woman's face was suddenly replaced by one of curiosity. Damon could see the figurative wheels in her brain churning.

She lowered her voice a decibel level. "Are you on a stakeout?"

Damon reflexively glanced in the direction of Clementine's row house. Light was visible through a front window, but Damon was too far away to see movement. "Mrs. Chenworth," he pleaded. "You still go to Cynthia's, right?" Damon knew she spent almost every morning at the salon, holding court.

Mrs. Chenworth nodded. Thick brown curls bobbed in front of her pudgy face. "Of course. You know I like to have coffee there with the ladies."

"Okay," Damon whispered. "I promise I'll come by soon and tell you exactly what I'm doing. But you have to go. Now. And don't tell anyone I'm here."

The older woman winked at Damon, then waddled off down the sidewalk.

Damon shut the car door and slumped down in his seat. He would have to ask Gerry for some tips on covert surveillance.

At eleven o'clock, the lights in Clementine's house went out. Damon waited but the man did not emerge. When Cynthia witnessed a shadowy figure meddling with crepe myrtles in her neighbor's yard, it had been just before dawn. Damon didn't know if he could stay awake that long. He longed for a caffeinated beverage. Instead, all he had was a center console full of hard candies pocketed from hostess stands across Arlington.

Damon spent the next two hours forcing his eyes open. Then, at one in the morning, he saw a figure emerge from Clementine's house. Street lights assisted Damon's vision. Beauregard "Clementine" Snead opened the trunk of his car and placed a duffel bag inside. The master gardener, dressed from head to toe in black, slid into the car and drove off slowly.

Damon let Clementine's car crawl two blocks ahead and then started the Saab's engine. Damon turned off his headlights to follow, careful to be less obvious than when he had trailed Shin Ho-Pyong.

Clementine drove less than half of a mile. He parked near a house with a pair of large crepe myrtles in the front yard. Given the late hour, Damon couldn't stop on the same street without looking conspicuous. He passed the house, turned the corner, and parked one block down. He crept through two backyards, then hid behind a nearby home's chimney. Peeking out, Damon could see Clementine Snead in the adjacent house's front yard.

Damon focused his binoculars on Clementine. The man was bent over in front of a crepe myrtle, reaching into his duffel bag. Damon expected to see him extract a canister of insects. But Clementine let him down. He pulled out a handheld mechanical instrument, flicked a switch, and held it against a leaf. It appeared as if he was taking a reading. Clementine jotted something down with a pen on a small notepad and took a second reading against a different leaf, then a third and a fourth. Damon longed to photograph Clementine, but he didn't want the flash to betray him. Instead, he turned off both the shutter sound and flash and surreptitiously snapped several pictures, even though he knew they would come out blurry.

After taking seven readings, Clementine moved to the yard's other crepe myrtle and repeated the process. Clementine examined an additional thirteen crepe myrtle trees in six other yards before returning home an hour later.

Exhausted and confounded by what he had observed, Damon drove to his duplex and dragged himself into bed.

Chapter 14

When Damon picked up Rebecca at nine-thirty on Saturday morning, a light drizzle was falling. Rebecca had accepted Damon's invitation to accompany him to Jeremiah Milk's funeral—she confessed that she was curious to see the other men and women he considered suspects.

Damon dressed in a black suit he inherited from his late father. Rebecca's outfit was drab but appropriate for a rainy-day funeral.

Jeremiah's body was laid to rest in an inexpensive, closed casket at the front of a large viewing room that was truncated by folding dividers. Damon could almost count the funeral attendees on his fingers. Other than himself, Rebecca, and the minister, the only other people in the room were Dottie Milk, the park employees apart from Emmanuel, Tripping Falls' two regular Park Police officers, Gerry, Margaret Hobbes, and a woman in her late sixties—presumably Dottie's sister.

Damon introduced Rebecca to Dottie who, after thanking her for coming, pointed them to a coffee urn. As they stood alone drinking bland java, Rebecca commented on the irony of serving coffee from an urn at a funeral home. Damon caught Gerry Sloman's eye and exchanged nods with the detective. With Margaret Hobbes at Gerry's side, Damon knew there would be no opportunity for them to speak with each other.

Instead, Damon and Rebecca made their way over to Veronica Maldive. Damon introduced Rebecca, who offered Veronica appropriate sympathies.

"Thank you for coming to the park the other day and asking me to see Dottie," Veronica said to Damon. Her face was plastered in heavy make-up. "She's a lovely woman."

"You're welcome," Damon replied.

"Dottie told me that you were at Jeremiah's house yesterday. She said you were looking for some records."

"That's true. Unfortunately, I didn't find any papers that were helpful."

"Were you able to get into the filing cabinet?" she whispered.

"Yes," Damon said. He lowered his voice. "It was open. I'm sure the police found the keys somewhere."

"What was inside? I don't mean to pry, but...." She trailed off, blushing.

Damon answered graciously. "Just run-of-the-mill files—credit cards bills, that sort of thing. Your boyfriend was a meticulous record keeper."

Veronica sighed. "I suppose Jeremiah never did come into money. It would've been nice for Dottie."

Damon paused, then said, "Jeremiah did have quite a windfall, Veronica." He provided a short narrative of his conversation with Glenda Atwater and then confided that Jeremiah had turned around and transferred the bulk of the money elsewhere.

"My goodness," she said. Veronica's eyes zoned out of focus for a moment. Damon imagined she was calculating the sum of Atwater money Jeremiah had left in his bank account.

"Veronica," Damon said sharply. "Did Jeremiah ever mention RDF Corporation to you?"

She snapped out of her reverie and thought for a full fifteen seconds. "No, I don't recognize that name at all. Is it important?"

"The police believe RDF is where Jeremiah transferred $1.6 million, but they can't find out anything about it. I was looking for records in Jeremiah's office that might shed some light on them."

"I wish I knew," she said and excused herself to meet with the minister, who was motioning to her.

"She seemed pretty interested in Jeremiah's money," Rebecca commented to Damon when they were alone.

"I suppose it's only natural," Damon said. "I know you're interested in meeting some of Jeremiah's other co-workers. Who else do you want to talk to?"

She leaned in close to Damon. "Even though I already met her, I want to speak with Aylin Erul and ask her about Lawrence Drake's non-existent attic."

Surveying the room to find Aylin, Damon's eyes met Drake's. The big man stared him down until Damon looked away. He shuddered, then spotted Aylin speaking with Alex Rancor, the park's operations manager.

Damon and Rebecca walked over to the pair of women. Alex greeted Damon pleasantly and introduced herself to Rebecca. Aylin was silent.

"With all of you here, who's running the park?" Damon asked.

"I asked Emmanuel to stay behind with a handful of our volunteers," Alex said. "And we didn't schedule any groups to come through this morning." She looked at the two U.S. Park Police officers. "If I knew they were coming, I might have stayed at the park, too."

After a minute of hackneyed conversation, Alex excused herself to use the restroom.

Damon looked at Aylin. She twitched nervously. "Why don't Alex and the Park Police get along?" Damon asked.

A look of relief passed over Aylin's face. She smiled. "Milt Verblanc told me they've been against each other since Alex started working at the park." She dropped her voice to a whisper. "Alex likes to smoke marijuana. She doesn't do it too often, but every once in a while you can smell it on her clothes. I think she smokes in the woods."

"And the Park Police are sticklers?" Damon asked.

"Oh, yes. They catch hikers smoking quite often and arrest them. They've smelled it on Alex but have never been able to catch her in the act."

"What about Emmanuel Alvarez?" Damon asked bluntly. "Doesn't he smoke pot as well?"

"Yes, but the Park Police love him. That's why they let him live in the cabin. Every so often, when one of the officers isn't up for doing the overnight patrol, they ask Emmanuel to fill in. He complies without complaint. In return, they leave him alone. Besides, Emmanuel doesn't represent the park in the same way as Alex. She and the rangers are the faces of Tripping Falls. So the Park Police feel she needs to have her head on straight at all times."

"Aylin," Rebecca cut in. "I heard some interesting news from the police."

Anxiety returned to the female ranger's face.

Rebecca continued. "We had to tell the police what you told us about Lawrence Drake. They checked his house. It doesn't have an attic."

"I know," Aylin admitted and cast her gaze to the floor. "The police told me the same thing. They even made me come down to the station to make a statement. Lawrence gave one, too. He hasn't spoken to me since."

Aylin wrapped her arms around her body. "I'm scared of him. I told Alex that I refuse to go into the woods alone with Lawrence. In fact, I started looking for a new job yesterday."

"So you didn't lie to us?" Rebecca asked directly.

"No," Aylin pleaded. "I just told you what he told me."

The minister announced that the service was starting. Aylin excused herself to find a seat.

Rebecca whispered to Damon, "I don't trust her. If she didn't have an alibi, I'd be on her like white on rice."

* * *

The service was brief. The minister spoke in generalities and was followed by Veronica and Dottie in turn. Both women had tears in their eyes when they spoke of Jeremiah.

All of the men present, including Damon, were asked to serve as pallbearers. Damon gripped a casket handle directly in front of Lawrence Drake. Damon could feel the man's breath on the back of his neck as they paced to a hearse. After they loaded the casket, a procession of cars drove three miles to a nondescript cemetery. Gray sky matched rows of small block headstones. At the gravesite, the mourners huddled under umbrellas to ward off misty rain. But a biting sideways wind made it impossible to stay dry.

Damon and Rebecca were standing beside Milt Verblanc when the burial proceedings ended.

"Such a sad day," Rebecca said to Milt as people began to disperse.

"Funerals are never fun," he said to Rebecca. Then Milt noticed Damon. "Still nosing around, I see."

"I'm here because Jeremiah's mother asked me to come," Damon retorted.

Milt held up a rain-soaked hand. "Sorry. If there's a killer roaming the park at night, I want the lowlife caught and hung before he comes after somebody else. And I could care less whether the police collar him or you do." Milt paused. "So let me give you my two cents."

Damon took a deep breath. "What are your thoughts?"

"I don't think he was killed by any of us," Milt said.

"By 'us,' you mean his colleagues at the park?"

"Correct. I heard the killer blew the light socket on the main floor of the shed but not the one in the basement. As a robotics junkie, I can say that slicing through a live power cord took a certain amount of panache and knowledge of the fundamentals of electricity. It's possible a person could figure it out by looking on the Internet, but it would take some planning and practice for a novice. Which means major premeditation." Milt cupped a hand over his mouth and blew hot air into it.

"The only person at the park who would have that kind of knowledge without conducting research is me," Verblanc said. "And I know that I didn't do it."

Damon was tempted to ask Milt about his alibi but held his tongue. He didn't want to set the man against him. Instead, Damon asked, "What about Alex? I know she was in the Air Force. Any chance she was an engineer?"

Milt's eyes sparked. "I hadn't thought of that. Alex has an electrical engineering degree." He paused. "But she told me she flew planes in the Air Force."

Milt stepped away from Damon and Rebecca, stating that he was due back at the park. Rebecca said to Damon, "Just because she told Milt she flew planes doesn't mean it's true. For all we know, she could have designed electrical systems for the Air Force."

"Or even if she did fly planes," Damon said, "with an electrical engineering degree, she could have easily figured out how to blow that socket."

"Let's get out of here. I'm cold, wet, and starting to get the creeps."

Only Dottie and Veronica remained. Damon and Rebecca offered last condolences and made their way to Damon's Saab.

Just as they climbed inside, a black limousine slowed to a stop behind them. Alistair and Glenda Atwater emerged, followed by a statuesque couple and a teenage boy.

Matthew Katz-Atwater was a sullen-faced youth with pock-marked cheeks and an expensive haircut. His hands were shoved into the pockets of a black trench coat that was designed for an adult.

Damon cranked on the engine of the Saab and activated the windshield wipers. He and Rebecca watched the Atwater clan ward off the rain with massive umbrellas. They approached Dottie and Veronica. Stiff handshakes were exchanged, and the younger woman, presumably Glenda's daughter Liliane, hugged Jeremiah's mother and girlfriend. Five minutes later, the group broke up. Dottie and Veronica went to a car on the opposite side of the burial site from Damon's Saab. The Atwaters walked back toward the waiting limousine. Glenda saw Damon and Rebecca through the Saab's windshield and motioned for them to join the family.

Damon turned off his car. He and Rebecca exited and climbed inside the limo. Hot air blasted from the vents. The pair sat near the rear door and Alistair Atwater made introductions.

"Please join us in a toast to Jeremiah Milk, Mr. Lassard and Ms. Leeds," Alistair said. He poured generous tumblers of scotch for the men, gin for the ladies, and sparkling juice for Matthew. Alistair raised his glass and praised Jeremiah Milk heartily. Matthew sat impassively while keeping his hands in his coat pockets. His drink remained untouched.

After perfunctory sips were taken, Rebecca faced Liliane and said, "This must be very difficult for your family."

"It is," Liliane replied. Her thin face was unnaturally tan and she wore a black pillbox hat with a pinned-back veil. "He helped Matthew and the rest of us through so much."

Damon watched Matthew as Rebecca and Liliane continued their small talk. The teen's facial expression didn't waiver, but Damon had the distinct impression that he was willing the ordeal to end.

At a pause, Geoffrey Katz said to no one in particular, "I still can't believe the man was murdered. He was so mellow. I can't imagine him upsetting someone so much that it would lead to his death."

Damon saw Matthew shiver.

"Who said he pissed someone off?" Alistair said to his son-in-law. "Maybe someone was after...." He cut himself short. Damon thought Alistair was going to say "after the money I gave him." Perhaps the family hadn't divulged to Matthew that they had compensated Jeremiah.

Damon took the silence as an opportunity to wish the family the best of luck, and then he and Rebecca escaped the suffocating heat of the limousine.

* * *

"What do you think of the younger set of Atwaters?" Damon asked Rebecca once they were driving back to Hollydale.

"Katz-Atwaters," Rebecca corrected. "They seem like they lost a family friend. Nothing remarkable."

"Not with Geoffrey and Liliane. Matthew struck me as a bit shell-shocked."

"Put yourself in his position," Rebecca said.

Damon acquiesced. "I suppose. But I wonder how much the kid knows about Jeremiah. They spent a lot of time together. It would be interesting to know whether the conversation ever veered from Matthew's problems to the details of Jeremiah's life."

"I hadn't thought of that," Rebecca said. Then she looked at him and her voice turned stern. "Damon Lassard, don't you dare talk to that boy. He needs time to grieve."

Damon colored. "I wish I knew whether Milt, Lawrence, and Alex had alibis," he said to change the topic.

"Veronica, too. But Jeremiah was killed at night. They could all just say they were asleep."

"True, but if I could cross one or two more names off of my list and just focus on a couple, it would be easier."

"Do you want me to call Gerry and ask him?" Rebecca asked.

"Do you think he'd come right out and tell you?"

"I don't know," Rebecca said. "Margaret hasn't banned him from speaking with me. And he knows you have a history of getting results. It's worth a try."

"All right, let's do it."

Rebecca invited Damon into her bungalow. Damon shook rainwater from his pants over a braided rug in the small foyer while Rebecca changed in her upstairs loft. Flowered 1980s wallpaper lined the entryway.

Minutes later, Rebecca bounded down the steps in a dry T-shirt and khaki shorts. Wet hair clung to her forehead. Rebecca tossed Damon a bundle of clothing—soccer shorts and a large sweatshirt. She microwaved hot chocolate while Damon changed in a downstairs bathroom.

Damon bundled his wet clothes into a plastic grocery bag, and the pair sat down at a rustic farmhouse table in the combination kitchen-dining room.

"Should I put it on speakerphone?" Rebecca asked.

"No, that's too obvious," Damon said. "I'll just listen in."

Rebecca dialed.

"Gerry Sloman here."

"Hi, Gerry. It's Rebecca Leeds. Are you alone?"

"Yes, I just left Margaret's office. Did you see something interesting at the funeral?"

"Not really," Rebecca said. "Alistair Atwater and his family came to the burial site just after you and Margaret left. But I wanted to ask you a question about the park employees."

"Rebecca, Margaret told me not to discuss the case with Damon, and I'm sure you're acting as a proxy for him. I told you both about RDF Corporation, but for my own sake, I really need to halt the flow of information."

Rebecca didn't respond directly to Gerry's comment. "Gerry, I just want to know about the alibis of the park workers. We know Emmanuel and Aylin were in Harrisonburg, but can anyone else be eliminated as a suspect?"

"So you and Damon can bother the rest of them like you harassed Lawrence Drake?" Gerry snipped.

Rebecca flinched from the barb. "I told you I was sorry about that, Gerry."

The phone was silent for several seconds. Then Gerry said, "I'll tell you what little I know about their alibis if you and Damon promise not to speak with the park employees anymore."

Rebecca looked at Damon who nodded. "Deal," Rebecca said.

"Please keep your word, Rebecca," Gerry said. "We questioned all of the park staff about where they were last Saturday after nine o'clock in the evening. Alex Rancor went with a group of friends to a late dinner and then to a dance club in downtown D.C. She was with them from eight-thirty until one o'clock in the morning. Then she took a taxi home and went to bed. We couldn't find the cab driver but we have statements from her friends, a restaurant waiter, and a bartender at the club. So she didn't pull the trigger on the pressure washer. None of the others have an alibi. Drake, Verblanc, and Veronica Maldive all said they were home alone, either watching television or reading before going to bed."

"How about the two Park Police officers?" Rebecca asked.

"We didn't come right out and ask them for alibis. It's too sensitive. But they both have stellar work records and no criminal history. It doesn't eliminate them, but our focus remains on the staff."

"I hadn't thought about criminal history. Do any of the park employees have a record?"

"A few years ago, Alex was arrested for smoking marijuana at a concert pavilion. But that's all we found on any of them."

Rebecca pressed on. "Did one of the Park Police officers do an overnight patrol last Saturday?"

"I thought you were only going to ask me one question," Gerry groaned. "Yes. Davida Harkins conducted her standard sweep at two o'clock in the morning. She didn't see anything, but she only checks the parking lot and visitor center. The medical examiner placed the time of death between ten o'clock at night and one in the morning—before Davida came to the park to make her rounds."

"Thanks, Gerry. I know you're going out of your way here," Rebecca said.

"Just keep your word that you and Damon won't question the park staff anymore."

Chapter 15

On his way home, Damon called Bethany. He hadn't spoken to her in almost a week and was excited to tell her about Clementine Snead.

Bethany answered on the second ring. She'd arrived back in Hollydale the previous day from her trip to tornado-ravished Nebraska and was anxious to hear Damon's update on the crepe myrtle saga. She invited him to her condominium for lunch. Damon decided his visit to the fitness center in Frederick could wait for a couple of hours.

Bethany lived in a twenty-story high-rise. A marble front desk and indoor waterfall highlighted the building's lavish lobby. Condominiums on the top floors had a distant view of the National Cathedral in Washington, D.C.

Bethany's fourth floor unit was tastefully decorated with cream-colored furniture and glass tables. After Damon shed his rain slicker, she invited him to sit on a three-seat sofa that balanced on sleek spindled legs in an open area that served as both living and dining rooms. She brought him a Snapple and settled into a loveseat. Between them stood a coffee table adorned with books on Italian architecture.

Damon told Bethany about the anonymous tip in general terms and recounted his exploits of following Clementine Snead the previous evening. "I'm busy this afternoon," Damon said, "but I'm planning to confront Clementine as soon as I have the chance. So please don't tell anyone in the meantime."

Bethany's brown eyes radiated with luster. She looked breathtaking, as usual. Her chestnut hair was a shade redder than when Damon last saw her, and she wore a fetching open-necked blouse coupled with a chiffon pleated skirt. "I can't believe you found the culprit," Bethany said. "What do you think he's doing?"

"I haven't figured that out yet," Damon admitted. "But I'll do my best to ferret it out of him."

"This is so exciting. Have you thought about joining the police, Damon?" She leaned forward and looked deep into his eyes.

Damon's insides tingled. Was she flirting with him? He couldn't tell.

"I've considered going to the police training academy," Damon said after a moment. The thought had been on his mind. "Speaking of crimes, have you heard about Jeremiah Milk?"

"A little," Bethany said. "Tell me about it over lunch."

As Bethany brought a mayonnaise-free Waldorf salad and turkey-with-pesto sandwiches from the kitchen, Damon moved to the dining table and asked her about Nebraska.

"It was so sad, Damon," she said. "Seven people died and almost a hundred homes were destroyed. I spoke with a lot of the residents. Most were strong and ready to rebuild their lives, but some were completely dejected. I can't blame them."

"I'm sorry to hear it," Damon said. "But it was a good assignment for your career, right?"

"Absolutely," she replied, setting down a pitcher of iced tea. "But I didn't relish the feeling of making personal gains when everyone around me had lost so much. My father told me to look at it objectively. If the station hadn't sent me to cover the story, the people in Nebraska would be no better off and another weatherperson would have reported on the horrific event. He's right, I know. But it was still gut-wrenching."

Until that moment, Damon hadn't realized just how compassionate Bethany was. She often came off to others as cool, but perhaps that persona didn't reflect her true nature.

The food was excellent, and Damon complimented Bethany on it. Then he told her he'd been investigating Jeremiah Milk's murder, and provided a synopsis, limiting the narrative to information available to the public.

"What happened to Jeremiah is awful," Bethany said. "But it's exciting that you're delving into it—maybe the police force is the right place for you."

"Did you know Jeremiah?" Damon asked.

"I could pick him out of a crowd," Bethany said. "But I never had any interaction with him directly. Only through my father." Damon recalled that Jackson Krims had been the person who introduced him to Jeremiah.

"How did your father know him?"

"Just by living in Hollydale, I think. Both of our families have been here for a long time. But Jeremiah was several years older than me, so he and I didn't overlap in school."

Bethany paused. She chewed a forkful of salad. Lines of concentration appeared on her brow.

"What's on your mind?" Damon asked.

"I just remembered a strange incident my father told me about years ago. It was at one of his Exxon stations." In addition to the Fish Barrel, Jackson Krims owned a handful of other properties in Hollydale, including several gas stations.

"Dad had just finished going through some paperwork with one of his suppliers," Bethany said. "After the supplier drove off, Dad realized they had missed a document that both men needed to sign. It was just a standard form that had to be filed with the state. He and the supplier signed them all of the time. But the form was due by the end of the day." Bethany stopped and took a small bite of a sandwich.

She finished chewing. "Dad said he tried to call, but the man didn't have his cell phone turned on. My father started swearing up a storm. Jeremiah Milk was filling his tank and asked what was wrong. After Dad explained, Jeremiah said he could help."

"How?" Damon asked.

"Jeremiah said that if Dad had a signature from the supplier on another document, he could copy it onto the form that needed to be signed. Jeremiah said he was an expert at replicating signatures."

"Huh," Damon said casually. His mind raced, but he couldn't think of anything related to the murder investigation that involved forgery.

"My father didn't take Jeremiah up on his offer. Fortunately, he was able to hunt down the supplier later in the day."

They finished lunch by discussing the prospects of Bethany being sent out on further weather-related assignments for the news station. As Damon departed, Bethany didn't offer him so much as a hug. He left the condominium, uncertain of whether the pair were beginning a courtship or just becoming closer friends.

* * *

The rain subsided as Damon drove fifty miles northwest to Frederick, Maryland. Rebecca had an afternoon filled with courses at The Cookery so Damon took the trek solo. As he drove, Damon thought about the key and sticky note bearing the number 47 he found in Jeremiah's coat pocket. Just because the two were in the same cufflinks box didn't necessarily mean they were related. Still, there was a good chance the key would open something at the fitness center in Frederick. Within seconds, he had it—a locker. Locker number 47 in particular.

Merriman's Health and Fitness Center was located in a large free-standing building in the newer part of Frederick. It shared a parking lot with a Best Buy and a Trader Joe's market.

Damon had changed into in a moisture-wicking athletic shirt, mesh shorts, and sneakers. He slung a duffel bag over his shoulder and asked for a one-day trial at the front desk. A man with a chiseled jaw and bulging neck muscles took down Damon's information and provided him with a temporary pass. When he gave his Virginia address, Damon told the man at the desk that he regularly traveled to Frederick for work.

Damon proceeded to the men's locker room. White fluorescent light reflected off of a shiny floor. Three men were inside, changing clothes. Two rows of lockers, one on top of the other, lined three walls of the room. About a quarter were secured by a variety of locks. Damon set his bag on a bench and made a show of searching it for a sweatband. With his head bowed, he cast his eyes up and scanned the lockers for number 47. He found it on the bottom row, secured by a padlock rather than a combination lock. Damon breathed relief. Another man came in from the shower area and opened the locker immediately to the right of number 47.

Damon donned an orange sweatband and made his way into the gymnasium. He spent thirty minutes on a treadmill and another thirty on weight machines. Damon scrutinized the swimming pool and exercise classrooms on the off chance that the man at the front desk was paying attention.

Back in the locker room, a single man was dressing. Damon left his bag on the bench near number 47. After showering, he wrapped a towel around his waist and returned to the locker area. It was empty.

Damon snapped into action. He removed the key from a side pouch of his duffel bag, said a silent prayer, and inserted it into the padlock securing locker number 47. The key slid right in. Damon popped the lock open.

Number 47 contained a small gray bag, half the size of Damon's duffel. Damon yanked clean clothes from his bag and deftly slid the gray bag inside, on top of his dirty clothes. He quickly zipped his duffel, dressed, and passed through the reception area with a courteous nod to the attendant at the front desk.

* * *

Damon drove toward the older part of Frederick and found an off-the-beaten-path coffee shop. He brought the small gray bag inside, ordered a hot apple cider, and planted himself in a rear booth.

The bag contained five inexpensive pocket folders, each of a different color and filled with paper. Damon quickly flipped them open in turn. The first contained bank statements and other details relating to the $2 million Alistair Atwater had given Jeremiah. The second contained a sheaf of papers on RDF Corporation. Damon smiled—finally, something tangible on RDF. Next was a folder dedicated to a single person, Mr. Dominic Freeze, CPA. Damon's brain lurched. Dominic Freeze was the name of the boy Dottie Milk said tormented Jeremiah Milk as a child. The contents of the fourth folder appeared to concentrate on a person named Kenneth Randolph. Was he another person who had teased Jeremiah? The final folder revolved around a corporation called Trident Gaskets, Limited.

Damon breathed out audibly. A treasure trove of information rested on the table in front of him. He sipped scalding-hot cider and started methodically to examine each of the folders.

The first folder was easy, as Damon already knew that the source of Jeremiah's wealth was Alistair Atwater. In addition to financial statements, there were a handful of photographs of Jeremiah with Matthew Katz-Atwater. Damon folded one of the snapshots in half and slipped it into his wallet.

Damon eagerly scoured the contents of Jeremiah's RDF Corporation folder. It contained official-looking paperwork from the Commonwealth of Virginia. The company was a sole proprietorship created by Jeremiah Milk one-and-a-half years earlier. It had no physical address. Upon RDF's creation, Jeremiah Milk deposited $1.6 million into the company's coffers. Shortly thereafter, Jeremiah transferred corporate control of RDF to Mr. Kenneth Randolph. Once Randolph had control of RDF, he promptly sent $100,000 from RDF to the savings account of a woman named Samantha Richter and the remaining $1.5 million to a bank account owned by Kenneth Randolph in his personal capacity. Two days later, RDF was dissolved. Computer printouts revealed records that Damon deduced were the results of a hacker's efforts to eradicate RDF Corporation's entire history. A handwritten note said: "RDF wiped. Virginia business registration files eliminated. Could not completely penetrate bank security. Only partial wipe of True Capital."

Damon's excitement grew as he processed the information. Only the record of the initial transaction from Jeremiah to RDF remained at True Capital, which was why the police were at a dead end. Damon wondered whether the Commonwealth of Virginia kept paper copies of new corporations or if he had the only physical evidence of RDF Corporation in his hands.

Needing more nourishment, Damon bought a second hot apple cider and a blueberry muffin. Sitting back down, he opened the folder on Dominic Freeze. The first pages detailed the man's biography and resume. Dominic was thirty-eight years old and lived in Havertown, Pennsylvania, near Philadelphia. He possessed an accounting degree from the University of Delaware and held positions with two other companies before his most recent stint with Trident Gaskets, Limited. At Trident he had the title "Chief Accountant."

The remainder of the Freeze folder contained records of exchanges between Samantha Richter and Dominic Freeze, including telephone bills, printouts of e-mails, and screen shots of text messages. The e-mails and text messages all went one way—from Samantha to Dominic—and they were graphic. Samantha Richter's phone bills suggested that over a year earlier, for a six-week period, she called Freeze's phone several times every day. Dominic's bills weren't in the folder, so Damon had no way of knowing how often he called her. The folder also contained snapshots of an attractive blond woman together with the same man in several places: on a park bench, at a crosswalk, and at a table in a restaurant. Finally, there were photos of the same woman and man entering the same motel room, albeit separately. Damon guessed that the woman was Samantha Richter and the man, Dominic Freeze. He wondered whether either was married.

Damon's head began to pound. He couldn't assemble all of the pieces yet, but he felt confident that the contents of the folders yielded information that would lead him to Jeremiah's murderer.

The fourth folder contained only two items—copies of a birth certificate and a social security card for Kenneth Randolph, the man to whom Jeremiah had transferred control of RDF Corporation and its $1.6

million. Randolph was forty-two years old and born in Macon, Georgia. The folder didn't contain any other identification, so Damon had no idea whether he still lived in Macon or what he looked like.

Damon peeled through the fifth and final folder, which was dedicated to Trident Gaskets, Limited, Dominic Freeze's employer. It provided some glue to the details swimming in Damon's head. The folder contained legal paperwork transferring a twenty percent interest in Trident to Kenneth Randolph in exchange for $1.5 million. The details of the ownership agreement made clear that Randolph was to be a silent partner. Trident Gaskets could use the $1.5 million for operations and expansion. In exchange, Randolph was entitled to twenty percent of all profits of the private company. Randolph wouldn't be known to the company's customer base or staff other than its board of directors and executive officers. The deal went through less than a month after Jeremiah and RDF Corporation passed the money to Kenneth Randolph.

Damon's brain itched with confusion. Jeremiah Milk had been plagued by Dominic Freeze as a child. When Jeremiah came into a fortune, he turned around and through an intermediary corporation—RDF—effectively gave Kenneth Randolph the bulk of it. Randolph took that cash and almost immediately bought half of the company that employed Dominic. Did Jeremiah know Randolph would invest in Trident Gaskets? There was no paperwork to suggest that Randolph kicked back any profits to Jeremiah. So why would Jeremiah just give that money away? Damon thought hard. It had to be tied to Dominic Freeze.

Chapter 16

By the time Damon returned to Hollydale, it was almost eleven o'clock at night. He booted up his laptop and brewed a pot of strong coffee. Damon closed his eyes and let the smell of freshly ground Columbian beans fill his nostrils.

Sitting at his kitchen table, Damon searched first for Kenneth Randolph. The name was too common to yield any significant results. Damon coupled it with "Macon, Georgia," and came up empty. Typing in Randolph's name with Trident Gaskets was equally fruitless. Apparently, the silent partnership had remained silent.

Damon tried Dominic Freeze's name alongside Trident Gaskets. This time he was rewarded with a host of references to newspaper stories. Damon clicked on a link to the *Philadelphia Business Journal*. The article, titled "Scandal Shakes Trident Gaskets," dated back one year. According to the writer, an unnamed informant notified the *Business Journal* that Trident had fired its chief accountant, Dominic Freeze, for embezzlement. When contacted by the press, a Trident spokesperson confirmed the termination, citing lack of trust and potential gross violations of the company's fiduciary and ethics policies. According to the informant, Freeze had worked his way up the corporate ladder at Trident and had been tapped to succeed Trident's chief financial officer after his retirement the following year. Once company executives learned of Freeze's theft, police searched his home, and found stacks of one hundred dollar bills hidden in his basement. Freeze claimed innocence to the press, asserting that he was the victim of a conspiracy designed to wreck his career.

The other articles Damon found had similar details. A follow-up in the *Philadelphia Business Journal* months later indicated that while Freeze maintained his innocence, he had plea bargained to avoid a trial and up to seven years in prison. By accepting the plea, Freeze relinquished the money found in his basement to Trident Gaskets and agreed to three years of probation. But the man's reputation was ruined. He would never work again as an accountant.

Damon refilled his coffee mug. Wired with adrenaline and caffeine, he searched for Samantha Richter. Damon found several women by that name but only one who lived in Philadelphia. The sole specks of information he could glean about her from the Internet were a phone number and a home address.

* * *

When he woke the following morning, crust caked Damon's eyelids like dried mud on tennis shoes. A full week had passed since Jeremiah's murder the previous Sunday. Damon called Rebecca. He passed along the information he found in the fitness club locker cache and summarized the accounts from the *Philadelphia Business Journal*.

"Jeremiah Milk set up Dominic Freeze to take a fall," Rebecca stated when Damon finished his report.

"You think so?"

"Absolutely," Rebecca said with confidence.

"It strikes me as a harsh form of retribution for grade school teasing," Damon said.

"True, but Dominic's mockery could've traumatized Jeremiah in a way that caused psychological damage."

"Maybe," Damon conceded. "But even if you're right, we're missing a link in the chain. Jeremiah didn't have a tie to Trident—Kenneth Randolph did."

"So the question is: What was Kenneth Randolph's role?" Rebecca asked.

"Exactly. If Jeremiah was out for vengeance, why wouldn't *he* become the silent partner?"

Through the phone's receiver, Damon could hear Rebecca tapping her fingers. After a moment, she said, "Probably because Dominic Freeze would've known if Jeremiah bought the twenty percent stake in Trident instead of Kenneth Randolph. Think about it, Damon. Randolph was silent. He may not have been known publicly or even to a majority of the staff. But surely the chief accountant for Trident would know who owned half of the company. Dominic probably wrote profit checks to Randolph every month."

"Well, if that's the case, Kenneth Randolph must have been a pretty good friend of Jeremiah's," Damon said.

"Or maybe Jeremiah was blackmailing him," Rebecca proffered.

"Possibly," Damon replied. He thought about the money trail: Two million dollars from Alistair Atwater to Jeremiah Milk, $1.6 million from Jeremiah—through RDF as a corporate shell that had all but disappeared—to Randolph, $1.5 million from Randolph to Trident for an ownership share in the company, and the $100,000 difference went to Samantha Richter. Four hundred thousand dollars remained in Jeremiah's True Capital account.

"What about Samantha Richter. Could she be Randolph's wife?" Damon asked. "And the $100,000 was payment for Randolph to act on Jeremiah's behalf?"

"I like that," Rebecca said, "except for the steamy messages she sent to Dominic." After a pause, she added, "Randolph's position as a principal investor in the company must have had something to do with Dominic's embezzlement. Do you know how much money was taken from Trident?"

"No. I was wondering whether it was the $1.5 million Randolph invested."

"I doubt it," Rebecca said. "If Randolph paid $1.5 million for twenty percent of the company, no one with half a brain could have embezzled that much and expected to get away with it. We're still missing some pieces, Damon."

"I know. Hopefully, I can fill in some blanks this morning. I'm going to see if I can talk to Dominic Freeze and Samantha Richter."

"Be careful, Damon," Rebecca warned. "And what about Clementine Snead?" she asked. Damon had recounted his clandestine efforts to Rebecca while they were at Jeremiah's funeral.

"That will have to wait. I'll be spending the day in Philadelphia."

* * *

Damon cleaned up and dressed neatly, then started the journey north to Philadelphia. He opted not to call Gerry. The detective would forbid Damon from speaking with Dominic and Samantha, just as he had barred Damon and Rebecca from having further contact with the park workers.

Damon knew he was crossing a line but his interest was insatiable. Besides, Damon reasoned, it was a Sunday and Gerry deserved a day of rest with his wife Trina. And if a detective started asking questions, Freeze and Richter might hire lawyers who would advise them not to answer. Damon would try to wriggle out some information first. He resolved to call Gerry on his way home and let him know about the stash of information he found in Jeremiah's fitness club locker.

Traffic was light. Damon arrived in Havertown, Pennsylvania, a middle-class suburb just west of Philadelphia, in two hours flat.

Dominic Freeze's address matched a 1920s stone Colonial-style home on a cul-de-sac. Children's bicycles, Razor scooters, and remote control cars littered the lawns on either side of the patch of yellowing, overgrown grass in front of Dominic's house. A black Ford Taurus with a dented rear bumper sat in the disgraced accountant's driveway in front of a closed one-car garage. An abundance of bird droppings covered the front porch railing.

Damon had spent the overnight hours and the greater portion of his drive to Havertown devising a plan to approach Dominic Freeze. He didn't want the man to know that he was investigating Jeremiah Milk's death. If Damon let slip that someone Dominic verbally tortured in his youth had been murdered, Dominic would infer that he was a suspect and clam up.

Damon had also seriously considered whether Dominic Freeze could be the murderer. If Jeremiah used Kenneth Randolph to frame Dominic for embezzlement, the loss of a career made for an ample motive. But, Damon countered to himself, Dominic Freeze wouldn't know that Randolph's investment money came from Jeremiah. And even though Freeze had grown up in Hollydale near the Milk family, it was doubtful that he would know the intimate details of Tripping Falls, like the location of Emmanuel's hedge trimmer and pressure washer or the park rangers' nighttime inspection schedule. Unless, of course, he had scoped out the park with a mind to murder.

Damon held a leather-bound notebook in his hand. He knocked sharply on Dominic's front door.

The man who answered looked physically ill. Loose bags under bloodshot eyes contrasted with his otherwise skeletal face. His complexion was the color of a weathered dollar bill. "Whatever you're selling, I don't want any," he said with annoyance.

Damon held up a hand. "Are you Dominic Freeze?"

The man didn't answer.

Damon pressed on. "I'm with the Gasket Fabricators Association, and I'm doing a follow-up story on Trident Gaskets for our newsletter." Damon had found the association's website earlier that morning and confirmed that the trade group did, indeed, publish a newsletter.

"I am Dominic Freeze, but I'm sure as hell not talking to a reporter about Trident Gaskets," he replied brusquely.

Damon wedged a foot in the doorway. "I'm not a newspaper reporter. I just want to tell your side of the story."

"And why would you want to do that?" Freeze asked skeptically.

"Because the trade association has a duty to make the truth known."

Dominic Freeze thought for a moment, then asked, "Why are you doing this story now? I was fired a year ago. It's been almost ten months since my plea bargain."

Damon had anticipated the question. "Because I just started with the Association a few weeks ago," he lied. "But I've been doing this type of work for a while—first with a bottling association and then with a group that represents silicone manufacturers. When I read the back issues of the Association's newsletter on Trident, I realized that there must be more to the story."

"Who's your boss?" Dominic asked.

Damon said a silent blessing that he had researched the Gasket Fabricators Association thoroughly. He rattled off the name of the trade group's executive director.

Dominic Freeze grunted and swept Damon inside with a flap of his hand. The gesture stirred a wave of dust in the foyer's yellow light. Damon sat on a navy blue fabric sofa that smelled of rose-scented air freshener. Arms crossed, Dominic leaned against a wall next to a stone fireplace.

"Can you start by telling me your side of the story?" Damon asked.

"I'll tell you exactly what I told the police a year ago," Dominic said. "Not that they believed me." He huffed in irritation at the memory. "The finance department at Trident is small. There was just the chief financial officer, me, and a few people who reported to me. The CFO handled all of the big items—financing new projects, working with the company's auditors, and preparing reports for the top brass, mainly the CEO and the Board. But he was never one for minutiae. I oversaw all of the day-to-day financial operations. So I was aware of every dime that came in and out of Trident. That's how I know someone set me up."

Damon took detailed notes. "Do you know what evidence the police found?"

"Of course I know," Dominic blustered. His face looked cadaverous. "It was a Monday morning. I had a dentist appointment so I didn't get into the office until about ten o'clock. The minute I walked in the door I knew something was wrong. Before I could even sit down, one of the administrative assistants told me that my boss—the chief financial officer—and Trident's CEO wanted to see me immediately. So I went to the CEO's office. They were both in there, waiting, along with the company's General Counsel. I was scared shitless. The CEO told me to sit down. Until that day, he had always been nice to me. But he was all business."

Dominic tugged at uncombed hair. "The CEO said they had a source who informed them that I made a series of withdrawals from the company's account two days earlier, on the Saturday. My boss handed me a stack of computer printouts. When I read through them, I couldn't believe my eyes. Someone used my corporate account to make three large cash withdrawals—one from each of Trident's three banks."

"I assume that as the go-to operations guy at Trident, you had access to the cash accounts?" Damon asked.

"Yes. Only two people could authorize a cash withdrawal—myself and my boss. But Trident has a strict policy that limits cash withdrawals to $25,000 per bank once a week. If anyone tried to take out more, it would trigger the bank's computerized security system and lock the account."

"So how were cash withdrawals made?"

"It's pretty straightforward. I'd access my corporate account online and make an authorization electronically. Once I did that, anyone could go to the bank and pick up the money as long as they had an authorization slip that I signed. Usually the administrative assistant did the gophering for our group."

"Did the banks do anything to verify the accuracy of the slips?"

"Of course," Dominic said with frustration, "A bank manager would take the slip and look up Trident's account on its data tracking system. The system would show that I had just authorized a withdrawal electronically. And each bank had a screenshot of my signature saved under Trident's account. The bank just had to verify my electronic authorization and match the signature on the slip to the screenshot in their files."

"And you claim you didn't electronically authorize any withdrawals that Saturday or sign any authorization slips?"

"I claim?" Dominic raised his voice. "I definitely did not make any authorizations. Whoever set me up took $25,000 from each of Trident's three banks. We never took out that much cash. It was only used for small events like company picnics. Any significant amount of money was always wired. And I'd never taken out money on a Saturday before."

"Should the banks have known that?" Damon asked, shifting in his seat.

Dominic considered the question. "I don't see why they would," he admitted. "They all probably have hundreds of corporate accounts. So as long as the process was followed, I doubt it would raise any red flags."

"I thought banks had cameras. If you didn't take the authorization slips to the banks, whoever did would be on camera," Damon offered.

"Unfortunately, you have to go to a manager's office to get cash from an authorization slip. Most banks don't have cameras in there."

"But they have cameras trained on the buildings' entrances, don't they?"

"My lawyer asked the same question," Dominic replied. "It was probably the only intelligent thing he did. But the security tapes from the entryway cameras didn't help. On the Saturday when I purportedly withdrew the money, there had been a storm. Umbrellas obscured the cameras from getting a good look at the banks' customers. Not to mention long coats and hoods."

"Sounds like the timing was unlucky for you," Damon said.

"Either unlucky or whoever took the money out had been waiting for a rainy day," Dominic said and rubbed his hands together. "You ask pretty good questions. Why are you working for a minor-league trade association instead of a newspaper?"

Damon shrugged his shoulders and answered with an open-ended question. "So the CEO had printouts of the electronic authorizations?"

"He did. They came from my account, all right, but I didn't send them."

"Did anyone else have your password?"

"Not that I know of. I'm sure someone hacked into my account."

"How about the authorization slips?"

Dominic wiped sweat from his forehead with the back of his arm. "The CEO had copies of the slips from each of the banks. I don't know how, but my signature was on each one of them."

Damon's mind shot back to his lunch with Bethany. Jeremiah Milk had told Jackson Krims that he could forge anyone's signature. He said, "That does sound like fairly damning evidence. Were you in the office on that Saturday?"

"No," Dominic Freeze shouted and balled his hands into fists. He took a deep breath and began to pace around the room. "I was fishing with a friend for most of the day. We were out at a lake an hour west of here—no rain there. I hadn't gone fishing in years, but...." He trailed off. "Don't put this in your article, okay?"

Damon bobbed his head.

"My wife had just moved out of the house and took our two children with her. This alimony and child support is a bitch without a salaried job. But going fishing saved me from prison. The time stamps on the electronic authorizations matched the time that I was fishing, and my buddy was willing to testify. That's why my lawyer thinks the prosecutor was willing to plea bargain. At a trial, it would have been a pile of physical evidence against me on one side and my friend's word on the other."

Damon held up his hands preemptively. "Speaking of physical evidence, the press reported that the police found stacks of cash in your house." Damon looked around the room.

"Yes," Dominic said with a deflated tone. He sat in a La-Z-Boy opposite Damon. "The police found $75,000. That's why I took the plea bargain—the evidence looked bad."

"You didn't know the money was here?" Damon asked.

Dominic picked up his head and suddenly became agitated. "Of course not! Do I have to spell it out for you? I was set up. The only reason I'm talking to you is that I want to clear my name. I didn't have an alarm system in here, so anyone could have picked a lock on one of the doors. For that matter, I never made a habit of securing my windows. Some of them don't even have screens. Anyone could have planted that money on me."

"The newspapers mentioned that the money was in your basement—"

Dominic cut in, "Hundred dollar bills stuffed into a shoebox. My basement's a mess. If the police hadn't searched the house, I probably wouldn't have found it for years."

"Do you have any idea who could've put it there?" Damon asked.

Dominic grimaced. "No," he said. "But it had to be someone at Trident. A computer hacker from the outside wouldn't know the details of our withdrawal system or that we have a limit of $25,000 per transaction. It wouldn't surprise me if one of the people I managed did it to get my job."

Dominic Freeze's story sounds remarkably plausible, Damon thought. He was convinced that Dominic was the victim of a well-executed scheme of revenge somehow perpetrated by Jeremiah Milk and Kenneth Randolph rather than a CPA-turned-criminal who had been caught with a shoebox full of cash.

Damon took a deep breath and plunged into unknown water. "Do you think Samantha Richter set you up?"

Dominic's face registered confusion, then turned to fury. "What? How the hell do you know about Samantha Richter?" He stood abruptly. "And now that I think about it, if you're from the trade association, why are you here on a Sunday?"

Damon leapt to his feet and back-pedaled slowly toward the front door. He had made a critical mistake. And then the realization hit him—Samantha Richter had nothing to do with Trident Gaskets or the embezzlement. And a trade association newsletter writer would have no idea who she was.

"There was a reference to her in the newsletter's files," Damon said weakly.

"Bullshit," countered Dominic Freeze with rage. "You're not with any trade association." The man stepped toward a mahogany credenza and gripped a drawer handle.

Was he going for a weapon? Damon didn't wait to find out. He yanked open the front door and sprinted to his car without looking back. He gunned the engine and tore out of the cul-de-sac.

Chapter 17

Nervous sweat dripped from Damon's face. He drank black coffee from a foam cup and ate a gritty cheeseburger in a garden-variety fast food restaurant ten miles from Dominic's home. Had Dominic Freeze seen his license plate?

Damon mentally shoved the thought from his mind, and his focus circled to phony signatures. Jeremiah could have forged the authorization slips as long as he knew what Dominic Freeze's handwriting looked like. As a twenty percent owner, Kenneth Randolph would surely have access to Trident's electronic database of files, including documents with Dominic's signature. He could have passed an image of the signature to Jeremiah. And Jeremiah would need to know the company's policy on maximum withdrawals; that pointed to Randolph, too.

Damon considered the embezzled money. Sophisticated companies didn't regularly use cash, and reimbursements for company picnics didn't call for a weekly allowance of up to $25,000. Times three. Dominic was probably lying when he said he never withdrew that much money. More than likely, Trident was dispensing cash under the table—perhaps to illegal immigrants cranking out gaskets on the factory floor or to grease the right wheels for lucrative contracts. As the facilitator of finances, Dominic would have been complicit in any such schemes. So even after he'd been fired, Damon concluded, Dominic wouldn't want to risk jail time by blowing the whistle on illegal distributions.

Damon choked down the last bites of burger and studied his directions to Samantha Richter's home. Dominic had mentioned a former wife. Had Samantha Richter married Dominic and kept her own last name? No, Damon thought—the messages she sent him were too salacious. Samantha had mistress written all over her. Were they still lovers? If so, Damon would be taking a huge risk by going to see her. Dominic Freeze could answer the door, gun in hand. But Damon still had unanswered questions and wasn't willing to leave Philadelphia yet. He didn't know the origin of "bite the bullet," but it seemed perilously apt to his situation.

* * *

Samantha Richter's white stucco apartment building in South Philly's Pennsport neighborhood resembled a cardboard milk carton. Her unit was on the third floor.

An attractive blond in her early thirties answered Damon's knock. She had good bone structure and long eyelashes that were offset by a vinegar smile.

"Yes?" she asked, appraising Damon from shoulders to waist. Damon could hear a television playing cartoons behind her.

"Are you Samantha Richter?" Damon asked.

"I am," she replied with hesitation.

Damon decided to be direct. "My name is Damon Lassard. I'm working with the police on some details pertaining to the murder of a man named Jeremiah Milk in Northern Virginia."

Samantha's face shifted from apprehension to confusion.

"I don't understand. What does that have to do with me?" A child cried out from the next room. "Hold on," she said to Damon and left him on the doorstep.

He took two steps inside. Samantha Richter retrieved a sippy cup for a toddler who was planted on the living room carpet six feet in front of a television set. She returned and pointed Damon to a stool in front of a breakfast bar, leaving the door to the outside hallway open. From the kitchen, she could keep an eye on the boy without him overhearing their conversation.

"Do you know who Jeremiah Milk is?" Damon asked.

Standing opposite a Formica counter from Damon, Samantha shoved unwashed plastic containers holding the remnants of mashed foods to a corner. Locks of wavy hair bounced as she shook her head from side to side.

"How about Dominic Freeze?"

Samantha froze. She narrowed her eyes. "Why do the police want to know about him?"

"I'm not a police officer," Damon clarified. "But I'm working with them and I need to know about Mr. Freeze."

"What does Dominic have to do with anything?"

Damon lowered his voice. "I know you had a relationship with him while he was married."

Samantha glanced at the two-year-old boy in the adjacent room. His eyes were fixed on the television set. "So what?" she said coolly. "That's between me and him."

Damon mentally checked a box—he had been correct about the extramarital affair. "I'm not accusing you of anything, Ms. Richter. I want to find out what happened to Jeremiah Milk, and I suspect that Dominic Freeze may have been involved. I just don't know how yet."

Samantha looked down at the countertop.

"What about Kenneth Randolph?" Damon tried. "He paid you $100,000 through a company called RDF."

"So you know," she said meekly, still not looking up at Damon.

"I have phone and computer records of you contacting Dominic Freeze, and photographs of the two of you."

"Hmmph," she snorted. "Those must be the ones Kenneth took. Did he give them to you?"

"Not directly," Damon said. "Please tell me what happened, Ms. Richter."

She tapped her fingers on the countertop and looked up. "You're really not with the police?"

"Not technically. But if what you tell me is relevant to Jeremiah Milk's death, I'll have to notify them."

She stood in silence for a moment, then said, "You keep mentioning this Jeremiah person. Who is he?"

"He was my neighbor, in Arlington, Virginia. He and Dominic Freeze went to grade school together. A week ago, Jeremiah was found dead at the state park where he worked as a ranger."

Samantha winced. "Well," she said, "If I tell you about Dominic, I may need the police to protect me and my son from him if word of this gets out."

Damon raised his eyebrows. "I'm sure my police contacts in Arlington can arrange that with the force up here," he said.

Samantha stepped over to the front door and closed it, then came back into the kitchen and brought a glass down from a cupboard shelf. She filled it with water. "I didn't sleep with Dominic. But his wife thinks I did."

She took a sip of water and set it and her elbows on the counter. Samantha looked Damon in the eye. Long lashes fluttered. "Kenneth Randolph paid me $100,000 to pretend that I was having an affair with Dominic."

Damon's breath caught. He blew it out slowly. "Pretend?"

She smiled. "Think about what you saw, Mr. Lassard. I called Dominic's phone incessantly. But almost all of the calls went one way, from me to him. At first, I tried to actually have an affair with him. For the money Kenneth paid me, I thought it would be easiest just to sleep with Dominic. Morals be damned— I'm a single mother raising a two-year-old and jockeying a cash register at Target." She glanced toward her son. "Kenneth trailed behind me for the first week and took pictures. I stalked Dominic and approached him several times. I pretended to run into him on accident—once on the street downtown and once in a park. I even sat down across from him in a restaurant when he was waiting to have lunch with someone else."

She straightened up. "I asked him to dinner, but despite my best efforts, he wasn't interested. He told me that he was flattered but married. So I started calling him. The first few times, I pretended to be a telemarketer. I tried to keep him on the line for as long as I could to create believable phone records. But he had caller ID and caught on quickly. He asked me what I wanted. I told him I was the blond woman he met by 'happenstance' several times and asked him out again. After another couple of calls, he realized I was stalking him and stopped picking up. But I kept calling and leaving messages on his voicemail so there would be a record. I started e-mailing and texting him, too. I made those hotter so Kenneth could have a good record."

"I don't have records of Dominic's calls. Did he ever phone you?"

"He did, but only a couple of times. He told me to stop bothering him. During the last call, he threatened to get a restraining order. But by then, I had records of almost six weeks of calls, e-mails, and texts. And

Kenneth had several photos of the two of us together from the first week."

"I saw pictures of you and Dominic going into a motel room," Damon said.

Samantha grinned. "That was Kenneth's idea. It was a good one, too. Before I even met Kenneth or Dominic, Kenneth had it planned out. Dominic collects antique toys. It's a little weird but no secret—his name is all over toy collection blogs and chat room sites on the Internet. Kenneth called Dominic and told him he was a toy dealer from Boston passing through Philadelphia on his way to a show in North Carolina. He said he was staying at a motel in town and planned to have a private showing. Kenneth dropped the names of a few other locals who are big into vintage toys—it wasn't hard for him to find the names online. Apparently, private showings aren't uncommon for hard-core toy hobbyists, so Dominic went to a motel where Kenneth had booked a room. Kenneth left the door ajar and the lights on inside. When no one answered Dominic's knock, he pushed the door open to look inside. Just then, Kenneth snapped a set of photos with a high-zoom camera from across the street."

"And you went through the same motel door on a later occasion," Damon said.

"Exactly. Dominic left when he saw that the room was empty. Weeks later, after Kenneth hired me, he booked into the same motel and asked for the same room so the numbers matched. All I did was walk inside while Kenneth took pictures."

"So it looked as if you and Dominic were meeting there for a tryst."

"I think that was the nail in the coffin for Dominic's wife," Samantha said with a sigh. "I hated to break up a marriage, but I have to look out for myself. I want my son to be able to go to college someday. I put half of the money in an account for that. Then I paid off my car loan and credit card debt, and I have enough to pay for my son's day care until he starts school. I stuck the rest in the bank. It may have been a despicable thing to do, but now I have financial freedom."

"You don't get alimony?"

Samantha laughed. "I'm not even sure who the father is." She shook her head. "My mother used to tell me to dot my i's and cross my thighs. I should've listened to her. But since I had Henry over there, I've settled down when it comes to men."

She offered Damon a glass of water, and he accepted it. "How did Dominic's wife find out?" he asked.

"That was easy," Samantha said. She walked around the counter and plucked a stool from beside Damon. She pulled it away several feet and sat down. "Kenneth sent her a series of anonymous letters."

"What did they say?"

"The first one informed her that Dominic was having an affair. The second contained the phone records and some of the pictures. The last letter contained the graphic text messages, e-mails, and the photos of me and Dominic going into the same motel room. Kenneth sent them each three days apart."

"I heard that it worked. Dominic's wife took their kids and left him."

Samantha lowered her eyelids. "I didn't know they had children."

I bet you didn't bother to ask, Damon thought. He concluded that Kenneth Randolph had used Jeremiah Milk's money not only to end Dominic Freeze's career but also to destroy his marriage and family.

"I really need to get back to my son," Samantha said. "I let him watch too much television as it is."

"Of course," Damon said. "But before I go, can you tell me about Kenneth Randolph?"

"Hold on a second." Samantha Richter spent the next five minutes changing her son's diaper and then setting him up at a table with crayons and a coloring book.

"I met Kenneth Randolph at the Target where I work," Samantha said when she returned. "I noticed him in my checkout line three days in a row. That doesn't happen by chance—there are about twenty cashiers at any given time. But it isn't too unusual, either." She batted her lashes. "I tend to have a lot of men in my line."

"What did he say to you?" Damon asked.

"On the third day, he asked me if I would be interested in making a serious amount of money." She lowered her voice. "I tried to blow him off. I thought he was a creep who wanted me to work at a strip club. But he read my mind. He said it had nothing to do with selling my body, and I could be $100,000 richer in a month. Of course that piqued my interest, but I was wary."

She wet her lips with her tongue. Despite her attractive features, Damon couldn't see past her complicity in knowingly wrecking a man's marriage.

She continued. "I met him after work at Target's café area, and he told me of his plan to split up Dominic and his wife. I didn't commit right away, so Kenneth wrote down his phone number and told me to think about it and call him in a couple of days. In the meantime, he gave me Dominic's address. Even before Kenneth walked away, I knew I would do it. I didn't tell him then, but I couldn't pass up the money. I drove to Dominic's house early the next morning and followed him to his office. I'm not sure why. I think I just wanted to make sure I could go through with it. And I realized that I could. I called Kenneth and told him so, and we went from there."

"Did you ask Kenneth why he was trying to break up Dominic's marriage?" Damon asked.

"Yes, but he wasn't willing to tell me. 'No questions asked' was part of our deal."

"Thank you very much for your candor, Ms. Richter," Damon said. "Would you mind giving me Kenneth's contact information?"

"Sorry, I can't. Ever since Dominic's wife left him, I haven't been able to get in touch with Kenneth. E-mails bounce back and the phone company said his number's been disconnected."

Damon grunted to himself in frustration. "Why did you try to contact him? Hadn't Kenneth sent you all of the money he promised?"

"Oh, I received every penny, but I was scared for my safety. Dominic left a nasty message on my voicemail. He said that his wife left him because of me and if he ever saw me again, he didn't know if he'd be able to control his temper. I almost moved. Instead, I added that big lock." She glanced at the door, then looked up at Damon with apprehension. "Now that I think about it, I probably shouldn't have let you inside."

"Don't worry, I'm not working for Dominic," Damon said. "But I really need to find Kenneth Randolph. Can you at least describe what he looks like?"

"That I can do," Samantha said. She unwrapped a stick of peppermint chewing gum and popped it into her mouth. "Late thirties or early forties. Tall and thin. And his fingers are disfigured."

Damon stared at her in disbelief. Was it possible that Jeremiah recruited another man with the same condition to help him destroy Dominic Freeze's life? Or were Jeremiah Milk and Kenneth Randolph the same person? He recalled the photograph of Jeremiah and Matthew Katz-Atwater he had found in the gym locker. Damon reached into his wallet, pulled it out, and set it down on the breakfast bar.

Samantha Richter looked down at the photo and placed a forefinger on Jeremiah's face. She said, "That's Kenneth, all right."

Chapter 18

Late afternoon sun scorched Damon's driveway when he returned home. David Einstaff was sitting on the front porch. He wasn't drinking, but the man's ashtray looked like a clew of worms that had overtaken a sand hill.

Damon nodded at David and went inside. He called Rebecca and filled her in on the day's events.

"Jeremiah Milk pretending to be Kenneth Randolph makes sense," Rebecca said when Damon finished. "It gave him access to Trident without allowing Dominic to know it was him."

"Right," Damon agreed. "Funneling the money for the stake in Trident through RDF Corporation erased the connection between Milk and Randolph." He snapped his fingers. "Marcus Pontfried must have been working for Dominic and figured out that Jeremiah was Kenneth Randolph. That's why Pontfried went to the park." He paused in thought, then said, "When Vanessa Maldive told Jeremiah that Marcus Pontfried questioned her, Jeremiah asked her if Pontfried had mentioned anyone else by name. I'll bet that Jeremiah was trying to figure out if Pontfried had asked specifically about Kenneth Randolph."

"So Jeremiah suspected he'd been found out," Rebecca said.

"Probably."

"Do you think Dominic Freeze is the killer?"

"I don't know if he wielded the pressure washer," Damon said. "But he sure had a strong motive.

Jeremiah destroyed his career and tore apart his family. He ruined Dominic's life."

"Ruined his life," Rebecca repeated pensively into the phone. She paused. "RDF. Ruin Dominic Freeze."

* * *

At seven o'clock in the following morning, Damon made his way on foot to Clementine Snead's home. It had been two days since he witnessed Clementine scrutinizing Hollydale's crepe myrtles. The walk took Damon ten minutes, and the crisp air against his face invigorated him.

Damon approached Clementine's row house from the rear. Each lot in the five-residence strip had a patch of backyard between the home and a detached one-car garage. Damon gingerly stepped around Clementine's garage. Along one side, he noticed a small window positioned above head height. Damon scanned his surroundings. The stretch of backyards was desolate. He dragged a black plastic trash can from a neighbor's lawn against the side of Clementine's garage, turned the can on its side, and climbed on top.

Morning sunlight streamed through the grimy window. Damon pushed aside a cobweb and peered inside. Mason jars lined a waist-high shelf. Damon pulled out the binoculars that were still inside his fleece pocket. He focused the lenses on the jars. They were filled with insects. Gotcha!

From his left, Damon heard a door slam and a voice shout, "I'm calling the police!"

Damon swung the binoculars down and rapidly twisted his head. He tumbled from the garbage can and landed on his backside. A wave of pain coursed through him.

Wearing a white, V-necked undershirt and tight tennis shorts, Clementine Snead strode angrily from the back of his row house toward Damon. "You're tr-tr-trespassing," he bawled.

Damon was still sitting on the ground in pain. Clementine hovered over him. "I know you. You were hanging around the garden center a few days ago."

"*I'm* the one calling the police," Damon retorted and stood up, rubbing his backside. "I watched you on Friday night. You're killing the crepe myrtles in Hollydale."

Clementine took a step back and forced a laugh. "I have no idea what you're talking about."

"Come on, Mr. Snead. I photographed you, and I just saw the insects in your garage." Damon knew the blurry pictures he had taken of Clementine during Friday's overnight hours would be useless as evidence, but it was enough of a threat to put Clementine squarely on defense.

The man hiked up his shorts. "I'm not killing any crepe myrtles," he countered. "I just needed test trees. Like lab rats. A-A-Actually," he stuttered, "not as bad as lab rats because the trees aren't in any danger of permanent harm."

Damon stared at him.

Clementine wiped sweaty palms on his shirt as seconds ticked by in silence. Finally the master gardener explained, "I'm developing a new product to treat crepe myrtle infestations. It's a major scientific breakthrough—completely organic but as strong as a pesticide. The organic sprays on the market are all weaker than pesticides, so you have to apply them more often. That makes it more expensive to treat your trees. My formula is just as strong as a pesticide but without the toxins."

"And you've been testing the solution on the local crepe myrtles?" Damon asked.

"Yes," Clementine admitted. "To perfect the combination of ingredients. I know which components to use but have to figure out the precise percentages of each to maximize effectiveness. And the solution I'm designing will work on all types of insects that eat crepe myrtle leaves. It'll be one-stop shopping."

"So you let loose a spate of bugs on your neighbors' trees to test different combinations of your solution?"

Clementine flushed. "I-I-It's for the good of the trees. And I'm not doing anything haphazardly. I have a methodology. One night, I populate a set of trees with one of three types of insects. Later, I spray them with a carefully calculated solution. Then on a third night, I take measurements to check the results. I'm only on my sixth cycle and already at the cusp of hitting the ideal ratios. My formula will revolutionize the organic tree spray industry." A rich glow came into his beady eyes.

"Weren't the owners of the trees spraying their own solutions as well?" Damon queried.

Clementine waived a hand in the air. "A minor impediment. Homeowners never seem to spray right away. By the time they do, my cycle's complete, and I just wait a few days for their chemicals to wear off before repopulating. Mind you, crepe myrtles are just the beginning. I'll be able to modify the core formula to take on all temperate plants and trees."

Damon was tempted to ask if Clementine planned to repeat his testing procedure for every species he had in mind. Instead, he pulled out his cell phone. "I want you to repeat everything you just told me to the police," he said and dialed the Arlington County police station.

He didn't ask for Gerry Sloman. Instead, he requested an officer who handled property damage complaints. After Damon summarized the recent history of crepe myrtle infestations in Hollydale and Clementine's story, the officer promised to come by and take Damon's and Clementine's statements and gather any evidence.

"The police will be here in fifteen minutes," he told the master gardener.

"Hey, no problem," Clementine said breezily. "Even if I have to pay a fine, that's a small price to pay for gardening immortality."

Later, after Damon returned home, he posted a note on the Hollydale listserv informing the citizenry that a perpetrator had been apprehended and the infestation would cease. The police had charged Beauregard Snead with destruction of property. Damon didn't name Clementine in his post but he was certain the man's identity would be all over town quickly—on his way home, Damon had stopped by Cynthia's salon and, as promised, regaled Mrs. Chenworth with his escapades in watching, tracking, and confronting Clementine.

* * *

Despite the bruise on his backside, Damon decided to take a late-morning run along the Custis Trail—a bicycle and pedestrian route that wound through Arlington's woodlands. The air had turned bitter and he felt a chill in his chest. But his mind, which was running on all cylinders, zeroed in on Jeremiah Milk.

Jeremiah had probably forged Dominic Freeze's signature on the bank authorization slips, retrieved cash from each of Trident's banks, planted it in Dominic's basement, and then tipped off Trident management and the press. At the same time, Jeremiah hired Samantha Richter to concoct an affair that would end Dominic's marriage.

Damon still had several questions, including how Marcus Pontfried had discovered that Kenneth Randolph was, in fact, Jeremiah Milk. He thought hard—had the private investigator spoken with Samantha Richter?

Damon also didn't know how Jeremiah penetrated Dominic's computer at Trident to make the electronic bank authorizations. Had Jeremiah stolen Dominic's password and broken into his office, or did he hack Dominic's computer? Someone had also wiped clean all references to RDF in the Commonwealth of Virginia's electronic business registration files. That fact suggested the work of an expert. Damon racked his brain. Did Jeremiah have that expertise? Perhaps he had assistance. Did Milt Verblanc's skills in robotics or Alex's engineering knowledge extend to computers?

Damon jogged the final stretch of a four mile trek in cool-down mode. He bent over on the sidewalk in front of his duplex to catch his breath. And then it came to him: the boy. According to Glenda Atwater, Matthew spent hours on his computer. No one except Matthew knew what he and Jeremiah talked about in the teen's room for considerable lengths of time. They must have been plotting a grand revenge.

Damon closed his eyes and pictured Glenda Atwater speaking with Jeremiah at Tripping Falls:

"Please help me," Glenda pleaded. "Matthew won't leave his room. All he does is type away for hours on end on his computer. I don't even know what he's doing up there. All I see on the screen is code."

Damon's thoughts moved to the initial conversation between Jeremiah and Matthew. He imagined the scene:

Jeremiah strode into the boy's bedroom and shut the door behind him. He held up his hands for Matthew to see.

"Going through some tough times, kid?" Jeremiah asked with avuncular charm.

Matthew nodded, staring wide-eyed at Jeremiah's hands.

"It's not going to get better for a long time," Jeremiah said. "Those boys who are teasing you are dirt. And the girls are no better—they're talking about you behind your back. You hate them, don't you?"

"More than life itself," Matthew said. "Who are you?"

"My name's Jeremiah. Your grandmother asked me to see you. She thought I could help get you out of your funk. Do you want to humiliate the kids in your class?"

Matthew nodded again. "I'm being homeschooled right now, but I don't like that either."

"Okay. We'll work on getting you back into school and come up with a plan for those bullies. But first I need you to help me. I hear you're good with computers. How good?"

"Very good," Matthew said with quiet confidence.

Jeremiah hesitated. "Could you hack into one? Say, the computer system of a company. Or a bank?"

Matthew nodded for a third time.

Jeremiah smiled and laid a hand on the boy's shoulder. "I have a feeling we're going to be great friends, Matthew."

* * *

Damon had to speak with Matthew before informing the police of his suspicions. Alistair Atwater would never let the teenager talk to a detective without an attorney present.

But first, Damon had another call to make. He dialed Samantha Richter.

"Samantha," Damon said into the receiver. "This is Damon Lassard. We met yesterday."

"Hello again, Mr. Lassard. Is everything all right?"

"Yes. I have one more question that I forgot to ask you. Did you provide a description of Kenneth Randolph to a man named Marcus Pontfried? He's a private investigator from York, Pennsylvania, that Dominic hired."

Damon could hear Samantha take in breath quickly. "I did," Samantha admitted. "A man by that name called about three or four months after I stopped bothering Dominic. But he didn't tell me he was a private eye. Or that Dominic hired him. He said he was with the IRS. He started by asking me questions about who had taken the photos of me and Dominic. I admitted it was Kenneth, and Mr. Pontfried said that the IRS needed to locate him. I told him the same thing I told you—that I didn't have any way of reaching him."

"But he asked for a description of Kenneth?"

"He did. I gave him the same description that I gave to you yesterday. Two weeks later, he came by my Target and showed me a picture. I verified that it was Kenneth."

Damon thanked Samantha and ended the call. Now he had a better sense of how Marcus Pontfried tracked down Jeremiah: Pontfried surmised that there was a connection between the embezzlement set-up and Samantha Richter and had squirreled Kenneth Randolph's name and description from Samantha. Recognizing Randolph's name as Trident's silent partner, Dominic would have realized that the man was trying to destroy him. And Dominic only knew of one person who matched Samantha's description of Kenneth Randolph and his malformed fingers— Jeremiah Milk. So Pontfried tracked down and photographed Jeremiah, then had Samantha confirm the person in the photo was the man she knew as Kenneth Randolph. Pontfried and Dominic would have concluded that Milk, acting as Randolph, also set him up on the embezzlement charges.

Damon was more convinced than ever that Dominic Freeze was involved in the murder of Jeremiah Milk.

Now, he just had to figure out if the man had done the deed himself or had help.

* * *

Damon showered, ate lunch, spent a few hours on mundane chores, and then looked up the address of the Katz-Atwater home in Potomac, Maryland. The house fronted a putting green on a private golf club. Gray shake siding covered the exterior. Grid-laced panes highlighted bay windows. White-railed balconies fronted French doors on either side of a second-story picture window. The house belonged in Nantucket.

Damon approached the front door, steadied his nerves, and rang the bell. He expected a housekeeper to answer, but Liliane Atwater heaved open the front door.

"Mr. Lassard," she said. "It's nice to see you."

Damon was surprised she remembered his name. With her long tan limbs, Liliane resembled a cricket.

"It's a pleasure to see you as well, ma'am," Damon said. "I was hoping to have a word with your son."

Liliane didn't express any concern at the request. *She's completely unaware of Matthew's activities,* Damon thought.

"Be my guest. Matthew just came home from school," she said. "My husband's at the office, and I need to set up for a late-afternoon tea I'm hosting. Do you mind showing yourself upstairs?"

"Not at all. Which room is Matthew's?"

Liliane pointed up a sweeping curved staircase and directed Damon to the last door on the left side of a wide hallway.

Damon climbed the steps and located the teenager's room. His closed door featured a vintage *Social Distortion* poster. Damon could hear pounding from a stereo. He curled his knuckles and thumped.

The music stopped. "Who's there?" a voice cracked.

"Damon Lassard. We met after Jeremiah's funeral."

Matthew Katz-Atwater opened the door and invited Damon inside with a jerk of his head. The boy wore a black *Dead Kennedys* T-shirt. Red and white pimples dotted his forehead like a topographical map.

Damon took in his shirt and the posters on the walls. "You have good taste in music," he said. "I'm a punk fan, too." Books, papers, and record jackets covered the floor.

"That's cool." Matthew sat in a swivel chair behind a wall of three computer monitors stationed on a glass-topped desk.

Damon shut the bedroom door and stood in front of Matthew. "I want to talk about what you and Jeremiah did to Dominic Freeze," he said plainly.

Matthew shrugged his shoulders. "I don't know what you're talking about, man."

"I think you do. I know that Jeremiah made up an identity and used it to infiltrate Trident Gaskets. I know that Jeremiah constructed a sham affair to ruin Dominic Freeze's marriage. And I'm fairly certain that Dominic was set up on embezzlement charges." Damon walked Matthew through the details he had uncovered.

"Why are you telling me all of this?" Matthew asked sheepishly, refusing to look Damon in the eye. His hands were buried in the pockets of black jeans.

"Because you helped Jeremiah," Damon said without hesitation. It was a guess, but given Matthew's reaction thus far, he felt certain he was correct. "I have a moral obligation to tell the police, but I wanted to give you a heads-up. I have my suspicions of how you helped Jeremiah, and seeing all of this computer equipment, I'm pretty sure I'm right."

The boy looked down at his feet. "The minute the police set foot in this house, my grandfather will hire a team of high-powered lawyers," he said with more regret than moxie.

"Look, Matthew, I'm not out to get you in trouble. I just want to find out who killed Jeremiah. I'll bet every dollar I have that Dominic Freeze had something to do with it, and I'm just trying to get as much information as I can."

Matthew pulled his hands from his pockets and covered his face. His misshapen fingers looked like a smaller version of Jeremiah's.

"How about this," Damon said. "I'll talk and if you want to jump in, you can."

"Okay," Matthew said cautiously as he picked at a blemish on his forehead.

"The plan was all Jeremiah's," Damon said. "But he needed help. He needed a computer hacker. And that's where you came in. First, you and Jeremiah created a false identity. Mr. Kenneth Randolph was conjured out of thin air. He had a birth certificate, a social security number, and a bank account." Damon paused.

Matthew stared at him, thinking.

Damon waited.

Matthew was unable to hold back the grin that slowly spread across his face. "Creating a false identity is simple as long as you're smart about it."

"How's that?" Damon asked.

"You don't want to take someone else's social security number, otherwise you'll get caught. So you just make one up and slap it on a forged card. A social security card is the key to getting a bank account."

"The bank doesn't check?" Damon asked in disbelief.

"Not initially. Banks only link up with the government systems when they send year-end notices for the taxes you have to pay on the interest from your account. So as long as you shut down the account by the end of the calendar year, there's no problem."

"Don't they need a driver's license or some other identification with a picture on it?"

"Sure, but that's just as easy to forge as a birth certificate. Of course, if a person made a driver's license, he'd want to destroy it right after he used it, because, as you said, it would have his picture on it." Matthew started laughing. It wasn't sinister; it was just the laugh of a teenager who had played a prank on someone.

"So now Jeremiah has a false identity," Damon said. "He transferred a large amount of money through a shell corporation, RDF, to Kenneth Randolph, who in turn bought a twenty percent share in a company called Trident. You wiped clean RDF Corporation's business registration files, scrubbed the bank's files as best you could manage, and then penetrated Dominic Freeze's computer at Trident. Jeremiah, as Kenneth Randolph, had access to Trident's internal systems, which I imagine would've made it significantly easier to get into Dominic's accounts. Then, once you hacked through his passwords, you electronically approved large withdrawals from three banks and printed out the authorization slips for Jeremiah to forge. You probably did everything from the very seat you're sitting in now." Damon looked pointedly at a high-end printer.

Matthew just smiled.

"So what was the deal, Matthew?" Damon asked. "Did Jeremiah agree to help you get even with someone who had victimized you?"

Matthew's face became serious. "I haven't said that I helped Jeremiah, and I'm not saying so now. But no, we never discussed specific plans to get even with anyone who hurt me."

"Hurt you? You mean emotionally?"

Matthew paused. "Yes, emotionally, that's what I meant."

"Matthew, has someone physically harmed you?"

The youth moved from his desk chair and took a seat on the edge of his bed. He retrieved a blanket, balled up in one corner, placed it in his lap, and sank his hands deep inside. "No. No one has physically harmed me."

Damon studied Matthew closely. He looked as if he was holding something back. Damon asked, "Matthew, was Jeremiah physically abused?"

Matthew curled his upper lip and sniffed back tears. After a minute, he whimpered, "Dominic Freeze."

Damon gave the teenager time to recover his emotions, then said, "I know Dominic teased Jeremiah a lot in elementary school, played tricks on him, things like that. Matthew, what else did he do?"

Matthew laid back on his bed and stared at the ceiling. His voice was almost inaudible. "He burned Jeremiah's fingers."

Damon moved to a corner of the bed and sat down beside Matthew. "Burned?" he asked gently.

"When Jeremiah was in fourth grade," Matthew replied. "He was ten. Jeremiah told me that Dominic and another boy grabbed him one afternoon on the way home from school. They took him to a cluster of trees near the schoolyard where some of the teachers used to smoke. Dominic tied Jeremiah's hands behind his back with a length of rope, covered his mouth with a bandana, and then shoved him to the ground." Matthew trembled. "Dominic pushed a boot into his back. The other boy got nervous and told Dominic to stop. According to Jeremiah, Dominic called the other boy a chicken-shit and told him to get lost. So the other boy ran off."

"Did the other boy know what Dominic was going to do?"

"Jeremiah didn't say. After the other boy cleared out, Dominic bent down and rammed a knee into

Jeremiah's back, holding him flat on his stomach. Dominic took a book of matches from a pants pocket, lit one, and waved it in front of Jeremiah's face. 'I want to know if you can feel pain in those *hooves* of yours,' he said and touched the flame to the tips of the third, fourth, and fifth fingers on Jeremiah's left hand."

Damon cringed, visualizing the scene.

"Jeremiah screamed out, but Dominic held his fingers to the flame until they started to char. Then he kicked Jeremiah in the side and left him wallowing in pain. The burns killed all of the nerves in the tips of his fingers," Matthew said. "Effing prick."

"Did Jeremiah go to the police?"

"No," Matthew said solemnly. "I don't even think he told his own mother the truth about what happened. He just gritted his teeth and moved on."

And vowed to take revenge, Damon thought.

Chapter 19

On his way home, Damon left Gerry Sloman several messages summarizing the destruction he surmised that Jeremiah wrought on Dominic Freeze's life. He hoped Gerry would appreciate his efforts: despite staying true to Rebecca's promise that neither he nor Rebecca would contact any of the Tripping Falls staffers, he had meddled in police business.

That evening, Damon walked to the Fish Barrel. Cynthia had reserved the back room of Hollydale's bar and grill to celebrate Mrs. Chenworth's sixtieth birthday. Cynthia wanted to surprise her salon's best customer.

At seven o'clock, Damon was crammed into a small but well-lit room. A knotted pine table stretched from one end to the other. More than twenty guests packed the open spaces between the table and walls. Damon scanned the room. He was the only man present other than Jackson Krims, owner of the Fish Barrel, and Doc Marley, who managed the local grocery store. Mrs. Chenworth's cohorts tended to be women.

Lynne Lassard-Brown snaked her way through a crush of bodies to her son. "Jackson needs your help to take away some of the chairs and move the table against the wall, Damon. Otherwise Mrs. Chenworth won't be able to fit into the room," she snickered.

Just after the furniture had been rearranged, Mrs. Chenworth arrived with Cynthia. A chorus of "Surprise!" filled the space.

Mrs. Chenworth put her hand to her heart and breathed in deeply. "Oh my! What a surprise, indeed!" She bustled forward like a corpulent Moses parting seas of people. "I had no idea anyone would throw me a party. But just in case, I made a dish for the occasion!"

Mrs. Chenworth pulled foil from the top of a pie tin and set the offering on the table among a crowd of plates laden with food. She turned to Lynne, who was standing beside her. "Apple pie and meatloaf are my two best dishes."

Lynne looked down at a flaky, lopsided pie crust. "Which is this?" she asked with a wicked grin.

Mrs. Chenworth's mouth shot open wide, but then she smiled and slugged Lynne's delicate left shoulder. "Oh, you kidder," the birthday girl said and turned to a cluster of chattering woman making their way toward her.

Lynne rubbed her shoulder. "That hurt," she said to Damon.

"You deserved it, Mother."

They helped themselves to plates of food.

"I heard you caught Clementine Snead," Lynne said.

"I did." Damon recapped the details, telling his mother about the hotline tip in confidence.

"Who do you think called it in?" she asked.

"I've been thinking about that," Damon said. "My best guess is one of his co-workers. You should have seen him boasting about his innovative genius. I don't think someone that arrogant would be able to keep quiet. He probably started bragging to his colleagues at the garden center about his special formula, and someone who knew about the Hollydale infestations put two-and-two together."

"That sounds pretty exciting, Damon," Lynne said. "Mrs. Chenworth told everyone she saw you on a stakeout."

Damon blushed. "Actually, she did. Clementine only lives a couple of blocks from here, and Mrs. Chenworth walked right by while I was watching his house."

"Was Rebecca with you?" Lynne had been trying to push Damon toward Rebecca romantically since he moved to Hollydale.

"No, I was on my own the night I followed Clementine."

"Too bad." Lynne said. She added with an impish laugh, "I was hoping that you and Rebecca were *staking out* in the back seat of your car."

* * *

"How's your niece's Labrador?" Damon asked Mrs. Chenworth later that evening.

"Just fine, no thanks to you, Damon," she responded. "You promised to walk him for me."

Damon assured her that he'd take the dog out the following morning.

"I can't wait until my niece comes back from Greece," Mrs. Chenworth said. "The dog's been sleeping in my bed!"

"Can't you put some pillows or a blanket on the floor for him?"

"I did," she said as she shoved a handful of macaroons from a nearby plate into her purse. "But he climbs up on the bed after I'm asleep. Last night I had a dream that I was in a straightjacket! I woke up in a cold sweat. I was under my comforter, but the Lab was lying on top of it, pinning me inside! It's a wonder more people don't suffocate because of their dogs!"

Damon tuned out Mrs. Chenworth's voice. His mind swept back to Jeremiah Milk's wife and infant son. They had both died in their sleep.

His thoughts were interrupted by Rebecca tugging at his sleeve. She towed Damon away from Mrs.

Chenworth with a polite, "Please excuse us for a minute."

"Thanks," Damon said to Rebecca once the two of them found a quiet corner of the party room.

Rebecca had on a crimped turquoise top and a black skirt that became increasingly sheer as it fell toward the floor. Her hair was swept away from her eyes with a series of barrettes.

Damon filled her in on his exploits with Clementine and his conversation with Matthew.

"I thought I told you to leave Matthew alone," Rebecca said.

Damon sighed. "I couldn't once I had an idea of how big of a role he played in Jeremiah's revenge scheme."

"I suppose you're right," Rebecca admitted. "I can't believe Dominic burned Jeremiah's fingers. That takes a sick mind. He has to be the murder. Or else, he hired someone to do it for him."

"I know," Damon agreed. "But I don't have any evidence. And I think someone else had to be involved. I can't see how Dominic would know Jeremiah's schedule at the park or where the equipment used for the murder was kept without inside information."

"I'm sure the police will find the evidence they need," Rebecca said. She touched his shoulder. "You've certainly found the lion's share of information for them."

Just then, Bethany Krims strode into the Fish Barrel's party room. Damon's heart lurched. She wore a modest but form-flattering black skirt suit. Emerald teardrops dangled from her earlobes. Her hair was freshly cut in short, blunt layers.

Damon caught Bethany's eye and she flitted her fingers toward him in a wave. Then she dashed over to her father. Bethany whispered something in Jackson's ear and danced out of the room.

Rebecca looked at Damon's wounded eyes. She put an arm around his shoulder. "I'm sure she's just going to a work function, Damon."

* * *

An hour later, on his walk home, a disappointed Damon passed the historic Hollydale Firehouse. After serving the community for ninety years, the volunteer station had recently been cast off into retirement in favor of a new base three blocks away.

Damon climbed the steps to his duplex. Gerry Sloman was sitting in a rocker alongside David Einstaff. David sipped whiskey. Gerry held a can of soda. The men raised their drinks to Damon.

"David told me about you cracking the case of the crepe myrtles," Gerry said to Damon.

"I ran into Mrs. Chenworth earlier today," David explained, then said, "You look down, Damon."

"I just saw Bethany a little while ago," he replied. "She was all dressed up to go somewhere. I think she landed another lawyer or consultant. She tends to go for the corporate types."

Gerry rose and slapped Damon on the back. "It sounds like you don't know where she was headed or with whom. So until you do, keep your chin up. Now, let's go inside and you can tell me all about the locker in Frederick and your trip to Philadelphia."

David's eyes focused briefly on the men through an inebriated fog but returned to his glass. "Okay, let's talk in my kitchen," Damon said to Gerry. "But first I'm going to make David some coffee." He turned to his neighbor. "It's Monday night, David. You need to go to work tomorrow."

After coaxing David to accept a steaming Thermos of coffee, Damon left his neighbor on the porch and spent over an hour at his kitchen table detailing his latest finds to Gerry. The detective took copious notes and, after Damon concluded his narrative, asked his friend to come to the station the following day to provide a formal statement. Damon also passed Gerry the folders he appropriated from Jeremiah's gymnasium locker.

"So you're pretty certain that the boy, Matthew, was involved in the set-up?" Gerry asked.

"Yes," Damon said. "I suspect the idea had been percolating in Jeremiah's mind for some time. When he met Matthew and found out he was a both computer whiz and a boy who had endured similar hardships, he knew the time was right to set his retaliation plan into action."

"And it didn't hurt that Alistair Atwater gave Jeremiah a heap of money he could use to buy his way into Trident," Gerry mused.

"I wonder if Jeremiah would've been able to carry out his plan without a bankroll," Damon pondered out loud.

"It doesn't matter. He had it. This is all great information, Damon. The problem is there's no concrete evidence linking Dominic Freeze to Jeremiah's murder."

"Trust me, I know."

"We'll bring Dominic in and push hard on him. I'll get a warrant to search his house, too. The prosecutors might try to make a case even if we don't find anything else. The motive is there." Gerry sipped hot coffee. "I suppose you bringing me this information now is fortuitous. Margaret was planning to arrest Lawrence Drake tomorrow morning."

Damon's eyes widened. "Lawrence Drake? What did you find out?"

"To be honest, it's just a combination of circumstantial evidence. Aylin Erul told you that she believed Drake had a shrine to Veronica Maldive in his home. We didn't find one, but we do have her statement. Drake would know Jeremiah's schedule, including when he would be in the shed by himself. Drake also knew where the pressure washer and hedge trimmer to cut the power cord were kept. He has no alibi for the night of the murder. Margaret wanted to look more closely at him as a suspect, so one of our junior detectives has been interviewing his family and friends. It turns out Drake's younger brother runs a painting company, and this past June, Lawrence Drake asked his brother to teach him how to use a pressure washer."

Damon put his elbows on the kitchen table and let the information sink in. "That's very interesting," he said.

"It is, but it's weak."

"So now that you know about Dominic, will you still arrest Drake?"

"I'll ask Margaret to postpone bringing him in for a couple of days," Gerry said. He tugged on the cross dangling from a chain around his neck. "I'd love to find a connection between Dominic Freeze and Lawrence Drake."

Damon stood and stretched his legs. "Will Margaret be upset at you for speaking with me?" he asked.

"Not for speaking with you. The information you found is vital, so you had to pass it along to us. But she'll be angry. You handled the folders from Jeremiah's locker, so we could have evidentiary problems. And by speaking directly with Matthew, Samantha, and most of all, Dominic, you've caused a boatload of other problems, not the least of which is that Dominic might have caught a fast train to Canada. And—oh, by the way—you could have gotten yourself killed. What were you thinking, Damon?"

"I don't know," Damon said ashamedly.

Gerry eyed his friend. "You really should consider signing up for the Northern Virginia Criminal Justice Training Academy. Once you finish the coursework and fieldwork, I could put a good word in the right ears at the Arlington station."

"Thanks, Gerry. I definitely need to think about it."

Chapter 20

The following morning, Damon woke up feeling despondent. He had convinced himself that Bethany found a suitor she preferred to Damon. And he didn't know whether the police would be able to find sufficient evidence to put away anyone for Jeremiah's murder.

Damon walked the yellow Labrador for Mrs. Chenworth, gave a statement at the police station as Gerry had requested, and then spent a quiet afternoon volunteering at the Hollydale library and an even quieter evening in the Crime Solvers' office. Not a single call came in, and his mind wandered. In addition to Jeremiah's unsolved murder, the circumstances surrounding the deaths of Dottie Milk's daughter-in-law and grandson still nagged at him.

The next morning, Wednesday, Damon walked to the Milk residence. Dottie was in front of the house, perched on the lowest rung of a metal stepladder. Armed with a wide putty knife, she scraped loose paint from wind-beaten wood siding.

Damon stopped on the sidewalk behind her. "Good morning, Mrs. Milk."

Dottie turned and looked at Damon. She smiled. "Good morning to you, Mr. Lassard."

"Are you planning to repaint?"

"I am. I'm going to sell this place now that Jeremiah's gone."

Damon offered to relieve her of scraping duty for a few minutes.

Dottie accepted and went inside to fetch lemonade. When she returned, Damon—who was three rungs high—gratefully accepted a glass. He took a long swallow and set the glass on a step of the ladder.

"When are you heading back to Arizona?" Damon asked over his shoulder.

"Probably next week," Dottie replied, sweeping loose fragments into a neat pile. "You know, the police contacted me yesterday. They asked me a number of question about Dominic Freeze."

Damon turned and looked down. "I've been talking with Detective Sloman," he said. "We think there's a good chance Dominic was involved in Jeremiah's murder."

"I should have known." Dottie shook her head in disdain. "He was an evil little boy then. I'm not surprised he turned into a monster of a man."

Damon provided Dottie with an abridged version of the harm Jeremiah had inflicted on Dominic Freeze. He told her that Alistair Atwater gave Jeremiah a substantial sum for working with Matthew but left out Matthew's involvement with Jeremiah's plans and the story about Dominic burning Jeremiah's fingers. He didn't want Dottie to go through any further emotional distress.

"The police told me the same thing," Dottie said when Jeremiah finished. "Shame on Jeremiah for not being a bigger person. But that didn't give Dominic Freeze the right to engage in vigilante justice."

"I couldn't agree with you more," Damon said. "Unfortunately, the police don't have anything that specifically links Dominic to Jeremiah's death."

Dottie frowned. "Between that terrible man's motive and his history of torturing Jeremiah, you'd think it would be enough."

Damon didn't agree with Dottie on that point but kept his mouth shut. He took a step up on the ladder and began to chip paint in earnest. It reminded him of sloughing off dead skin from a sunburn. With his back to Dottie, Damon said, "Mrs. Milk, there's something that's been bothering me." He paused, then pushed on. "Can you tell me about the night your daughter-in-law and grandson died?"

Damon heard Dottie stop sweeping. After a moment, she said, "I didn't know whether you had heard about Kathryn and Samuel."

"I did," Damon said, still facing the house. "They both died of natural causes, hours apart."

"It sounds like you already know the story then," she said timidly.

"Most of it, yes." He scraped a chip of paint the size of a playing card from the woodwork and watched it flutter to the ground. "But I've been wondering why you didn't call 911 or take Samuel to the hospital after you found him."

Damon heard a shuffling movement behind him and turned his head. Dottie was dragging a wooden rocker from the front porch. She lugged it to near the base of the ladder and settled herself on it. "I suppose I can tell you. I told Lieutenant Hobbes yesterday. She had the same gut feeling as you do—that there was a bit more to the story, something only Jeremiah and I knew. I've always felt so guilty about it."

Damon turned back to the house. He suspected it might be easier for Dottie to speak if she didn't have to face him.

"Two days before their deaths, I was taking care of Samuel while Kathryn was shopping and Jeremiah was out here, shoveling snow. The baby just wouldn't stop crying. I don't know why. So I...." Dottie choked back tears. "I shook him in frustration. I only did it one time, and it wasn't hard. But I did it."

"And you told Jeremiah?" Damon asked.

"He saw me do it. I was upstairs with Samuel in his nursery, and I hadn't heard Jeremiah come in from outside. As soon as I shook Samuel, I felt Jeremiah's presence in the doorframe behind me. I explained to him that I'd never done it before and I wouldn't ever again. That was the truth. I regretted shaking Samuel as soon as I'd done it. Jeremiah gave me a tongue lashing, but I'm fairly certain he didn't tell Kathryn—her attitude toward me didn't change in the days between the incident and her death. At the time, I wasn't worried about Samuel's health. Babies get jostled around in strollers all of the time without any long term harm. As long as I never did it again, I was sure Samuel would be just fine."

"And then he stopped breathing two nights later."

"Yes," Dottie said. "Jeremiah had gone to the hospital with Kathryn. When I went to check on Samuel and found him dead, I panicked. I had no idea whether or not he died because I shook him. Every time I think about it, which is quite often, I tell myself that one small shake couldn't have caused his death two days later. But of course, I have no idea if that's really true, and I never will." She sniffed. "My first inclination was to call 911, then I thought about the consequences. Jeremiah could be temperamental. If I called for an ambulance and went with Samuel to the hospital, Jeremiah might react on the spot and scream out in front of anyone who was around to listen that I was responsible for the baby's death. I was scared of being sent to prison for my mistake. And Samuel was already dead, I reasoned. I might not be a doctor, but there was no doubt in my mind that he'd passed any point of being saved."

"So you waited for Jeremiah to come home."

"I did. He didn't accuse me as I feared. Rather, in a voice resigned to fate, he said that he was taking Samuel to the hospital, and I should start packing my things. After the funeral, he wanted me out of the house."

"That's why you moved to Arizona?"

"Yes. The house was in my name, but I didn't push Jeremiah on the matter. The whole ordeal was incredibly hard on me. I moved into a retirement community for older adults. I have friends there now, so I've decided to stay in Arizona. Between selling this house and the money Jeremiah had left in his bank account, I can comfortably live out my days there."

"Jeremiah left his money to you, then?"

Dottie laughed nervously. "He didn't have a will, so I think it'll pass to me through probate. I must say that I was quite surprised when Cameron Williams from True Capital told me Jeremiah had $400,000 in the bank."

"It was from Alistair Atwater," Damon said.

"I suppose so. I believe Jeremiah had forgiven me, you know. We never stopped talking, even after I moved to Arizona. At first our conversations were stilted, but time and distance healed a lot of wounds."

Dottie rose from her chair and moved it back to the porch. Damon took that as his cue to leave and descended the stepladder. As he stepped to the ground, the image of Dominic Freeze burning Jeremiah's fingertips reentered his mind. He focused his thoughts on the other boy, the one who had been with Dominic while he bound Jeremiah's hands but had been too frightened to go any further.

"Mrs. Milk," Damon said and approached the front porch. "Do you remember the names of any of the other boys who were in Dominic's childhood clique? The ones who teased Jeremiah?"

"Not specifically," Dottie said. "But if you gave me some names, one might ring a bell."

One by one, Damon walked Dottie through a list of men, including Lawrence Drake, Milt Verblanc, the male Park Police officer, and even Emmanuel Alvarez despite his advanced age.

"I'm sorry, Mr. Lassard. None of those names is familiar to me," Dottie said.

Damon sighed. He tried Matthew's father, Geoffrey Katz, for good measure, but Dottie hadn't heard of him either.

Damon finished his lemonade and handed the empty glass to Dottie. "Does Dominic Freeze's family still live in Hollydale?" he asked. Despite his position with the citizens association, there were numerous families he didn't know.

Dottie shook her head. "No. They moved just after Jeremiah and Dominic finished ninth grade. I heard Sebastian, Dominic's stepfather, got a job at a commercial apple juice mill down in North Carolina. He started in the winter and moved down south a few months before the rest of the family. Jackie Freeze didn't want to uproot Dominic or his stepsister in the middle of the school year. I remember, some of the other women in Hollydale helped Jackie pack boxes. Not me."

Damon's ears tingled. "Dominic Freeze had a stepsister?"

"He did," Dottie said. "Is that important?"

"I don't know," Damon admitted. "Were they close?"

"Michelle and Dominic? I have no idea. She was quite a few years younger than him."

"Do you remember what she looked like?"

"Unfortunately, Damon, I don't recall anything about Michelle's appearance that would stand out. She had straight brown hair. She must have looked similar to half of the girls her age."

"Thanks, Mrs. Milk. I don't know whether it'll help, but it's good information to have. You said Dominic and Michelle were stepsiblings. Did Michelle go by the name Freeze?"

"I don't think so. I'm pretty sure she went by her father's last name: Walczak."

* * *

Dominic made a beeline to the Hollydale branch library. He ran a search of newspaper articles for Michelle Walczak using his Lexis account. No hits. A Google search for Dominic's stepsister was equally fruitless.

Damon closed his eyes and thought. Might she have a connection to one of the park workers? Damon was convinced that Dominic Freeze had worked with an insider at Tripping Falls to murder Jeremiah. If Dominic's stepsister was several years younger than him, she would probably be in her early thirties. Pretty young to be dating Lawrence Drake or Milt Verblanc, he thought. Was Michelle the lover of one of the *women* at the park? Or perhaps Michelle Walczak could *be* one of the female staffers. After all, Jeremiah had created his own false identity. Both Alex Rancor and Aylin Erul appeared to be in their late twenties or early thirties. Veronica was a few years older.

Damon longed to have a photograph of Michelle Walczak from her youth. But where could he find one? Damon's brain clicked and he briskly walked a half mile to the elementary school that served Hollydale.

* * *

Diane Ridgeway, Ashbury Elementary's assistant principal, exuded vivacity. She pumped Damon's hand when he entered her office, and before Damon even sat down she was touting the school's attributes.

Diane finally sat behind her desk and gave Damon a wide grin. "Now, how can I help you, Mr. Lassard?"

Damon returned her smile. Diane was in her late forties and had a pinched nose that didn't fit her outgoing personality. "I'm looking for old yearbooks from Ashbury. Ones that date back twenty to twenty-five years ago."

Diane beamed. "That's easy. We have a shelf full of yearbooks in the school's library. I believe they go back at least thirty years." She looked at Damon inquisitively. "May I ask who or what you're looking for?"

Damon hesitated. He mumbled something about genealogy research for a friend.

Diane eyed Damon curiously but didn't comment. Instead she gave him directions to the library.

As Damon stood to leave the assistant principal's office, he noticed that the fourth finger on Diane Ridgeway's left hand was bereft of a ring. Inspiration hit, albeit on a matter completely unrelated to his mission to track down Michele Walczak.

"Ms. Ridgeway," Damon stammered. "I know this may seem a bit unconventional, but I was hoping to ask you something on a personal level."

Diane squinted at Damon. "Go ahead," she said with caution.

Damon plunged forward. "I noticed that you aren't wearing a wedding band. I have a neighbor. His name is David. I think you two would make a great match, if you're not seeing anyone and are willing to go on a blind date."

Diane Ridgeway threw her head back and laughed. "I thought you were acting a little strange. Sure, why not? I'll go out with your friend." She gave Damon her phone number and shooed him into the hallway like a mischievous third grader.

Damon smiled to himself. Now he just had to convince David Einstaff to take a leap of faith.

He found the library, which was situated in the center of the pentagon-shaped school. Damon asked a tired-looking library aide where he could find the shelf of old yearbooks. They were located in a corner reserved for discarded computer equipment and a beautiful wooden card catalog with brass knobs. Damon pulled open one of the small drawers—it was still stocked with cards.

He spent twenty minutes scanning the pages of dusty hardbound albums. Damon quickly located photos of Jeremiah Milk and Dominic Freeze. Then he found a school picture of Michelle Walczak. Given the yearbook dates, she was six years younger than her stepbrother Dominic. Damon peered closely at the photo of the plain-looking brown-eyed, brown-haired girl, then shut his eyes and conjured the faces of the female park workers from his memory bank.

Aylin Erul had large green eyes. The shape of her eyes resembled those in the photo but nothing else seemed to match. Of course, Damon thought, features change over time.

Damon shifted his focus and imagined Alex Rancor. The girl in the photo and Alex had nothing in common other than skin color. The curve of the nose was wrong as was the shape of the girl's mouth.

Finally, Damon considered Veronica Maldive. The education specialist's eye and hair color matched Michelle's, but the shape of the girl's face was much more narrow than Veronica's. The difference could be due to weight gain, Damon thought.

Based on Michelle's photograph, Damon ruled out Alex Rancor as Dominic Freeze's stepsister. But he couldn't unequivocally conclude that Michelle Walczak was neither Aylin nor Veronica.

Damon located a handful of other yearbooks with photos of Michelle but none shed any more light on her current identity. For good measure, and with the library aide's permission, Damon made photocopies of Michelle's pictures. He folded them into his jacket pocket alongside a newspaper photo from the *Philadelphia Business Journal* of an adult Dominic Freeze that he had printed at the Hollydale branch library.

* * *

Damon made his way to Tripping Falls State Park. Rebecca had vowed to Gerry that neither she nor Damon would speak with the suspects again, but Damon pushed the promise to the nether regions of his mind.

As he was driving, his mother called. "Hello, Damon," Lynne said. "You left Mrs. Chenworth's party in a hurry the other night. Is everything all right? Bethany's appearance must have upset you."

"I'm fine, Mother," Damon said through clenched teeth. His mother always knew exactly what he was thinking when it came to women. He summoned inner fortitude. "Did you happen to find out where she was going?" he asked.

"I did, Damon. That's why I'm calling. I went to Cynthia's salon yesterday to get my nails done. Mrs. Chenworth was there, of course. As you could expect, she knew exactly where Bethany was going when she stopped by the Fish Barrel."

"Mrs. Chenworth must have cornered Jackson Krims," Damon said.

"I'm sure that's what happened."

"So where was Bethany going?"

"Damon, I don't think you want to know."

"I can handle it, Mother. Just end my agony."

"She wasn't going to see another man, Damon. She had an audition to be a weather broadcaster on a national cable network. According to Bethany's father, they saw her coverage of the tornado aftermath in Nebraska and loved it."

"That's wonderful news," Damon said into the phone. "Why wouldn't I want to know?"

"Because the job's based in Atlanta."

Chapter 21

The visitor center was bustling with activity. A dozen hikers of retirement age formed a semicircle around Lawrence Drake, who was standing in front of a large park map. Drake spotted Damon and glowered in his direction.

Damon steered his way around Lawrence and through the doors to the management wing. Veronica Maldive's office door was closed, but Alex Rancor's was wide open. She was filling out forms longhand. Alex looked up and waved Damon inside.

"I was hoping I'd see you again, Damon." She twisted hair around her forefinger. "I was wondering if you'd like to take me out to dinner sometime. I wanted to ask when I saw you at the funeral, but I didn't think it was an appropriate time."

Damon considered the woman in front of him. Alex was a no-nonsense woman, appealing in a businesslike way. She had been pleasant with Damon every time they had spoken, and her delicate features were objectively attractive. But Damon still held out hope for a romance with Bethany, and he didn't feel a spark with Alex.

"I'm actually seeing someone right now," he replied. It wasn't completely true but made letting Alex down significantly easier.

"No problem," Alex said with bravado. "You're looking for Veronica, right? She should be in her office."

Damon stepped across the short hall and knocked on Veronica's door.

"It's open," the teaching specialist said.

Damon pushed his way inside. Veronica was up to her elbows in glue, popsicle sticks, and cotton balls. Her dark hair was mussed. Brown eyes under lashes heavily caked with black mascara widened when she saw Damon.

"Sorry I'm such a mess," Veronica said with a smile. "Please, sit down, Mr. Lassard. Thank you for coming to Jeremiah's funeral. That meant a lot to me."

On his way to the park, Damon had decided that Veronica was just as likely a candidate to be an accomplice of Dominic Freeze as Aylin Erul. She started dating Jeremiah earlier in the year, and Damon didn't know if her motives were pure. Damon had also been led to the private investigator, Marcus Pontfried, by a single person—Veronica Maldive. According to the teaching specialist, she'd been the only person to see Pontfried at the park. What if he had never even come to Tripping Falls? Of course, if Veronica and Dominic were co-conspirators, why put Damon onto Pontfried's track?

Damon looked closely at Veronica. He longed to pull out Michelle Walczak's photo and do an on-the-spot comparison. Instead, he tried a roundabout approach. He unfolded his copy of Dominic Freeze's picture and laid it on Veronica's desk.

"I was wondering, Veronica, if you've seen this man around Tripping Falls?"

She looked at the photo. "No, I haven't. Detective Sloman showed me a picture of the same man yesterday."

Damon thought she sounded genuine but couldn't be sure.

"He must be a suspect in Jeremiah's murder, right?" Veronica asked. "The detective wouldn't tell me."

"I believe the police are looking at him very closely," Damon said. He decided to take a shot at Veronica's background.

"Have you seen Jeremiah's mother, Dottie, since the funeral?" he asked.

"I took her out to dinner two nights ago."

"That was really nice of you. When I saw her this morning, she said she planned to sell the house in Hollydale."

"She'll be all right in Arizona," Veronica said. "She's dealt with family tragedy before."

Damon agreed. "Still, it's hard to leave behind a home you lived in for so many years. I was born in Michigan and sometimes I miss it." Damon paused. He longed to know where Veronica had spent her formative years. Was it in Hollydale as Dominic Freeze's stepsister?

As if reading his thoughts, Veronica said, "I know how you feel. I grew up in Maine and don't get back there very often."

Now Damon had an answer. Of course, Veronica could be lying.

* * *

Damon checked the rangers' lounge for Aylin, but it was empty. He stepped outside and cut through the woodlands to Emmanuel Alvarez's cabin. The maintenance man had been keenly helpful the first time Damon spoke with him.

Emmanuel was in his garage, cutting sheet metal. He looked up and waved as Damon approached. Damon shook his hand.

"I'm about ready for some snow," Emmanuel said genially. He wore a checked flannel shirt and dirty jeans.

"You'll probably have to wait another couple of months. I didn't know people from the Caribbean were fond of cold weather." Damon leaned against the garage's refrigerator.

"I think I'm wired differently than the rest of the folks down there. That's probably why I never moved back."

"Makes sense," Damon said. "Any chance I could pick your brain again about Jeremiah's murder? You were right on the money when it came to the method the killer used."

"I was, wasn't I?" The older man smiled. "The police came around yesterday asking about someone named Dominic Freeze. He and Jeremiah must have had quite a history."

Damon filled Emmanuel in on the pair's childhood interactions and his understanding of Jeremiah's schemes to discredit Dominic professionally and to ruin his marriage.

"Sounds like Jeremiah had a lot of rage," Emmanuel said. "I suspect he kept it bottled up for a long time."

Damon nodded his agreement.

Emmanuel said, "If this Dominic is the killer and is as malevolent as he sounds, their history would go a long way toward explaining why he spent time with the pressure washer on Dominic's fingers and toes."

"That sounds logical," Damon said.

"But you know all of this already." Emmanuel lit a cigarette. "So, what's really on your mind?"

"A link to Tripping Falls," Damon answered without hesitation. "I think there's someone on the inside who's either Dominic's hired gun or who showed him the location of your tools and told him precisely when and where Jeremiah would be alone."

Emmanuel took a hard drag from his cigarette. "And who do you think that might be?"

Damon pulled out the photocopy of Michelle Walczak's yearbook picture and handed it to Emmanuel. "She'd be a grown woman now."

Emmanuel studied the photo. "You think this girl is one of the female staffers at the park?"

"Possibly. She's Dominic's stepsister."

"I'd say it looks a little like Aylin, provided she started wearing green contact lenses. But it could be Veronica—it's hard to tell with her weight. Alex is less likely, unless she had a whole lot of plastic surgery."

Damon handed the picture of Dominic to Emmanuel. "This is Dominic Freeze. Have you seen him at the park?"

Emmanuel looked at it carefully then passed it back. "The police showed me a similar photo. I haven't seen him here. Of course, that doesn't mean much. The park has a lot of acreage." Emmanuel took another puff on his cigarette, then said, "If he was working with an insider who knew the schedule of the Park Police officers who do the overnight checks, Dominic could have come in afterwards to do his reconnaissance. He'd be able to roam about freely until the break of dawn."

The rotors in Damon's head started to hum. *The break of dawn.* He recalled the tall, elderly man who had interrupted his conversation with Alex Rancor and Jeremiah in the visitor center lobby the day before Jeremiah was murdered. His property backed up to the parklands, and Jeremiah said he regularly hiked in the early morning hours.

"What is it?" Emmanuel asked, sensing Damon's change in expression.

"Do you know of a man named Bertlemann? He lives near the park."

"Frederick Bertlemann, sure," Emmanuel said. "Do you think he's Dominic's inside man? The guy thinks he owns the place, but I've always considered him harmless." The maintenance man paused, then said, "Oh, I see your line of thinking. He walks the trails before the park opens. He might have seen something."

"Exactly. Do all of the staff know that he comes onto park property in the predawn hours?" Damon asked.

"Good question. Alex knows because she works with him on fundraising. I know because I've been at the park forever. Same with Lawrence Drake and Milt Verblanc. And Jeremiah for that matter. Aylin hasn't been here too long, so I'm not sure about her. And I don't know whether Veronica would know as the teacher: she spends more time inside her office than out in the park."

That's it! Damon thumped a palm against his forehead. The obvious had been staring him in the face all along.

"You have something?" Emmanuel asked.

"I think so," Damon said. "Can you show me where Mr. Bertlemann lives?"

Chapter 22

Frederick Bertlemann's house was hidden in the woods surrounding Tripping Falls State Park. Only the narrow mouth of a gravel driveway was visible from the road. Emmanuel pointed it out through the passenger's side window as he rode along with Damon.

Damon let Emmanuel out of the car. The maintenance man cut through the woods on foot to make his way back to the park. Damon turned into Bertlemann's driveway and followed it thirty yards. The drive stopped in front of a home that resembled an enormous birdhouse. Its exterior was constructed of wide horizontal boards punctuated by circular windows and topped by a steep pitched roof.

BOOM!

The tremendous sound cracked the air and shook Damon's car. Enormous splinters of wood sailed like missiles from the second story of the birdhouse. Damon ducked under his steering wheel. Sounds of wood crashing into the windshield pierced his ears. After a moment, the air fell silent. Damon looked up. One side of the top of Bertlemann's house had been blown apart. Flames lapped up oxygen and shot skyward.

Damon pushed open the door to his Saab. Shards of glass, shingles, and burning wood littered the yard. Fiery pieces that vaulted into the surrounding woods lit masses of leaves nestled under the trees. Damon envisioned the small flames growing into a forest fire. He jerked the cell phone from his jacket pocket, dialed 911, and urged the dispatcher to send fire and ambulance rescue immediately. "Also, please contact Detective Gerry Sloman with the Arlington County police force about this right away," he added rapidly. "I think it's related to a murder he's investigating."

Damon ran toward the front of the burning home. He saw someone emerge from a screened-in porch at the side of the house and sprint into the woods between Bertlemann's house and Tripping Falls. The person was dressed from head to foot in black and wore a ski mask. A backpack bounced behind the figure's shoulders.

Damon's mind raced. Was Frederick Bertlemann inside the house? Should he track down the runner or look inside? Saving a life was paramount. Heat scorched Damon's face as he opened the front door.

Damon heard a shout from behind him. He turned to see Emmanuel Alvarez emerging from the woods and hurrying toward him.

"Did you see him?" Damon shouted.

"Who?" Emmanuel called back. The maintenance man stopped on the porch in front of Damon and wiped sweat from his face.

"Someone just ran from the house. That way." Damon pointed. The person in black had entered the woods twenty yards from the spot Alvarez had exited.

"No," Emmanuel said quickly. "You go after him. I'll go inside and look for Bertlemann."

"I called 911," Damon shouted and dashed into the woods.

Damon raced hard in the direction he had seen the figure run. Although in excellent shape, he was close to a minute behind, and he wasn't familiar with the terrain. A quarter of a mile into the woods, Damon came upon a narrow trail. Bertlemann probably used it to traverse from his home to the park every morning. Would the arsonist risk taking a trail? The chance of being spotted rose if he or she followed it, but it also allowed for a faster and quieter escape.

Damon put his hands on his knees to catch his breath and to listen. Other than the sound of birds, the air was silent. He started to move down the path, treading at a moderate pace. One minute later, Damon caught a glimpse of movement. He quickly ducked behind a fallen oak. Poking his head up for a peak, Damon spotted the culprit. The person in black was perched on a wide flat stone twenty-five feet ahead and to the right of the path. Thick tree trunks obstructed Damon's line of vision. Staying crouched behind the oak, he crept five paces to his left to improve his view.

Gloved hands removed the black ski mask. Damon breathed in deeply, waiting to confirm his suspicions.

Bingo! Straight blond locks splayed when released from the mask's constraints. Aylin Erul unstrapped the backpack, set the mask inside, and pulled out a ranger's uniform.

Damon watched Aylin don her uniform. His brain jetted through possible actions to take. If he left now to fetch Gerry, Aylin would be back at the park, dressed as a ranger by the time the detective arrived. But Damon's eyewitness account of Aylin fleeing Bertlemann's house had to count for something, didn't it? Another option was to tackle her and call Gerry once he had her pinned to the ground.

The loud chirp of an incoming call on Damon's cell phone resolved his dilemma. Damon fumbled his hand into his jacket pocket but not before Aylin looked up. Her glimmering green eyes locked with Damon's.

Aylin took off in a dead sprint. Damon raced after her. She weaved among the trees, dodging thickets of spiny brush and fallen limbs. Aylin knew the wooded area better than Damon, but his legs were longer, and he quickly closed the gap between them. Twenty feet, fifteen, ten.

Arrgh! Pain seared through Damon's ankle as his foot caught in a hole obscured by matted leaves. He collapsed to the ground. Aylin glanced back then disappeared into the trees. Damon tried to jump back up, but his throbbing ankle refused to cooperate.

He cursed out loud. Damon pulled out his traitorous cell phone. No signal. Blaring alarms from fire engines in the distance reached his ears.

Damon stood and tried to keep weight off of his injured ankle. But he couldn't hop more than a few feet at a time. He sank to his knees and crawled back toward Bertlemann's house. When he reached the spot where Aylin had changed clothes, he spotted her backpack. She had left it behind in her haste. Damon hefted it over his shoulder and continued to plow in the direction of the sirens.

As he dragged his body forward, Damon smiled to himself. His conclusion as to the identity of Dominic's accomplice, albeit late in the day, had been spot on. Not only had Aylin concocted a motive for Lawrence Drake to throw off the police, but she had conveniently been in Harrisonburg on the night of the murder, taking along Emmanuel to ensure that he was nowhere near his cabin when Dominic Freeze needed access to his garage. With Aylin in Harrisonburg, in Damon's mind, that cemented Dominic Freeze as the man who pulled the trigger on the pressure washer.

The clincher that had finally registered with Damon was that Aylin had started work at the park only six months earlier. Every other Tripping Falls employee had been on staff before Jeremiah implemented his plot to ruin Dominic Freeze. Aylin, on the other hand, started three months after Dominic hired Marcus

Pontfried to find the man who framed him for embezzlement.

Damon suspected that if anyone looked closely at Aylin's prior work history as a ranger, the information would turn out to be falsified. It would be too coincidental that Dominic's stepsister happened to be a park ranger. More likely, once Dominic knew where Jeremiah worked, he and his stepsister Michelle waited until there was a job opening at Tripping Falls. Michelle gave herself the name Aylin and created a resume that would fit the position to a tee.

And Damon had no doubt that Aylin Erul was indeed Michelle Walczak. The shape of the eyes of the little girl in the yearbook photo were the same as Aylin's. She learned the intricacies of the park, including where tools that could be used as implements of death were kept, and most importantly, when and where Jeremiah would be alone in the park. She just had to get Emmanuel out of his cabin, which proved to be a simple task. Damon didn't doubt that Aylin's mother had plumbing problems—either created by Aylin or real—but Damon suspected Aylin had identified exactly which date Emmanuel would be "available" to assist.

The only thing that didn't make complete sense was Aylin's motive. Stepbrothers and stepsisters could be close, he supposed, but asking a sibling to participate as an accomplice to murder was over the top.

* * *

When Damon finally reached Frederick Bertlemann's house, the fire department had snuffed out the blaze. The second floor had collapsed onto the first, destroying all but the foundation. Smoke rose from firehose-soaked clusters of charred trees and piles of leaves. Emergency personnel buzzed around two massive fire engines, three ambulances, and a half dozen police cars parked on Bertlemann's lawn.

Paramedics were tending to a man on a stretcher. Gerry Sloman and Emmanuel Alvarez hovered behind the caregivers.

"Gerry!" Damon cried out as he crawled across the lawn.

The detective turned sharply. He and Emmanuel ran to Damon's side.

"What happened? Are you all right?" Gerry shouted and reached down to help his friend to his feet.

"It's Aylin, Gerry!" Damon shouted "It's Aylin! Ten minutes ago she was headed toward the park."

Gerry nodded his head and relayed the information via radio transmission. Then Gerry and Emmanuel hoisted Damon between them and carried him to an empty stretcher. A paramedic rushed to his side, but Damon waved him away. "I'm okay. I just twisted my ankle. Or I might have broken it. But I need to talk to the detective first."

The paramedic reluctantly backed away.

"Don't worry, Damon," Gerry said. "We'll get Aylin. And we arrested Dominic Freeze this morning. I'll tell you about that, but first, tell me what you saw." Emmanuel stepped in close to listen.

Damon relayed his story. He had convinced himself that Aylin was Dominic's stepsister, Michelle Walczak. Recalling that Frederick Bertlemann regularly took hikes before the park opened, Damon wanted to show him Dominic's picture and find out if he had ever seen Dominic at the park, either alone or with Aylin. Damon recounted watching the house explode, seeing a figure flee, and tracking down the arsonist, who turned out to be Aylin. He handed her backpack to Gerry. The detective delicately unzipped it and looked inside.

"An explosives kit," Gerry said. "Between your testimony and this bag, we should have enough evidence to bring her up on charges for the attempted murder of Frederick Bertlemann."

"Attempted murder?" Damon asked. "So Bertlemann is alive?"

Gerry smiled and lifted his chin in the direction of a nearby stretcher. Then he turned toward Emmanuel. "He is, thanks to Mr. Alvarez. Emmanuel rescued him. Bertlemann inhaled a substantial amount of smoke and has a few burns, but they aren't life threatening."

Damon reached out and shook Emmanuel's hand.

The maintenance man smiled. "Mr. Bertlemann was smart. He was taking a bath when the explosion went off. He said he opened the bathroom door and saw flames engulfing a guest bedroom and the top of the stairs. So he stoppered the tub and submerged himself in the water."

"Bertlemann was lucky, too," Gerry said. "Lucky that the second floor didn't collapse until after Emmanuel helped him out."

"You went up the stairs through the fire?" Damon asked.

"Thankfully, I didn't have to." Emmanuel grinned. "I went inside and it was scorching hot and smoky. Flames hadn't reached the downstairs yet, but the staircase looked impassable. I called upstairs and Mr. Bertlemann responded—said he was in the bathtub. Fortunately the bathroom door was right at the top of the steps." Emmanuel wiped his brow. "Mr. Bertlemann really saved himself. I had no idea what I could do other than wait for the fire department, but then he yelled down that there was a fire extinguisher in the cabinet under the kitchen sink. Bertlemann opened the door to the bathroom and I threw the extinguisher up the steps. A lucky shot—it rolled right to him. He dipped his clothes in tub water, put them on, and then used the extinguisher to fight his way through the flames down the stairs."

Damon had to hand it to Frederick Bertlemann. He thought through the situation with a level head. But he was also extremely fortunate that Emmanuel was on the scene.

"Were you able to speak to Mr. Bertlemann?" Damon asked Gerry.

"Yes," Gerry replied.

Gerry, Damon, and Emmanuel watched as the paramedics loaded Frederick Bertlemann into a waiting ambulance. The vehicle sped away from the smoldering remnants of the man's home. A paramedic tugged on Emmanuel's sleeve. Emmanuel didn't have any burns, but he'd inhaled quite a bit of smoke, and the paramedic insisted on transporting him to the hospital as a precaution.

"Frederick Bertlemann was well enough to speak after he and Emmanuel escaped from the house," Gerry said once he and Damon were alone. "He just returned from visiting his daughter in Colorado and didn't even know Jeremiah Milk had been killed until I told him."

"So the police hadn't shown him Dominic's picture?"

"Not until now. None of the park staff had ever mentioned Bertlemann's name. I showed him a photo of Dominic a few minutes before you crawled in from the woods."

"And Bertlemann had seen him?"

"He had. With Aylin. About a month-and-a-half ago, he was taking his daily walk before the park opened. His route that day led him past the Tripping Falls parking lot. Daylight had broken, and Bertlemann saw Aylin and Dominic Freeze standing near a vehicle. Bertlemann said it appeared innocuous: he figured

Dominic was a boyfriend dropping her off at work a little early."

"But Aylin and Dominic saw Bertlemann?"

"Yes. Bertlemann waved to the pair of them. And Aylin, flustered, waved back. My guess is that she was too new to know Bertlemann flouted official park hours."

"So Aylin knew that Bertlemann could link her to Dominic, and that made him a threat."

"Exactly. A threat she had to act on when we arrested Dominic this morning. She couldn't risk Bertlemann seeing Dominic's face on the news and recalling their early morning encounter. I put out an APB on Aylin right after Bertlemann told me about it. Your eyewitness account of Aylin as the arsonist and the evidence inside her backpack will seal her fate."

"What about Dominic?"

"With the information you provided me the other night about Dominic, we found a judge to issue a search warrant for his home. We acted on it last night and unearthed a stack of printouts on electrical wiring. We confiscated his computer, too. Our tech team will tear apart his files and search history. My guess is he taught himself how to blow the circuitry on the main floor of the shed."

"Will that be enough to convict him?"

"To be honest, I'm not sure that alone would be enough. But once we catch Aylin, I'm willing to bargain with her in exchange for her testimony against Dominic. After we charge her with an attempt on Bertlemann's life and as an accomplice in Jeremiah's murder, hopefully she'll open up to save her own skin." Gerry paused, and then added, "I'll let you know what happens."

Damon allowed an ambulance driver to take him to the hospital. After a multitude of scans and probes, he was given a clean bill of health and a set of crutches. His ankle was badly sprained but not broken.

Chapter 23

It was early evening when Damon arrived home. His Saab was parked in the driveway—he'd given Gerry his keys before getting into the ambulance.

David Einstaff pointed at the open chair beside him on the porch. Without having eaten since breakfast, Damon felt famished. He managed a weak smile and sat.

"Rough day?" David asked, glancing at the crutches. David poured his neighbor a tumbler of whiskey to match his own. The man always seemed to have an extra glass on the porch.

"Painful but fruitful," Damon said. "I'd rather not talk about it if you don't mind."

"Not at all." David clinked the two glasses together and handed the fresh one to Damon.

"David, I know it hasn't been too long since you and your wife divorced," Damon said.

"Not since it was finalized," David corrected him. "But the marriage has been over for a while now."

"Would you have any interest in dating someone?"

"Your mother?" David asked with a hint of hope.

Damon wasn't surprised at the question. "No," he said. "It would be a blind date."

David sipped whiskey and studied Damon over the rim of his glass. "But you know her, right?"

"I met her for the first time today. Diane Ridgeway. She's the assistant principal at Ashbury Elementary, and she's full of life."

David closed his eyes and titled his head back into his patio chair. His Adam's apple bulged. "Okay," he said quietly. Then he perked up. "I mean, yes. Thank you. I can't remember the last date I was on, but it's time I started getting out there."

"Great," Damon said. He set his drink on the small table between their patio chairs, rose with the help of his crutches, and clapped David on the shoulder.

Damon left David on the porch and went inside to fix himself a sandwich. The answering machine in the kitchen blinked with bright red pulses. He punched "play," and Bethany's voice filled the air, asking Damon to give her a call "whenever he had a chance."

Damon picked up the phone and dialed. After exchanging pleasantries, Bethany apologized for not speaking with him at Mrs. Chenworth's party.

"I was in a major rush," she said. "I had a job interview."

"I heard through Mrs. Chenworth's grapevine," Damon said.

"I'm not surprised. One of the network producers had just flown in from Atlanta and squeezed me in for a nighttime coffee at her hotel."

"How'd it go?" Damon asked nervously. He wanted Bethany to succeed but certainly didn't want her to move to Atlanta.

"Oh, Damon, I think it went really well," she said with excitement. "I wanted to share the good news with you. The producer and I hit it off, and someone from the network called a few hours ago. I'm going down to Atlanta to interview with some of the executives!" Bethany made a sound that sounded like a tire screeching on wet pavement—it was one of pure exhilaration.

After hanging up, Damon sank into an armchair. He was physically and mentally exhausted. The chase after

Aylin and long crawl through the woods had drained his body, while Bethany's news deflated his spirits.

* * *

Damon spent the following day at home, recovering. Rebecca and his mother paid separate visits and lauded his efforts to track down Aylin. He spent the evening alone, watching back-to-back television movies. Ten minutes after crawling into bed, there was a knock at his front door. Damon roused himself, wrapped a loose-fitting robe around his body, and hobbled down the stairs. Gerry Sloman was standing out front with a big grin and a six pack of longnecks.

Damon invited him inside.

"Sorry I woke you," Gerry said. He set the beer down on the kitchen counter and started to rummage through Damon's drawers for a bottle opener.

"I hadn't fallen asleep yet. Is this a final celebration? You found Aylin?"

"Yes. She was holed up in an apartment thirty miles east of here. Near Annapolis. Her real name of course is Michelle Walczak, and she lived for several years right here in Hollydale with her stepbrother." Gerry upcapped two beers and handed one to Damon. "We found fingerprints all over the explosives kit in her backpack. They're sure to match hers."

"Did you speak with her?" Damon asked.

"Yes," Gerry said and raised his bottle in the air. "She flipped on Dominic."

"So you'll be able to put him behind bars for sure?"

"I just spoke with the prosecutor. He's aiming for premeditated murder. With Aylin's testimony, I have no doubt Dominic will not only be convicted but get a life sentence."

"And Aylin er, Michelle?"

"As I expected, the prosecutor agreed to knock down the charges against her. But she's still looking at twenty years."

Damon set down his bottle and shook Gerry's hand. "Well done, Gerry."

The detective laughed. "You did all of the hard work, Damon."

The men sat at the kitchen table. "So what did Aylin say?" Damon asked.

"She basically confirmed everything you discovered. After Dominic accepted the plea bargain on the embezzlement charges, he went to work on finding the person who set him up. Dominic hired Marcus Pontfried. At first, they were both stuck. But then Pontfried asked Dominic about his fishing excursion on the day his computer at Trident was hacked. When Dominic relayed the details of his marital trouble as the impetus for the outing, it struck the private eye that there might be a connection."

"So Pontfried went to interview Samantha Richter," Damon said.

"Exactly. Samantha admitted that a man she knew as Kenneth Randolph contrived the sham affair. Pontfried recognized Randolph's name. Dominic had given him a list of everyone who worked in Trident's office as well as its Board members and silent partner."

"And Samantha told me that she described Kenneth Randolph to Pontfried, including his disfigured fingers."

"Right," Gerry said. He started to scrape the label from his beer bottle. "Pontfried passed along that description to Dominic who knew of only one person with fingers like that: Jeremiah Milk."

"So Pontfried hunted down Jeremiah to confirm Dominic's suspicions."

"Yes. He found out where Jeremiah worked and went to the park. Veronica Maldive confirmed that the Jeremiah Milk at Tripping Falls had malformed fingers, so later Pontfried surreptitiously snapped a photo of him and went back to see Samantha Richter. When she verified that the man in the photo was Kenneth Randolph, Jeremiah's goose was cooked, so to speak. Even though Dominic didn't have much evidence, he was confident that Jeremiah was responsible for wrecking his marriage and his career."

"Did Marcus Pontfried know Dominic was going to kill Jeremiah?" Damon asked.

"I doubt it. That's why the prosecutor isn't going after him."

"Seems like Pontfried's getting off scot-free."

"He is," Gerry said. "As will Matthew Katz-Atwater."

"Did you get anything else out of Matthew?" Damon asked.

"No. We tried to speak with him, but Alistair Atwater hired a top notch legal team. Plus, the boy's a juvenile. He won't even get a slap on the wrist. But I suspect that Jeremiah's death has scared him straight."

Damon smiled. Despite acting in complicity with Jeremiah, he wished the teen well and hoped he could get his life back on track.

Damon finished his beer and opened a second. He went to the refrigerator, pulled out the remainder of a blueberry crisp courtesy of Rebecca, and set it in front of Gerry with a fork.

"No need for a plate, I suppose," Gerry said with a smile. He began to eat from the tin.

"So were Dominic and Aylin so close that she just went along with his plan to murder Jeremiah?" Damon asked. "That seems pretty far-fetched."

"They couldn't have been too close. She just ratted him out to save herself a longer sentence." Gerry wiped his mouth with the back of his sleeve, then frowned at the blueberry stain on his shirt.

As Damon rose to retrieve a washcloth, Gerry continued. "Aylin had been financially dependent on her stepbrother. Dominic earned a good living at Trident and he sent Aylin—or should I say Michelle—a check every month to supplement her income. She'd been working as a hostess at an Olive Garden and the extra money was invaluable. So when Dominic lost his livelihood, she took a financial hit."

"That would've been tough," Damon said. "But—"

Gerry held up a hand. "And, Aylin told me that Dominic offered her a six-figure payoff."

"But he'd lost his job and was already paying alimony and child support," Damon protested. "Was he lying to his stepsister or did Dominic have a horde of money somewhere?" He passed a damp cloth to Gerry, who scrubbed vigorously at the stain on his sleeve.

"Neither." Gerry frowned at the stain which refused to go away. "But Dominic had access to a huge revenue stream. He only brought Aylin into his confidence after he learned that it was Jeremiah, acting as Kenneth Randolph, who set him up. In fact, I'm not sure whether Dominic would've killed Jeremiah if he hadn't masqueraded as Kenneth Randolph—a man who only existed on paper, yet owned twenty percent of a midsize company. According to Aylin, once Dominic learned that Randolph and Jeremiah were one and the same, he realized that he could fulfill two goals with a single act. By killing Jeremiah, he could not only satisfy his lust for vengeance but also turn murder into a financial windfall."

Damon shook his head in amazed understanding. "Jeremiah might be dead, but the fictional Kenneth Randolph lived on."

Gerry tipped his beer bottle in Damon's direction. "You got it. Dominic figured that not a soul on Earth knew anything about Kenneth Randolph other than himself, Marcus Pontfried, and Samantha Richter, who didn't count in his book. Matthew Katz-Atwater knew, of course, but Dominic was unaware of him. Aylin said Dominic planned to lay low for a while after he killed Jeremiah. Kenneth Randolph, as twenty percent owner of Trident, received profit checks every month. And Dominic, the former chief accountant, knew exactly where those checks were sent. Dominic planned to create identification in the name of Kenneth Randolph, just as Jeremiah had, and cash the checks himself. After all, there'd be no one to complain. A year or two later, he'd sell the stake in Trident for a mint. Aylin didn't have all of the details of Dominic's plan, but that was his general idea. And he was going to give Aylin a cut."

"Wow," Damon said in disbelief. After a moment he asked, "So who's entitled to the twenty percent stake in Trident now?"

Gerry chewed a mouthful of blueberry crisp, then said, "Dottie Milk. She's Jeremiah's sole beneficiary since he didn't have a will or any other immediate family. Someone from our financial crimes unit is going up to Philadelphia tomorrow to explain the situation to the folks at Trident. And I've spoken with Alistair Atwater. He said he doesn't want the money back. He gave it to Jeremiah for bringing Matthew 'back to life' and didn't care how he had spent it."

"Have you told Dottie about her rights to the stake in Trident?"

"I did this morning. She was beside herself. But I have to hand it to Dottie. After it soaked in, she told me that she was going to sell the stake in Trident. Dottie plans to live in Arizona on the $400,000 left over at True Capital but pass along the enormous sum from Trident. She said she'll donate the majority to Tripping Falls, and use the rest to set up a fund to help provide for Dominic Freeze's two children. Much as she hates Dominic, she recognizes that his children are collateral victims. When Dominic goes to prison, they'll be left without his financial support."

"That's extremely magnanimous," Damon said.

"I suspect it's Dottie's way of washing her hands. I don't think Jeremiah's lack of innocence sits well with her."

Damon nodded in agreement. "What did Aylin have to say about Bertlemann?" he asked.

"It was just as we suspected. Aylin was relatively new to Tripping Falls when she showed Dominic the shed near Cherubim's Run and Emmanuel's garage. She didn't know Bertlemann walked the grounds before the park opened in the morning, so she was caught off-guard when he waved to her and Dominic in the parking lot. When she found out Dominic had been arrested, Aylin knew she had to take action. As long as Dominic kept his mouth shut about Aylin, Bertlemann was the only person who could place them together. She calculated that taking out the old man was a safer bet than waiting to see whether the police would show him Dominic's picture."

"I wonder if she planned to continue working at the park after torching Bertlemann's home or would have vanished into thin air."

"I don't know. Either approach would be risky. The police hadn't given up on a connection to the park staff, so she and a handful of others would've been in our crosshairs. On the other hand, if she disappeared, we'd square our focus onto her. It doesn't matter, once you spotted her in the woods, she knew she had to run. I suspect that she hightailed it out of the park just minutes before our convoy arrived."

Damon rubbed his eyes. "Did Dominic torture Jeremiah before killing him? It looked like he focused on obliterating his fingers and toes before finishing him off."

Gerry grimaced. "Aylin said she didn't know, though I suspect Dominic took his time and made Jeremiah suffer. What Jeremiah did to Dominic Freeze wasn't right, but I have no qualms about sending Dominic away for life."

The two men finished their beers in silence. Damon closed his eyes and reflected on the extreme highs and lows in the extraordinary life of Jeremiah Milk, filling in the blanks with his imagination. Born with a disfigurement, Jeremiah endured a childhood riddled with mockery. He became a shell of a boy. His life took a turn to the positive when he landed a fulfilling position as a park ranger and was free to spend hours alone with nature. When he fell in love with Kathryn, he hit an emotional high. Jeremiah had convinced himself that no woman could ever love him, but he had been wrong. Kathryn had seen past his physical imperfections and into his heart, which hadn't yet turned to stone. And when their son was born, Jeremiah decided that life wasn't so bad after all. The years of agony started to fade from memory.

But then the unthinkable happened and fate crushed Jeremiah Milk like a sledgehammer. Kathryn and Samuel were swept out of his life in an instant. Not with a single stroke, but with two swift blows in rapid succession. He took out his frustration on his mother—the one person who had cared for Jeremiah his entire life—and banished her to Arizona. Jeremiah removed himself from society and anger bubbled to the surface.

He returned to Tripping Falls, as he needed the income. All the while, he sought an outlet for his ire. He didn't harbor animosity toward his co-workers and wasn't the type to spray a crowd of innocents with bullets. No, his ill will was reserved for those who had exacerbated his feelings of inadequacy. And who better to target than the ringleader of his childhood tormenters: the boy who had literally burned him.

Damon imagined that Jeremiah was a planner. Jeremiah formulated a host of potential schemes that would bring shame and financial ruin to Dominic Freeze. But his best-laid plans required a combination of money and computer skills.

On the day Glenda Atwater walked into the Tripping Falls visitor center, the die was cast that would lead to the downfall of Dominic Freeze and the death of Jeremiah Milk. With $2 million in his back pocket and the services of a pimpled computer pro who was in a vulnerable and combative state, Jeremiah had the tools he needed.

Damon envisioned Jeremiah relishing every word of the *Philadelphia Business Journal's* account of the embezzlement he engineered. He had crushed the marriage and career of Dominic Freeze and still had $400,000 in the bank plus a stream of monthly Trident checks thanks to his self-created doppelganger, Kenneth Randolph. He had a new girlfriend as well. Damon wondered whether Jeremiah started to look over his shoulder after Veronica told him that a private investigator had come to the park.

Gerry interrupted his thoughts. "I'm heading home, buddy," the detective said. "Go get yourself some sleep."

Chapter 24

At nine o'clock the following morning, Damon was just starting to rouse himself from slumber when he heard the sharp rapping of the brass knocker on his front door. With sleep still in his eyes, Damon wandered downstairs and opened the door. Alistair Atwater stood before him in a double-breasted suit and four-hundred dollar shoes.

Damon was surprised to see him. "Can I make you some coffee?" he asked after inviting the billionaire inside and leading him to the kitchen table.

"No, thank you," Alistair said briskly but politely, taking in Damon's robe and slippers. Alistair looked down at his thumbs and drummed them on the tabletop. "I have to be honest, Mr. Lassard. I have mixed feelings about you."

"I'm sorry for speaking with your grandson without disclosing the nature of my visit," Damon said. He felt intimidated and had to muster inner resolve. "But I didn't believe that Jeremiah had acted alone."

Alistair Atwater held up a hand. "My attorney isn't present, Mr. Lassard, so let's not speak about Jeremiah or what Matthew may or may not have done. You shouldn't have spoken to my grandson. You should have gone to the police instead and let them take action." He looked Damon in the eye. "That being said, you delivered results. I've been in the corporate world for a long time. Sometimes you need to act on instinct to achieve the desired outcome."

Damon met his gaze. "I couldn't agree more, sir."

"That's why I'm here, Damon." The CEO relaxed his posture. "I'd like to offer you a position with Atwater Enterprises."

Damon blinked with astonishment. He hadn't expected to see Alistair Atwater ever again, let alone be offered a job from him.

"I don't have any experience in commercial real estate," Damon said cautiously. "Or much corporate experience at all."

Alistair waved a hand in the air. "No matter. I plan to make you the junior person on a team of investment analysts. You'll learn all you need to know on the job. I'll have our finance department fix you up with a small starting bonus so you can go out and buy a few nice suits. Be in our corporate office downtown at eight o'clock on Monday morning." Alistair Atwater set his business card on the kitchen table.

Damon was still in shock. "Mr. Atwater, to be honest, I've never thought about this line of work."

"I can assure you that you want this position," Alistair said curtly. "I expect to see you three days from now, on time." The billionaire walked out of Damon's house without another word.

Damon staggered to the kitchen sink and splashed cold water on his face. He wasn't sure whether he wanted to modify his laid-back lifestyle. But maybe he needed a change—now that the murder of Jeremiah Milk had been solved, would boredom creep into his days of volunteer activities?

* * *

Later that morning, Damon called on Rebecca at The Cookery. He filled her in on the police's capture of Aylin and the details of Gerry's interview with her.

"I can't believe you did it again, Damon," Rebecca said. Her arms were covered in flour up to the elbows. "Over the summer, you tracked down the killer of that traveling carnival owner, and now you figured out who murdered Jeremiah Milk. You've solved two major crimes in three months. And that doesn't even count catching the crepe myrtle culprit."

"All I did was talk to people," Damon said with humility.

"Well, I think it's about time you joined the police force, Damon. You really should start the training classes. You could probably work your way up to detective in no time."

Damon sat down on a stool in front of a long stainless steel counter. "Actually," he said, "someone just offered me a job."

Rebecca shot him a satisfied look. "I bet it was Lieutenant Hobbes. Did that woman finally see the light of day and realize how big of a help you are to the police?"

"No, not her. Alistair Atwater offered me a position as a junior investment analyst with Atwater Enterprises."

Rebecca set down the ball of dough she was kneading. "Seriously?"

Damon nodded.

"That's a real opportunity, Damon. Are you considering it?"

"I am. Alistair expects me to start on Monday. In fact, he basically told me to show up. He didn't wait for an answer."

"I suspect that's how he's gotten as far as he has," Rebecca said. "By not taking 'no' for an answer. But of course, you could decline if you wanted to."

"I have to think about it. An opportunity like this one may never come my way again. But I'm not sure I'm cut out for the corporate world."

"Well, you have an entire weekend to choose your career," Rebecca said with sarcasm.

As Damon walked home, he cogitated over Alistair Atwater's offer. He also considered the police force. The paths were so different, but Damon knew deep down that he should choose one. Volunteering at the library and taking on the role of citizens association president were enjoyable. And his few stints with the County Crime Solvers had temporarily charged his adrenaline. But Damon suddenly felt a void inside that he needed to fill—a real vocation that he could sink his teeth into. His thoughts flip-flopped. The money, status, and credentials he could achieve by working at Atwater Enterprises would be enviable. And Bethany tended to gravitate toward corporate professionals. On the other hand, solving crimes was exhilarating, and the police genuinely helped people in need.

Standing in front of his duplex on a clear, late-September afternoon, Damon decided that he would choose one road or the other. In the meantime, while he still had the opportunity, he went inside to take a midday nap.

THE END

ABOUT THE AUTHOR

 STEPHEN KAMINSKI is the author of *Don't Cry Over Killed Milk,* the second book in the Damon Lassard Dabbling Detective series. The first was *It Takes Two to Strangle.* He is a graduate of Johns Hopkins University and Harvard Law School. Stephen has practiced law for well over a decade and currently serves as General Counsel to a national non-profit organization. He is a lifelong lover of all types of mysteries, including cozies, and lives with his wife and daughter in Arlington, Virginia.

Select reviews of *It Takes Two to Strangle: A Damon Lassard Dabbling Detective Mystery*

"I found a winner in Stephen Kaminski. Mr. Kaminski has delivered one of the most intriguing plots I have come across in quite a while.... [T]he plot just rockets along with us guessing 'whodunit' every page along the way. In a way Damon Lassard is similar to a male Jessica Fletcher, from TV's 'Murder, She Wrote'."

—Vic's Media Room

"If you enjoy cozy mysteries such as the Hamish MacBeth and Agatha Raisin series by M.C. Beaton ... and the Coffeehouse series by Cleo Coyle, you'll definitely enjoy your time with *It Takes Two to Strangle.*"

—Dreamworld Book Reviews

"Using a laid back writing style, with subtle humor, [Kaminski] engages his reader through carefully delivered dialog, plot preview, revealing nuances, and clues that fortify the storyline. Frequent unexpected plot developments, romantic innuendos, and interaction among the key players engage the reader from the early pages right through to the dramatic finale."

—Reader Views

"This is a good cozy mystery, easy to read. The background and descriptions seem very real. The author keeps you guessing, but in the end all the loose ends come together. This is the first book in the Damon Lassard Dabbling Detective series—and I look forward to reading the next installment."

—Meritorious Mysteries

"The mystery is complex with plenty of suspects and I must say I was surprised by one of the culprits. He was totally off my radar until the evidence was spelled right out for me. I will be looking forward to more adventures with Damon Lassard and Detective Gerry Sloman."

—Escape with Dollycas into a Good Book

"Wrap up in your blankie and start reading this Dabbling Mystery Book and you'll not set it down until you are done."

—Books, Reviews, etc.

"Stephen Kaminski has crafted an impressive debut mystery…featuring protagonist Damon Lassard. Kaminski has plotted a complex case, with clearly defined suspects and lots of clues that will keep the reader guessing until the end."

—Raymond Flynt, Author of the Brad Frame mystery series

"A well-crafted cozy mystery! Kaminski moves the story along at a good pace, with believable characters, and a tight plot. Kaminski's prose is eloquent without being pretentious, and he uses his strong command of the English language to create wonderful descriptions of his characters and the places they frequent."

—Debra Trueman, Author of "Advice of Counsel"

"I LOVED THIS BOOK. I enjoyed the characters and the plot. I like a book that surprises me with twists and turns, and this one did exactly that. The only downside is that this book is the first of the series and I have to wait for more. Rats!"

—Leslie Matthews Stansfield, Author of "Mr. Tea and the Traveling Tea Cup"

www.ingramcontent.com/pod-product-compliance
Lightning Source LLC
Chambersburg PA
CBHW050420260626
47156CB00003B/1087